HÉLÈNE PICARD

SABBAT

TRANSLATED AND WITH AN INTRODUCTION BY
BRIAN STABLEFORD

AND WITH A PREFACE BY
COLETTE

THIS IS A SNUGGLY BOOK

ISBN: 978-1-64525-110-1

SABBAT

HÉLÈNE PICARD (1873-1945) published her first book, the lyrical drama *La Feuille morte*, in 1903, which was followed by a number of volumes of poetry, including *L'Instant éternel* (1907) and *Les Fresques* (1908). The author was briefly employed as Colette's secretary while the latter was working for Le Matin in 1920, and, in 1924, she published, as part of a "Collection Colette," her only prose work, *Sabbat*, one of the great works of literary Satanism.

BRIAN STABLEFORD's scholarly work includes *New Atlantis: A Narrative History of Scientific Romance* (Wildside Press, 2016), *The Plurality of Imaginary Worlds: The Evolution of French roman scientifique* (Black Coat Press, 2017) and *Tales of Enchantment and Disenchantment: A History of Faerie* (Black Coat Press, 2019). He has translated more than three hundred volumes from the French, mostly in the genres of *roman scientifique*, *contes de fées* and Romantic and Symbolist fiction. His recent fiction includes the visionary science fiction novel *The Revelations of Time and Space* (2020) and its sequel *After the Revelation* (2021); the last in his long series of "Tales of the Genetic Revolution," *The Elusive Shadows* (2020); and the comedy fantasy *Meat on the Bone* (2021), all published by Snuggly Books.

SNUGGLY BOOKS

CONTENTS

INTRODUCTION

Sabbat by Hélène Picard (1873-1945) was first published by J. Ferenczi et fils in 1923 as part of a "Collection Colette." The author had been briefly employed as Colette's secretary while the latter was working for *Le Matin* in 1920, having met her the previous year, and they remained good friends thereafter. The book is dedicated to Colette, who also provided the preface, the brief text of which implies strongly that the book was commissioned by her. Colette might also have assisted with its editing, perhaps in the organization of its fragments, which give the impression of not having been written in the order in which they appear in the printed text.

Sabbat followed half a dozen volumes of poetry—including *Souvenirs d'enfance* (1913)—issued after Picard's first publication, the fantastic lyric drama *La Feuille morte*, in 1903. *Sabbat* was not quite her last publication, but she produced little more thereafter,[1] being chronical-

---

1 The preliminary material in *Sabbat* advertises two more prose works: *Tatahouin, souvenirs d'enfance* as "*pour paraître*" and *L'Abbesse aux enfers* as "*en preparation*," but I can find no evidence of the actual existence of either.

ly ill and bedridden for the last two decades of her life, suffering from a condition described as "neurasthenia," a then-fashionable term for debilitating illnesses for which doctors could not find an attributable cause within their conventional vocabulary.

The Toulouse-born Hélène Dumarc had married Jean Picard, the sub-prefect of Privas in 1898, the year in which she won her first prize at the prestigious annual *jeux floraux* held in the city. Initially happy, the marriage eventually ended in separation and angry divorce, leaving a residual bitterness that is obvious in some sections of *Sabbat*, to the extent that anything can be considered obvious in such a surreal and deliberately enigmatic work. Although inevitably marketed as a novel, it is really a collation of prose poems, of a kind not without precedent in the annals of Symbolist literature; contemporary readers would probably have noticed affinities with Adolphe Retté's *Thule des brumes* (1891; tr. as *Misty Thule*), but it has more interesting echoes of the similarly surreal *Histoire du roi de bohème et ses sept châteaux* (1830; tr. as *The Story of the King of Bohemia and His Seven Castles*) by Charles Nodier, written in a self-indulgent mood while the author was ill and finding it very difficult to publish his work under the oppressive regime of Charles X.

Nodier's work is formulated as an opium dream experienced by a character named Théodore (the familiar name by which several authors associated with the Romantic Movement called one of their heroes, the German writer of hallucinatory fantasies E. T. A, Hoffmann) and it consists of a series of internal dialogues between three distinct fragments of the notional author's personality. *Sabbat* similarly consists, in the main, of a series of dialogues between the notional author and an imaginary Satan, but the narrative voice frequently slips between the first and third person and it is not always obvious where items of dialogue begin and conclude, or who is supposed to be addressing whom.

Nodier admitted, slightly reluctantly, self-medicating with the aid of opium, and *Histoire du roi de bohème et ses sept châteaux* is, to some extent, an attempt to explore, explain and capitalize on the drug's hallucinatory effect, in the spirit of Thomas De Quincey's *Confessions of an English Opium Eater* (1821; loosely translated into French by Alfred de Musset as *L'Anglais mangeur d'opium*, published in 1828). The hallucinatory aspect of the various sections of *Sabbat* varies, but it reaches a peak of indulgence in the subsection entitled "Sabbat," where the author appears to be mimicking, and perhaps mining, her fever dreams, and also trying to exert a measure of control over her delirium by transforming it into poetic imagery and supplying it with a unifying theory of sorts.

Nodier always remained uncertain as to the precise nature of his illness, although his daughter Marie recorded in her memoir of his life that once, in desperation, he swallowed a concoction of turpentine and other noxious substances after a doctor told him that he must have a tapeworm, but that the cocktail would kill it if he managed to survive its poisonous effects himself. Unlike Picard, he recovered a measure of health, and he was able to keep writing until the eve of his death, muffling the delirious aspect of his work but never suppressing it entirely. Picard did not have a tapeworm, but like Nodier, she undoubtedly suffered the fate of all victims of undiagnosable illnesses, who always find it a trifle difficult to persuade others that they really are very ill and that their symptoms are not "all in the mind." There is no record of the medication she took, but it would be astonishing if it did not include opiates, and it is surely significant that she insists in *Sabbat* that few poets can have failed to see Satan "emerging from a poppy."

As its title declares, *Sabbat* belongs to the rich French tradition of "literary Satanism," and it is one of the most forthright contributions to that tradition. It occupies a very particular place therein, and pays oblique tribute to some of its ancestors and precursors. It is undoubtedly significant that in 1903, Colette had been the only person of note to speak out in defense of Jean Lorrain—a lifelong invalid who mined the hallucinations induced when he had tried to self-medicate with ether, in numerous short stories—when he was sued for defamation by the artist Jeanne Jacquemin after he incorporated a disguised depiction of her in "Victime," a story published in *Le Journal* in that year. The story repeated and elaborated an analysis begun in a two-part article in the same newspaper entitled "Les Princesses des ténèbres" (1896; tr. as "Princesses of Darkness"; tr. in *Princesses of Darkness and Other Exotica*, 2021), which had coupled Jacquemin with Lorrain's former protégée Rachilde as type-specimens of a modern species of *sorcière* [witch]. Lorrain intended that judgment as a compliment, although Jacquemin took it amiss; Colette obviously had a similar analysis in mind when she wrote the preface to *Sabbat*, and had surely discussed the argument with her secretary before commissioning the work for publication, thus helping to provide Picard with an important aspect of the fundamental rhetoric and symbolism of her novel.

The first part of Lorrain's article is a straightforward exercise in literary criticism, arguing that the protagonist of the recent novel *La Princesse des Ténèbres* (1895) "by Monsieur Jean de Childra"[1] is a representative of a new type of witch "for the occultism of which the atheistic *fin-de-siècle* has an unhealthy curiosity"—a type partly inspired by Charles Baudelaire's *Litanies de Satan* (1857). Lorrain finds other examples of the type in Madame Chantelouve, in Joris-Karl Huysmans' *Là-Bas* (1891), which popularized the notion that Satanism was thriving in contemporary Paris, and important characters in two novels by Paul Adam, *Être* (1888) and *Mystère des foules* (1896). In the second part of his article, however— seemingly a hasty afterthought, the article being part of a weekly series written to a deadline—Lorrain claimed to have been personally acquainted with two *sorcières* of the type in question, Rachilde and an artist he does not name but is clearly recognizable as Jeanne Jacquemin.

---

1 Lorrain improvised this name, knowing perfectly well that the novel was by Rachilde (Marguerite Eymery), under which pseudonym it was swiftly reprinted. Because of a typesetter's error, however, the first edition is actually credited to "Jean de Chibra" and Alfred Jarry contended, plausibly, that Lorrain must have made a mistake and that Rachilde had actually intended it to be signed "Jean de Chilra," that name including a perfect anagram of her usual signature.

The Baudelaire poem referenced by Lorrain—an aggressive renunciation of Catholicism—did not initiate the French tradition of literary Satanism, the nineteenth-century revisions of which had been launched, obliquely, by Alfred de Vigny in "Eloa, ou La Soeur des anges" (1824) and continued by Alphonse de Lamartine in *La Chute d'un ange, episode* (1838) but it did mark a watershed in its development; it was swiftly supplemented and elaborated by Jules Michelet's remarkable scholarly fantasy *La Sorcière* (1862). It is Michelet's characterization of witches that is employed by Lorrain, with due credit, as a justification for his own. French historians had had a certain difficulty in chronicling the great witch-panic of the sixteenth and seventeenth centuries, in which "inquisitorial" methods (i.e., torture) were widely employed, mostly by Dominican monks, to extract confessions from people—mostly women—accused of witchcraft. Those programmatic "confessions" routinely forced them to admit that they had attended meetings of witches—sabbats—at which their tacit or explicit pact with the Devil was confirmed, in an obscene caricature of Catholic communion. Although a few French historians committed to the faith of the Church felt obliged to believe that the confessions were accurate, most took the view that they were entirely fantastic, but Michelet differed, also for ideological reasons; he suggested that some accused witches must have been heroic rebels against the oppressive tyranny of the Church, who really had made a tacit pact with an imaginary and symbolic Satan, and sometimes even went as far as inventing rites of "worship" (of which he obligingly supplied a wholly fictitious example markedly akin to Baudelaire's *Litanies of Satan*).

The defense of Satanism as a heroic rebellion against Catholic oppression formulated by Baudelaire and Michelet inevitably became a significant inspiration to anticlerical poets of the Symbolist school that originated in the 1880s and reached the peak of its fashionability in the Belle Epoque, especially in the sector of the school labeled "Decadent"—initially as an insult, by hostile critics, but soon adopted as an ironic badge of pride by such pugnacious adherents of the movement as Jean Lorrain. Théophile Gautier argued in the introduction that he wrote for a posthumous edition of *Les Fleurs du Mal* that Baudelaire's "decadence" was not a species of moral degeneracy but a matter of literary style, the exotic elaboration of which was a natural concomitant of the "cultural decadence" of societies reaching a kind of historical terminus, thus licensing works of art that exemplified the decadent consciousness as well as those that railed against it, like *Là-Bas*, whose ambiguous title refers both to the literal Underworld of the Dantean Inferno and to the corrupt streets of Paris as viewed from the height of a church bell-tower.[1]

Hélène Picard was not a "decadent" Symbolist at the outset of her career, her early poetry tending strongly to

---

1 Huysmans' work is preoccupied with literal as well as moral pollution, understandably in an era where the Parisian sewer-system was still under construction and the air at the altitude of a bell-tower really would have been much cleaner than the air at street level. Picard has a similar sensitivity, but her epitome of environmental pollution is the incense of churches—which was, of course, intended to cover up the stink of unwashed congregations.

the sentimental and the nostalgic as well as being very conventional in form, but time, experience and illness soured her outlook very considerably and it is perhaps not surprising that she not only abandoned her commitment to conventional form but turned against it. Like the Romantic poets who first turned the accusation of "decadence" on its head, she elected to invert accusations of moral failure made against her—on weak grounds, if the first subsection of *Sabbat* can be trusted—in no uncertain terms, accepting Satan as her poetic savior, and then setting forth to unpack that notion and specify its real implications. Seen as an ensemble, that is what *Sabbat* does, with a surreal flamboyance that is typically "decadent" in terms of Gautier's apologetic analysis. Baudelaire would surely have understood and approved, just as Colette did.

Simply by virtue of its strategic employment of symbolism, Symbolist poetry and prose became an essential precursor of Surrealism, which championed a minimization of conscious intervention in the creative process and the extraction of raw material as directly as possible from the wellspring of the unconscious mind—a process normally accomplished by dreaming, which numerous writers who were gifted with a natural extravagance attempted, at least briefly, to assist with the aid of psychotropic substances—but in Picard's case, that methodology was greatly assisted, and effectively compelled, by her existential circumstances.

Much critical attention has been paid to the contribution of psychotropic substances to the literary creativity of such writers as Samuel Taylor Coleridge,

Thomas De Quincey, Charles Baudelaire and their fellow members of the Romantic Movement, not least by the writers themselves; Coleridge was among the English Romantics supplied with nitrous oxide by Humphry Davy and Baudelaire among those fed with hashish by the protopsychological researcher Joseph Moreau. As Baudelaire concluded in his quasi-scholarly study of *Les Paradises artificiels* (1860), however, those who attempted to use psychotropics strategically in order to stimulate their creativity soon became disenchanted with the method, and it is important to remember that they all began using such substances as medicaments because they were suffering from illnesses that undermined all their activities cruelly. Hélène Picard's *Sabbat* is no more a straightforward product of her illness than it is of opium or her poetic vocation, but it would be foolish not to recognize that if she had not been chronically ill, and somewhat disenchanted with life—in spite of her declared determination to remain positive, constructive and hopeful—her later poetry, including and perhaps quintessentially her poetry in prose, would be very different in tone, manner and rhetoric. It is not at all surprising that, like many other poets of her medically-disadvantaged era, she found Satan emerging from a poppy, and it is greatly to her credit as a writer, thinker and dreamer that she contrived to interrogate him so extensively and to reach such an elaborate understanding of him, in frank opposition to the conception invented and popularized by the Church.

The notional author of *Sabbat* is not delusional; her work makes no bones about the fact that her Satan is an imaginary product of her own consciousness and her own art, but she considers, rightly, that that only serves to make him more interesting. Her depiction of him is confused and sometimes self-contradictory, but the confusions and contradictions that she highlights are intrinsic to his satanic nature and a subject of interest themselves. Her poetic prose sometimes resembles angry ranting, and often gropes for meanings that it does not succeed in grasping fully, but that too is intrinsic to the nature of the exercise and a subject of interest in itself. Her characterization of the eroticized Sabbat is a long way from Michelet's, let alone the classic representation concocted by the French witchfinder Pierre de Lancre in his *Tableau de l'inconstance des mauvais anges et demons* (1612), with the aid of the children who dutifully nourished his fantasies with the substance of their own, but that distance is a kind of progress, and *Sabbat* is entitled to credit for reaching an extreme of Satanic conviction that extrapolates the French tradition of poetic anticlericalism into wildernesses previously untrodden by the human imagination. It is an unrepentant study in inventive heresy, but it is also a stylishly delirious exercise in Symbolism, possessed of a distinctive sarcastic and wrathful wit. Critics often overlook the comedic aspect of Decadent prose, none of whose exponents would have had any sympathy with the common adage that sarcasm is the lowest form of wit, and it is worth emphasizing here that the surreal components of *Sabbat* were written in a sarcastic spirit fully cognizant of the extreme unimportance of being earnest.

Hélène Picard's friendship with her contemporary Colette (Sidonie-Gabrielle Colette, 1873-1954), was, by necessity, mostly conducted by correspondence, and some of Colette's letters to her have been published, as have letters written to her by another friend, the actress Marguerite Moreno (1871-1948), who had been the wife of the Symbolist writer Marcel Schwob (1876-1905)—a friend and colleague of Jean Lorrain[1]—between 1895 and his premature death. Schwob had also been a chronic invalid whose illness physicians were initially unable to specify—although he eventually died of tuberculosis—and whose outlook on life, reflected in his work, became increasingly lachrymose as his career progressed. Colette had been a chronic invalid too in the era in which she wrote the novels that eventually made her famous when their true authorship was disclosed.[2] Nor was Picard the

---

1 Lorrain loved to tell the story of an occasion when he persuaded Schwob to bring Oscar Wilde to dinner at his house in Passy, an occasion so auspicious for him that he invited Anatole France to join them. According to Lorrain's "Lui" (1901; tr. as "Him" in *Princesses of Darkness and Other Exotica*), Wilde told a story after the dinner in which Lazarus, having been resurrected, tells Jesus that there is nothing but oblivion after death, to which Jesus replies: "I know—don't tell anyone." Anatole France's contributions to the French tradition of literary Satanism include, as well as the titles cited below, the intensely lachrymose "L'Humaine tragédie" (1895).
2 Colette's husband at the time, Henry Gauthier-Villars (1859-1931), recruited writers from his social circle to pen slightly risqué novels that were issued by his family's publishing company under the "house pseudonym" Willy. Colette's four Claudine novels (1900-1903), written while she was ill in bed (Gauthier-Villars claimed to have commissioned them in order to distract her, although Colette represented the situation differently, saying that he locked her in her room until she had finished them to his satisfaction) were initially issued under that name, and then reprinted under the signature "Colette Willy" before she went to court to reclaim her copyright and sole credit, always disputed by her husband and editor.

first "neurasthenic" with whom Colette had formed a sympathetic friendship; she left behind an affectionate memoir of her one-time neighbor Pauline Tarn (1877-1909), who wrote Symbolist poetry and prose-poetry under the pseudonym Renée Vivien. The latter preferred to employ pagan imagery in her heretical fantasies, but her own version of Satan is featured in "Le Genèse profane" (1902; tr. as "The Profane Genesis") and "Lilith" (1903) and one of her last works was "Christ" (1907), which presents the story of the gospels sarcastically, as it might have been reported by the tabloid press. Although they were also her contemporaries, it is unlikely that Picard ever met Schwob or Vivien, but she surely read and appreciated their work even before she formed relationships with Moreno and Colette.

Picard was a voracious reader, and she was undoubtedly familiar with the work of numerous other "neurasthenic" and "hypochondriac" writers, as well as with the overlapping population of writers who produced landmark works of literary Satanism, including Gustave Flaubert, in *La Tentation de Saint Antoine* (written 1840, revised 1856 and further revised for the published version of 1872), Anatole France, in a similar story of Satanic harassment, *Thaïs* (1890) and in *La Révolte des anges* (1914), and Rachilde in *La Princesse des Ténèbres*. Her response to them was, however, very distinctive; we can only speculate as to whether it had any further influence of its own, although there are clear similarities between the final section of Picard's text and the libretto that Colette penned, allegedly in a week, for Maurice Ravel's opera *L'Enfant et les sortileges* (1925). *Lolly Willowes;*

or, The Loving Huntsman (1926) by Sylvia Townsend Warner can easily be seen as part of an eccentric set with Rachilde's novel and Picard's collage, penned with an ostentatious English decorum rather than a Baudelairean flamboyance.

Sabbat remains a much more obscure work than the other titles cited; at the moment of writing it is impossible even to access the list of Picard's titles contained in the Bibliothèque Nationale, but if it is there it was probably consigned to the library's *enfer* at the time of publication; it is not presently available on *gallica*. That does not alter the fact that it is a very intriguing work, of considerable importance as a late addition to the canon of Decadent prose, which deserves to be much more widely read and appreciated.

I have appended to the present text a translation of an item published in the "Mille-et-un Matins" section of *Le Matin* two years before the book's publication; the section in question was then being administered by Colette, who was married at the time to the newspaper's editor, Henry de Jouvenel. Although it is obviously not a fragment escaped from the collage, it has some affinities with the items assembled in the "Sabbat" subsection of the text, and is interesting in juxtaposition with the text of *Sabbat*, as the other prose works mentioned in the preliminary material of the Ferenczi volume would undoubtedly have been, if the author had ever managed to prepare them successfully for publication.

※

The translation of *Sabbat* was made from a PDF file of the Ferenczi text kindly supplied to me by the publisher of the present volume. The translation of "Les Génies chagrins" was made from the 3 août 1921 issue of *Le Matin* reproduced on *gallica*.

—Brian Stableford, March 2021

PREFACE

I have thrown you to prose, Hélène, with regret and scruples, as if I were harnessing a thoroughbred to a tumbrel. To humiliate a proud neck that has only ever had rhyme for a master, to constrain to the straight rut winged hooves that have trodden the clouds . . . I trembled more than once at my daring . . .

I have even more reason to tremble now that I have read your book. A witch is born, as lustrously demonic and new as a kitten as yet unlicked. She knows herself, via Poetry, to be a daughter of Satan. Scarcely emerged from her unctuous and blind darkness, she speaks and signs, and remembers all that she has not known. She pronounces great speech that fumes like a firebrand: "There is a certain salivation of the spirit that can only be demonic. Poets know it particularly . . ."

Better than knowing him, that Satan necessary to their pure Sabbat, they are great enough to invent him.

She also says: "If, from the poppy, you do not see Satan emerge, as naked as original sin, as crimson as splendor and crime, you are very unfortunate . . ." Ah, shepherdess, I know what you mean. Forever bucolic, in spite of your nuns, your victims of cancer, your burned towns and your possessed little girls in the shadow of provincial boarding-schools, have you not led your sabbat of ideas amid wild flowers and beneath a shepherd's crook? Here you are, standing up against Catholicism, in truth, from your full height of a cicada. Severe and gigantic, many others have been seen . . . many others, but not this one. You attain him, so well that he retains, stuck to his inflexible forehead, the petal of a burning rose that you have thrown to him with the invectives that most terrible of nightingales might trill in its throat.

Many others have been heard . . . many others, but not these.

Perhaps, black and gigantic, he leans over you with consideration. "She also knows herself in sin . . ."

But he will not stigmatize you, Hélène, as much as you hope; for he is subtle.

"She has had, in sum, an idea of God and it is not certain that her joy, her dance, and her mildness, by which she thinks to escape us, are as pantheistic as she believes . . ." He has seen the horns that you have attached to your crook, the diabolical antennae that you wear, your forked tongue, the maleficent signs that you design, in pollen and in dew, on your forehead—and you take care lest your irreverent dance reveals to your somber antagonist a hoof—*the* hoof, ha ha, the hoof of Belzébuth, Lucifer and Asmodeus . . . But your old adversary has not made the sign of the cross at that sight. He is subtle, I tell you. "Let her dance," he will say. "Have you not noticed that her hoof is not cleft in the middle, and have you not recognized—by its golden tap and its divine arch—the foot of Pegasus?"

—Colette

SABBAT

A POET

A POET

When I was born, my mother never ceased murmuring, for three nights in succession; "that black cat, that black cat, that black cat . . ." And her pale bed-ridden gesture designated my cradle. I cried and agitated there extraordinarily, it appears, already full of a strange vitality, and the mysterious black cat, in my mother's parlance, reigned against my cheek, sitting on my pillow, not taking its eyes off me, testifying in my regard a jealous, terrible and fervent solicitude.

My mother's condition caused anxiety; she had a fever, but her gaze did not express any terror when, under the muslin curtain, it fell upon the satanic animal and the little girl who manifested herself tempestuously and who was as pretty as an evil flower. Health covered me with its gilded venom . . . a curl danced on my forehead.

Then my mother recovered her spirits; the black cat no longer watched over her new-born, but the latter—at the age of three days!—was suspected by her nurse-maids. And one of them whispered to the other: "It's not astonishing that the Devil has taken possession of that innocent. Can you imagine that, in the family château, they had the imprudence, while Madame was pregnant, to dig in the cellars where the late grandfather, who was reputedly accursed, was said to have buried heaps of gold. And what cellars! A hell of darkness. Of course, in the meantime, the Devil had hastened to put his hand on the treasure. When they tried to extract it from him, what did he do to avenge himself? He turned toward the child. It's quite simple. And the baptism couldn't do anything, you know. The child is forever in the possession of the Devil. For myself, I won't remain much longer in the presence of that monster; have you ever seen anything so beautiful?"

On the morning of the fourth day, suddenly ceasing to wail, I burst out laughing, for I resembled a rosebud that draws its little perfumed dagger and I grew in wrath, twittering, malice and strength.

As soon as I had two teeth—and I was precocious!—I tested them on my mother's breast, while interrogating her with my sly and brilliant gaze. "Well . . . ?" she said to me, annoyed and amazed that I was attempting a bite with two teeth. Then, doubtless content to have revealed my intelligence to her, I suckled, purring like a cat.

At six months, I merited that my father whipped me because I was already showing signs of stubbornness and reason. At fourteen months, when I was put in the presence of zoo animals, I gave the spectacle of amorous folly; tears of affection ran down my cheeks. Since then, I traveled the world, and I returned therefrom every evening on my little bare feet.

At three years I possessed the gift of second sight and no one around me lost a jewel, a duster or their mind without my saying, immediately: "It's over there . . ." and I ran straight to the ruby that was gleaming in a gap in the floorboards, to the duster mingled with the thieving maidservant's dirty washing, or to the mind wandering over a flower; I brought back a butterfly and returned it to the demented brain.

Later, already hostile to the physical dolor and the plaint that I scorned, I declared to my doll: "You have a stomach ache; well, I'm going to give you a lick of the belt," and I left her for dead with a thorn planted in her heart. Then, amid a great deployment of dances, a great debauchery of songs, joyous cries and a metallic racket, I buried her, and with cymbals on my fingers—two saucepans—I stamped on the grave with a victorious foot. Then, in the sacred transfiguration of the sibyl, I cried: "There she goes, off to heaven!" And truly, I saw, laughing in the azure, the blue eyes of my doll.

Alas, the Devil was still in me, utterly divine. I felt his living claw on my cheek and his luminous and passionate tongue on my eyelids. Nothing had diminished the power, damaged the beauty or offended the fervor in my soul for my amorous Devil. Toward my fifth year I began to become a charming little girl like all the rest, so it is easy for me to say that from birth to the age of five I was a supernatural marvel. Who afflicted, who wounded and who caused my adorable Demon to pale within me? Was he jealous of my alphabet, having already taught me to read the stellar secret in his eyes? Was he scornful of my toys, having rocked me in his arms against the black sun of his heart? Did he snigger at my games, the one who, having made me mobile necklaces of ants, sonorous crowns of cockchafers, palpitating girdles of dragonflies, and who, one evening, in a mountainous desert, as my nursemaid was carrying me, shut the main door of the château on me, and threw into my face an extraordinary quadruped whose cool inflamed breath I can still feel on my cheek?

"The Devil! The Devil!" cried the maidservant. "Lord Jesus . . . !" But the unicorn looked at me ineffably and fled into the marshy heath, a star on its forehead . . .

Did he criticize the lessons in morality that were given to me—to me, who was at my commencement rapacious, proud, combative, undisciplined and completely unsociable, as violent in color, perfume and aggression as a carnation, as insatiable and malevolent as the chicks of swallows, who are always hungry and have the desire for wings in their sparkling eyes?

Could he suffer that they would not leave me as he had made me—which is to say, as graceful as a flexible wasp, overflowing like a cup weeping over its limpid crystal, and so inspired that my gazes were hymns, my gestures incantations and my dances sabbats?

Was he indignant when there was talk, one day, of sending me to school, of making me sit down on a servile bench, of teaching me to make use of wool and canvas, he who, one morning when I found myself alone, snatched me amorously from my bed, carried me away, cooing singularly like an invisible turtle-dove, to an abandoned room where I was put in communication with some of my future strange divinities: poisons, phantoms, grimoires, memory, portraits, flowers with the lazy gestures of ancient strollers, and the winged dance of golden brodequins, as mild and funereal as ash?

Did he protest when my most fervent amour was stolen from me: Solitude, the pensive and powerful mother who was, alas, the fortunate rival of my own; who had foliage and the wind for tresses and the great plaint of moonlight in her savage owl's breast?

Oh, my Devil what have you become? How has the progress of your genius been arrested within me? I was born, I know, for its perfect realization, possessed from my first hour, marked for the exotic divinity that crowns, in its origin, the infernal rose. And, remembering your dark and lustrous pelt, the satin of your aristocratic ears, O Satan-Cat, with your ambiguous and savant eyes, your throat that already initiated mine with the devouring sign of the great accursed, your mouth in which the blaze of my future inferno already glowed, your mute laughter that left a fiery trail over mystery and the invisible, and the despotic paw that you placed upon my temple in the cradle where my destiny as a poet awoke, I declare that you were not merely a rhapsodic and singular vision of my delirious mother, for the blue gaze of my pure mother always communicated with unexplored worlds.

But universal Devil, infinite Devil who subsequently divinized my infancy and the rebellious sun of my hair, why, why, have you quit me?

"It's you who abandoned me, creature! When you began to understand, you lost consciousness, and, dishonored by acquired knowledge, it was necessary to say goodbye to innate wisdom. Of your demonic virtues, which were called 'faults,' they tried to make deadly qualities, and my fallen Masterpiece wept . . .

"All poets, in humanizing themselves, kill the Lucifer within them, more or less. But whatever they do, whatever happens, they always remember the terrible primal Presence, and sometimes, when you feel me quivering in your soul, and even in your entrails . . ."

"Oh, shut up . . . it's too magnificent . . . Seized by modesty, eyes maddened by light, I hide in my arms my face in flower and fire. And yet, how I look, how I listen, how I see, how I hear! The bones of the dead sing like flutes, and creation salutes, once again, the serpent that is told like rosary beads over the tempted hands of men . . . But I must have been so beautiful!"

"You were more so than you believe, better than you were told, you who never stopped looking at the sun, who never let the hours crumble in your heart made for eternity, who only aspire to one glory: Ascension . . ."

"Bonds retain me, walls made of shadow are around me still . . ."

"You only think of escape. That is the commencement of your second divinity, the one that you poets acquire . . . And those of you who never cease to say: 'It's necessary to depart!' are already en route."

"Yes . . . the moral summit of the lyrical world . . . I can see it. Perhaps I shall reach it . . . But expression, as tight and flamboyant as the hammer that one brings down in the forge . . . the sober and pure Victory who drapes her white sheet . . . the eagle planted by its thousand ruby claws in the heart of the dream and revealing therein, by the beating of harmonious wings, the infinite meaning . . . the impossible poured into a cup and offered to human thirst! Alas, what I want to engender, like a she-wolf lost in a desert of stars, is nothing on my cheeks but moist Silence. And the Genius has only left in my soul the perfume of his braziers and his . . . adieu."

"Eh! Do you believe that your desire does not animate Desire, that your torment does not aliment the sacred Furnace? Poets, you have solidarity, and sometimes, miraculously, the sigh that trembles on the lip of one of you suffices to provoke a tempest in the breast of another. The tears that you think vain irrigate celestially the meadow of one of your brethren, and you do not know the extent to which he owes its flowering to you, to you who have wept.

"Collectively, you poets are a great vibrant fatherland, and what does it matter whether the divine Voyager advances this way or that? All the echoes of his mysterious footsteps awake and cast mutually the cry that is the recompense of the living sun: 'He has passed this way! He has passed this way!'"

"Fraternity of dazzled souls! And yet, the songs of an individual cannot live if we do not want to kill within us the eternal Song. I have never marched outside of myself, without myself. A marvelous simplicity has always surrounded me with pride. 'I am,' I have said, at every hour of my existence. 'The universal harmony has welcomed me and enrolled me.' Strong in that thought, I have lived, my absolute nailed to the soul like a sun. And afterwards? Too bad."

"Go on, poet, go on. Delight is with you. Go on . . ."

"Sorrow seems to me to be a wound in infirmity. Among poets, is it not inconceivable and impossible that Initiates, accursed or fortunate, are not tempests of joy and avidity, that we—the tongues of the mouth of Miracle, a dancing and flamboyant dragon—should lament! It is impossible that those living on lyricism feel that they bear their future decomposition within them, and drag their skeleton like an eyeless witness looking into the void. That is not true! Our tombs, poets, we shall cover with roses and decorate with a veiled urn, but we will not admit it, and we will always see our coffins rising up, in order to launch them into the chaos of chaos on our shoulders full of stars."

"A moving fresco! But the poet never knows whether the symbol rises toward the Divinity or whether it descends. No matter! An image is already another world . . ."

"What! You're resuming the form of the imperious and charming cat, of the black and pure Presence . . ."

"You've just merited it. All hope casts you back to your primal spirits, poets. I salute you . . ."

THE WITCH

THE WITCH IN THE CONVENT

The lay sister left us in presence, my grandmother, me and Jesus.[1] The last-named, as fresh as a rose with forget-me-not eyes, smiled in the blond crop of his beard. He and I cast a glance at one another understood one another. The lay sister, who fatally lacked elegance, and her formidable and puerile abbatial keys, her candid and aggressive snout, her gray robe that recalled the odor of the humble mouse of the corridors, did not astonish unduly the ten-year-old witch who had still been pursuing the day before, from rock to rock in the Ariège,[2] the

1 The feminine noun *converse*, which I have translated as "lay sister," refers to affiliates of a Catholic religious community who are not ordained members of it. The daughters of upper class families, especially orphans, were often sent to be educated in convents in the nineteenth century, which served as convenient prison-camps until they reached marriageable age.

2 The Ariège is a département in the Occitan region of France, centered on the town of Foix. The area was ravaged during the so-called Albigensian Crusade, justified by its propaganda as a persecution of heretics known as "Cathars" [i.e., *katharoi*, or "puritans"], although it was really a cynical political land-grab, which concluded with the siege of Monstségur in 1244 and a subsequent massacre: an infamous item of history not forgotten or forgiven even in the twentieth century and surely not entirely

siren with the heart of snow, the intrepid and fugitive daughter of the Pyrenees.

Holy Madame Angélique, who came as I entered, placed her desiccated parchment hand on my shoulder and said in her shrill voice while introducing me to her rapacious and pompous face: "This child is ours. We will make a little saint of her."

My grandmother bowed with all her plush, extravagantly black mantle, and made no apology to the ten-year-old witch who was being snatched from nature, recommending her to order, assiduity and manual labor, particularly the mending of stockings, and finally, if possible, to learning Latin.

The little door closed on the little grandmother, and the tall Holy Madame Angélique with the eye of an ageing imperial eagle hurried the sister of the mandrake into the catechism hall.

"Tell yourselves firmly, my children," moaned a lanky black-clad man, "that those tortures will last forever and ever and ever. Hell, that place of unimaginable punishments into which a single mortal sin will plunge you . . ."

The sister of snakes opened her golden eyes very wide. She could smell the hay and the sunlight, and, nudging her neighbor, a paltry little fruit of the bourgeois espal-

---

irrelevant to the particular anticlericalism of the heroine. The "crusade" in question gave birth to the Dominican Order, which was subsequently given authorization to conduct heresy-hunts, employing the methods of Inquisition, and was thus ancestral to the image of the witch popularized in the sixteenth and seventeenth centuries and deliberately transfigured by Jules Michelet in *La Sorcière*.

ier, with her elbow, she said to her, too loudly: "When do we get to play marbles?"

A nun with the suspicious and scrupulous face of an old ape approached. "New girl, know that one does not speak during catechism. Monsieur the almoner will give you a bad mark!"

In fact, he shouted: "A drop of blood in the brain—bang!—and it's done! In what state will you appear, my children, if death surprises you between one moment to the next, before the terrible judge? What will you place on the right-hand plate of the balance? On the left—O terror!—I see your lies, your disobedience, your laxness, your greed . . ."

The sister of foxgloves and scorpions took a piece of dry bread from her pocket and devoured it gluttonously.

"New girl, get out!"

That phrase was often repeated in the convent and the religion that it taught. Nothing was more natural. Witches are faggots for the pyre, and when witches have approached nuns and priests they understand the fundamental antagonism that renders a breviary so suspect to a horn, and *vice versa*.

Unfortunately, the excessively lucid eyes of child witches who, full of candor, play with owls and the Devil, can only see with terror the majority of men in soutanes and women in cornettes. Among their ancestors, doubtless, walked numerous black penitents, jailer nuns with eyes at prison loopholes, and how could I have accepted, without protest and rebellion, that limited and persecutory population—me, whose maternal grandmother was a beautiful brunette mountain-dweller, a green-eyed witch who, in her savage park, recited the verses of Desbordes-Valmore, the celestial damned woman of the midnight owls?[1]

As for the nuns of my adolescence, here are a few of them: Holy Madame Paul, the imbecile gossip with the deep boyish voice; Holy Madame Eustache, so gluttonous and so pious—in the convent, fervor and bulimia go together—whose burps were as zealous as her rosaries; Holy Madame Rosalie, grotesque and apoplectic, with an enormous neck and a falsetto voice, stifled by plethora, hypocrisy and holy water; Holy Madame Pascal—the superior—with the head of a worldly Jesuit and a prudent, spoiled smile, soft, mild and dubious, an overripe and wormy fruit of the celestial grain-lofts; Holy Madame Augustine, inhabited in the belly by fibroids and in the soul by elegiac perfidy; Holy Madame Bernard, the "Voltaire" of the convent, an "encyclopedist" suspected by the superior, but such a picturesque compound of an Etruscan vase, a gendarme and a shark, that the sympathy she inspired in us caused us to burst into irreverent laughter in her wake.

Could I forget Holy Madame Roch, brutal and obtuse, punishing *en masse* like Jehovah, the Good Pastor's

1 Marceline Desbordes-Valmore (1786-1859) was the only female poet included by Paul Verlaine in his catalogue of "poètes maudits." Although resident in the far north of France she befriended the young Honoré de Balzac and his associate Samuel Henri Berthoud, and helped them to further their careers; the latter, in particular, made significant contributions to the burgeoning tradition of literary Satanism. Desbordes-Valmore's melancholy poetry reflected her troubled life and she was an expectable inspiration and role model for Picard.

surly dog, a fanatical conductress of the tribe, having—the unfortunate woman!—hair and keys everywhere? Her heavy jaw, her heavy crucifix and her heavy bell made her a permanently angry Dominic, but from time to time, as she was passionate about the Eucharist, she bellowed the name of Jesus with a desperate immodesty, and we perceived then that she possessed ravishing blue eyes.

Could I forget, too, Holy Madame Maurice, cordial, intelligent and generous everywhere except in the dormitory in the evening? There, when we undressed and it was a matter, for us, of precipitating ourselves toward the secrecy of the "little room," and the trumpet of Absaroth[1] resonated in her ears, she extinguished the gas abruptly, struck her hollow breast with a sonorous fist, and vociferated litanies to chastity that, by reflex, made us think of libertinage.

I ought also to cite Holy Madame Agathe, a mummy and she-ape, yellow-eyed and yellow-skinned, correct and insensitive, posing the same fixed and shiny gaze on the monstrance and the children's footbath in the wash-house; and Holy Madame Lucien, so harsh to orphans, pug-faced, sylvan and brown but covering with white and blue frills her niece, the sanguine and choleric Marie-Thérèse, consecrated by her faunesque stepmother to the "good Mother of all."

And make room for Holy Madame Marie of Jordan, or Lebanon—I can no longer remember—with the eyes

---

1 Absaroth is an eccentric variant of Astaroth, the name of a grand duke in the hierarchy of Hell, popularized by the witch-hunter Johann Weyer; it is presumably derived from the name of the Phoenician goddess Astarte.

of a tortured calf and a nasty odor, fifty years old in her flabby rotundity and excessive height, who satirized in a rondeau the "unfortunate" thirty years of one of her sisters in religion, celebrated in a madrigal a novice still slightly restive and a Lamb enraged by amour, rhyming "*ange*" with "*fange*" twice over, and recounted in a villanelle her transport to the divine meadows where, with a lily-of-the-valley at her waist and the harp of David on her fingers, she danced for the Lord in the midst of her "young companions." In the meantime, with a terrible urgency, she pursued us into every corner, a crucifix in one hand and a portrait of Marie Alacoque[1] in the other, her manuscripts in her pockets and under the bib of her lugubrious apron. And when she had passed by furtively, what did we find on our lecterns? Incendiary confessions in the form of images in which there was no question of anything but hearts transpierced by swords and lilies over which apostolic tongues were distributed by a dove with an implacable eye.

But as we rejected all her advances she fell into a languor that rid us of her, for, having gathered the whole community around the distinguished acne of her large morose features, the superior, justly alarmed, sent her to exalt with verse the retired nuns in a house of retreat in the country and the pig that the daughters of Sion were fattening for the feast of Sainte Catherine.

Finally, I certainly ought to introduce that other

1 Marguerite-Marie Alacoque (1647-1690) was a mystical nun who promoted reverence for the Sacred Heart (of Jesus). After suffering official disapproval while she was alive her visions of Jesus eventually acquired a great posthumous popularity; she was canonized in 1920.

"bride of the Lord," Holy Madame Savinien, the mistress of the boarding-school, with the terribly beautiful dark eyes, and the perfectly scrupulous dental pronunciation, and bad, bad, bad—oh, the slut!—like the silence of a cell that one no longer loves, a veiled viper manufacturing poison in the glands of her flat jaw, in the shadow of the cross.

Soulless, almost all of them, those saints, as well as those who only worked for their own eternal salvation. No loins and yet obese, balloons of brown cloth. No bones, and yet skimpy, phantoms of black cashmere.

And yet, among those cicadas of canticles, those mosquitoes exasperated around burning candles, those moles of the road of the cross, those ants devouring the supreme crop, those caterpillars of the morning rose, those termites of the sacred parvis, there was Holy Madame Joséphine, who dreamed of all her expansive and weary whiteness, and Holy Madame Anne, who was nothing but mystical aristocracy, youth and wisdom, but also despair. I kissed the hands of the one I called "Sainte Dolor." I watched the one I called "Sainte Cécile" dying of regrets, music and her large black eyes. Poor vases of election filled with tears by failed lives!

Two or three nuns, harmonious in their vocation, loved children, forget-me-nots, meditation, smiles, rays of sunlight on their white cornettes and the footsteps of Jesus in their cells . . .

Grace, poetry, prayer of monastic captivity, I have nor forgotten you. But the others? The twenty others? The thirty others? All the others? Do you remember them, vibrant and pretty Holy Madame Claire, you who wept over against my rebellious hair so many times?

The convent succeeded, at first, with the perfection that it brought to little things, in rendering its paltry and ostentatious God incomprehensible to me.

Furthermore, in the idolatrous churches of the Midi in which the sumptuous playfulness of the nuns paraded us, I was only capable of terror or poetry. There, very pale, I respired the damp odor of corpses and catacombs; there I was inflamed for those imbecilic and charming preachers who have the neck of a bull amid the stained glass, and the great agitation of wild horses under their brown robes.

Sometimes I flowered, a lily corrupted by desolation and penitence, over the branches of pompous candlesticks; sometimes, bunches of myrtle seemed to me to be agreeable whips for which the impetuosity of little fifteen-year-old saints ought to wish.

I fled the miserly cloths, the ephemeral candles, the chairs that groaned in bearing morose prayers, the humiliations in woolen skirts of those poor relatives in vainglorious chapels, the devotees with lowered eyes, but I was smitten by the occasional satanic blue Gabriel in the rose-window of an apse.

Gradually, the appetite for a special kind of dissipation took possession of me; I put all the church into "imagery," which frightened me and enchanted me—and I experienced the joy of a little Satan, playful, sinful and avenged. And then, the victorious red color of the windows always predisposed me to games of inspiration, slaughter and desire.

I was a poet. Poets ought not to be confined. It is dangerous for them and for what surrounds and limits them. They escape as best they can, those convicts, and as I am equitable, I shall say that the nuns were nuns, but that the witch was a witch.

Soon, I was extraordinarily astonished, here by the funerary drapes, the icy boxwood, the sinister aspergillums, the obtuse officiants, suppliants and avengers of the dead—the living among the living!—the entire Carnival of Fear, and there by the greedy saints who were incessantly at grips with the avarice of widows and the small coin of orphans; they always ended up robbing the former and making the latter sniff a little hellfire. It's true that those fabulous rogues signed, in return, fabulous assignats: *indulgences*, and I don't know what stupefied me more: the humble collecting box of that petty trader Antoine or the rutilant heart of the flashy foreigner Judes, who, in his quality as a good fellow, extracted emeralds and rubies from the adventurers of devotion.

However, I admit that those frightful demonstrations and interested idolatries did not prevent me from swooning before the angular sweetness of Philomènes and Roses de Lima,[1] or making my infantile communion of the plaster of their innocence, or throwing myself into the furnace of beatific topazes invaded by the rising sun, with a heart ravaged by gold and folly, or absorbing

---

1 Saint Philomena was an allegedly-consecrated virgin whose remains were discovered in a Roman catacomb in the early nineteenth century. Rose of Lima (1596-1617) was a Dominican lay sister canonized in spite of never having taken Holy Orders.

myself in the adoration of one of those reliquaries that contain apotheosis and damnation, and around which are crystallized, in insolent jewels, the sweat and fear of Christian slaves, or of cherishing the white Virgin at the starry hours of litany . . . but was that piety? And I shuddered with a strange and prodigious sadism in contemplating the eternity of saints in crimson robes, saints armed with distaffs or ornamented with the excessive femininity of doves, roses avid for perfection with the sulky lips of tempted virgins, poppies that, determined not to pass thorough purgatory, solemnly renounced, with a scapular around their neck, the sensualities of the vale of tears, penitent buttercups who died of repentance on pyres of thorns, hearts full of a provocative and sinister passion, exceedingly weary Good Shepherds, the young Louis de Gonzagues,[1] anemic, green, atrabiliary and shady, the elegantly funereal pansy at the foot of the obliquely frivolous cross, the unleashed confessor coiffed with a sage turtle-dove, the decent Hermit delivered to the goatskin and the litter of golden hay, I sensed that all those splendors that reign over the vellum and the gelatin, with too much candor to be pure, were perhaps inspired—who knows?—by the Devil, but surely not by the God of whom I had a vague, amorous and formidable conception.

Thus, in churches, when I was not stifled by anguish, everything delighted me in drawing me away from

---

1 Aloysius de Gonzaga (1568-1591) was a chronically ill Italian Jesuit canonized in 1726; several schools are named after him in various countries, including a famous one that preserves the French form of his name.

the God they revealed, including the Biblical brutes in stained glass who made me sparkle with lyricism: Abraham armed with the sword, Jacob tempted by the golden ladder, Moses streaming with the bitter sweat of the predestined of Jehovah, and the hysterical eater of locusts who, launching famished and insipid beasts into the terror of agonizing worlds, condemned Creation, opening furious and terrible eyes upon it, one of which is a red moon and the other a sun gone mad.

But God? But God? But God?

Those delirious deformations provoked and excused my own: the beautiful Proserpine, the mad unicorn, the resuscitated witch, the miraculous Lady with the cloven hoof. Poetry no longer quit the wild and exalted child. One day, she threw the violets of Thaïs over the enormous horny feet of a prophet, a rock inhabited by penitence, devouring crickets and perfumed southerly winds . . . One evening, in the sensitive crystal of a pure vase dreaming on an isolated little altar, she heard Cleopatra's pearl tinkle . . . Another time, she saw, falling adorably, the obol of Saint Mary of Egypt, who was accessible, by dint of sanctity, to the concupiscence of passers-by . . .

But God? But God? But God?

As for the confessional, that dungeon in the darkness of which the drains of human misery and mediocrity splashed, that box coiffed with dust—and what symbolic sculpture!—I held it in horror. No confidence fell from my lips there at which I can blush, but I was . . .

delicate, and I believe that my delicacy was the primary reason for all the revolts of my life. I abominated the priest in that ridiculous sad prison. He reeked of the sacristy and ugliness, he looked at me through troubled and curious spectacles, he sighed continually, offended me with his questions, and then, the "how many times" that followed the confession always seemed, to my quickly diverted mind, the leitmotiv of a frivolous society game.

One day when I went into the chapel in order to salute some culpable azure Gabriel, suddenly, sitting in the confessional, attentive and amused, his finger lifted and his beard dancing, the Satan appeared to me who knew, like me, that ingenuousness and malice are two gracious twin sisters when they frolic in the pure air and mingle their games—which, for the former, consist of picking roses, and for the latter of sniffing them.

How would I have been able to say my catechism that time, in all innocence, replete with so many precepts, laws, threats, rigors, when I myself had such a rudimentary and touching notion of what you call "good" and what you call "evil"? But I was, as yet, only an extravagant and dreamy little girl, and the monastic proof only burst upon me later, in all its violence. It lasted for years. I had performed that charming and empty act, my first communion, with a desperate and rhapsodic fervor, but the Hell with which people never ceased to threaten me, in that epoch, remained in my soul terrible and poetic.

Soon, I felt tears of anguish crowned with thorns falling on my head. I heard the play of bones and chaplets in the fingers of the nuns. I felt burning and sulfurous breath in the curtains of my little schoolgirl's bed, already touched by Javel water. I knew the depravities of fasting, of the road of the cross, of confidences made in a whisper to a black robe which sinned in listening to sin moan, of the examination of conscience inspiring secret manipulations that, between the hysterical plaster and the panting wood of obscure chapels, breathless as much by virtue of concupiscence, was fear of the Devil.

The incessant inquisition of the God of the terrible *de profundis* no longer quit my soul, which the smallest garden had once rendered so free.

The sister of violets, those demonic sweetnesses, paled, became tall and serious, no longer smelling of sunlight and hay but of alpaca wool and the degenerate soap that Holy Sister Mercanti de Jesus sold between picking rhubarb and papal benediction. The sonority of her joyful spirit had long been cracked against the iron door of Catholic tribunals. Poor seventeen-year-old witch! Already, that receptacle intoxicated by suns believed in the tears and tortures of the reproved. Barking priests and mewling nuns invaded her.

"You are lost, dreaming in the Lord's meadows? But consider yourself then, excessively gracious witch with dimpled cheeks and chestnut-colored tresses under the autumn sun: Your gilded eyes? Damnation. Your velveted breast? Corruption. Your cheek attentive to the miracle of the moment? An offense to the saints with faces corroded by ulcers and the fear of God. Your innocence? An ambush. Your modesty? All malice. Your silence? All sin.

In that crisis, an Oblate came to preach a retreat to us. He was not light-hearted. He must once have planted a few perishable tulip bulbs at Port-Royal[1] while meditating on predestination. Père Olivier was a man of forty, fat and devoid of strength, dying of sanctity, and implacably brown. He wore a ferociously polished copper crucifix over his breast and his large bruised eyes were those of a heavily made-up martyr.

When I implored him, one evening, in the parloir where he put himself at the disposal of "souls in torment," he reassured me in approximately these terms: "Run toward lust, young woman, and you are doomed; but kneel your fifteen years on our cold tiles and not one of your prayers will not say to you: 'You are saved.' If you clutch the perfume of life in your burning girdle, our rigor will condemn you; but if you wear a cilice on your lacerated loins, the infinite silence of monastic stones will no longer cease to torture you, for know this: in the labyrinths of Grace, one seeks, one finds, one follows, one loses God . . . one encounters him again . . . suddenly, he escapes you . . . he extends his arms to you . . . you speak to him . . . who responds? Oh, too often our tears are more vain than the droplets of funerary candles . . . the cry of a saint who no longer dares to die . . .

"Your health? An evil spirit animates it. Detest therein the insolent and mocking temptation. But if you merit the humble estate of malady, fear therein the tremulous

1 The abbey of Port-Royal-des-Champs, associated with a number of highly reputed schools became the center of the stern Reformist movement known as Jansensim in the 1660s, by which time the movement was under fierce attack by the Jesuits, which concluded with Jansenism, like Catharism before it, being declared heretical; the abbey was closed and its buildings razed in 1708.

and plaintive temptation. You see, whatever you do in mortal life, one only changes demons. Who are the most proven among our brethren? The flourishing or the desiccated? Is joy more tempting than dolor? Is the flesh more fallible than the bones? Does fasting not damn us as much as bread? Is the eternal snare not extended in the silk of chasubles and the coarse cloth of monastic habits?"

Ah! "Poor!" as one says among us, and with an accent that would have disarmed Jehovah himself!

It was necessary after that conversation of the Oblate and the witch, to see the latter's seventeen years!

One evening, she saw the fleshless Pascal of Jansenius[1] on the threshold of her eternal destiny. From then on she refused the milky Sunday bread, and the Thursday walk when, while going to visit the "Solitaries," grim cloistered nuns, she and her fellows bought a sou's worth of peanuts in the suburb corroded by light and sometimes flowery with an infantryman's trousers.

Crushed by the idea that she was an infimal but very responsible eternal question mark before Olivier's divine Hurluberlu, the sterility of his love, the arbitrariness of his predilections, his tyrannies, his disgrace and his thunder, she finally knew—O Catholic perversity!—the scruple more corrosive than a wound, the anxiety more

---

1 The great mathematician Blaise Pascal (1623-1662), a pupil of the Port-Royal school, became the most important apologist for the beleaguered doctrine of Jansenism; his philosophy, summarized in his posthumously-published aphoristic *Pensées* (1670) became one of the accepted classics of French though in spite of its heretical taint.

disorganizing than a fever, the doubt more arid than the soil of vanquished Judea. That was the "good work." Poor seventeen-year-old witch! She became thin, no longer slept, avoided communion and appealed in whispers to her mother.

"A damned soul!" said the old nuns, adjusting their spectacles and their false teeth and passing around their neck scapulars of their own manufacture, whose blue and green silk seemed to have been vomited by some angelic gastritis, and Holy Madame Eustache's burps became as reproving as the thunder of Sinai.

But the seventeen-year-old witch who had sought God in fortunate nature, and who was presented instead with the God of monks and obsessives, fell into a disquieting melancholy. "Crisis of the eighteenth year," diagnosed the practicing doctor, a prolific devotee who, unctuous, modest and fervent, was reminiscent of a church candle father of eleven tallow candles.

Poor seventeen-year-old witch! God, for her, was what remained to her of the ever-absent maternal smile, all that she hoped for when she raised her eyes, as she was accustomed to do, beyond the horizon . . . but she was condemned to a God that was passed through a burette to become a vengeful cloud that bloodied, it was said, the hands of Marie Alacoque and set fire to the loins of Dominics and Torquemadas.

She had, in fact, her crisis of the eighteenth year. She was shut away, alone—the reprobate—in the infirmary, which being above the wash-house was also the fatherland of cockroaches. Then, after various proofs, she descended therefrom fresh, vigorous, sly and alive . . .

Faith—that of the convent—she had left on the mantelpiece of the sinister little room, at the feet of an indescribable savior of men who, with a dusty finger, presented his tomato-juice heart, while, devoid of a cornette, with a black shawl over her shaven head, regularly, at eight o'clock in the evening, the head nurse—Holy Sister Indifference to Death—leaned over her bed.

THE WITCH AND
MONSIEUR COMBIENDEFOIS

Without a soutane or a tonsure, Monsieur Combiendefois[1] is very widespread. When he is truly convinced,
how can one expect tolerance from him? Dogma is dogma, a canon is a canon.

Then, with casuistry under his nose like a snuffbox
and orthodoxy on his belly like a cataplasm, frightfully
sanguine between the monumental inkwell—*vanitas
vanitatum!*—and the humble conjugal nightlight—
Madame, let us make a Christian—he would lead
Torquemada himself to the pyre. What amused the
witch was that the marshmallow fanatic in question,
who reeked of the papal antechamber and the cotton
handkerchief, the heater and the devotee, pectoral syrup and pious maxims, would have escorted the grim
Inquisitor not in a hood but in a . . . nightcap.

Oh, that fury of worldly relationships and windows
overlooking the street! Like people sure of their facts he
always speaks in the name of the community: "You? You

---

1 i.e. "Mr. Howmanytimes," echoing a standard formula of the
inquisition of the confessional.

will roast eternally. Sins of the flesh? They are so swiftly expedited by us, they are so discreet, poor things. Those sins? Pooh!"

"Of course. They're yours."

"But the sin of pride . . . ! The sin or revolt . . . !"

"I have suffered terribly from your religion. In the name of what do you expect me not to protest?"

"It combated your detestable mind."

"Possibly. But what funny apostles it raised up against me. They tortured me even more by their examples than by their threats."

"What do you expect? They're men like others."

"Indeed . . . indeed . . . but in sum, it's not so much their weaknesses that I reproach, even though their sacerdocy ought to maintain them in grace and dignity, as I am maintained in dignity and race by my sarcerdocy, Poetry. What I hate in them is the excessively frenetic appetite for the grinding of teeth, for the torture and the eternal despair of others.

"One surrenders, in the end, to that delirious imagery, but think about the oversensitive children who no more lose their eyes at the age when one tries to enable their salvation with blows of the fist than the sun on their back. What a drama for those who have known that obsession! A holy ministry? Would you like one? To employ religiously, and render worthy of the research and possession of God, young souls who, fatally—but later—are hungry for God."

"A religion for everyone, then? We have been brought up in that one. We observe it, and remark that it is incompatible with the care that our household demands, responsible for three domestics, the establishment of our sons, the bad character of our daughters-in-law, the consideration that we obtain from our landed property and our defunct titles, with the prosperity of our factory or the renown of our notariat . . ."

"Dear predestined notaries!"

"What we know is that *we ought to damn you*, we who do not have . . ."

"Those devouring suns in the soul. *You ought to damn me*, you who once a year, at least, in order to be in regulation . . ."

"Precisely: in order to be in regulation."

". . . Go to recount your meager turpitudes to the robe that is always the same on the man who puts it on, eats too much, sins, wounds the purity of virgins, opens Gehenna to the souls of schoolboys, jokes with puerility and bonhomie or assists, indifferently and mechanically, those who carry out the hard labor of sweat one last time . . ."

"Our directors of conscience cannot all be François de Sales . . . But there is no salvation . . ."

"Outside the Church. I know . . . I know . . . as soon as a child of seven opens his catechism he falls upon that fundamental declaration. It's charming. But you, you will be saved, you who, once a year—at least—in order to be in regulation . . ."

"Precisely: in order to be in regulation."

". . . Receive on your tongue, withered by the bile of envy or the phlegm of intemperance, the bread of the Angels. Once, as a young virgin kneeling at the immaculate table, I fainted every time, in dread, before my share.

And yet, every time, too. I bounded when one of your ministers, in bureaucratic formulae, like a collector demanding that one pay taxes, *demanded* that I have faith."

"It's so easy!"

"Children without God? A sad thing, doubtless, but do you know what becomes of the children who have had *yours*, truly and fundamentally, when they do not bury themselves in cloisters, demented and desperate? Simultaneously outré and abulic, like you, or in revolt, like me, recklessly wanting something else, with burning tears on their faces . . ."

"You will roast eternally."

"Why?"

"Because you wanted something else."

"Yes . . . since my first hour, I had the Devil in me—which is to say, liberty. I exalt that predestination."

"Satan in you! Since your first hour! Wretch, wretch! You are one of those that the divine Savior . . ."

"I know: yours."

". . . Has marked for reprobation for all eternity."

"Why?"

"That is an unfathomable mystery. But, you see, the wings that lift you up and carry you away, which humiliate us, which slap us, which frighten us . . .

"They torture me most of all. The flight is such a great anguish when it commences! Those who have passed through baptism require so much courage—if you only knew!—in order not to be Catholics, for, as you say, it's so easy! But it's a matter of you, at present, you who are saved, who will have, forever and ever and ever, the certainty—and you experience a certain coquetry in it, fortunate privileged!—of a crown of roses on your head, powdered with the pellicles of functionalism, peeled in places, elegantly, by atherosclerosis and slightly dishonored by your security as taxpayers—for, in sum. Heaven is your retirement, my dear Monsieur Combiendefois . . ."

"We earn it."

"Yes, by not eating meat on Friday. I'm sick of hearing that you prefer salmon to beefsteak."

"Blasphemer! Heretic! Impious and doubtless lapsed!"

"Call me, simply: Poet. That's sufficient for my shoulders."

"You will roast eternally, but we, forever and ever and ever, face to face with the Spirit, will sense the nameless felicity bathing . . ."

". . . Your greedy mouth, of course. Each of us, will we not, will present to him our little notebook. On one He will write 0 and it will be Hell. On another 20/20, and it will be Paradise. On another, the average, and it will be Purgatory. There will be the cancerous, the mediocre, the strong in essay-writing and . . . the Teacher . . . as always. That, God? Oh, what was made of my adolescence, of my youth? I know what stupidity and what despair are dispensed among the holy patronnes of ulcers, the protectresses of convents and congregations, among the beadles who light the route to Eternity with fifteen-sou candles. I did not go to sleep once, when I was beautiful, chaste, avid for the noblest life and the greatest dream, without hearing myself menaced with sudden death, the vengeful God, and Hell—Hell!—by some nun, sickly or bloated with blood like an executioner. Among the eighty boarders of the convent of ***, if there were only me who was martyrized, since I was the most innocent, the most mystical, by that religion, of which I only knew the sensual snares and only retained the implacable condemnation, it would too many, too many, too many."

"You never cease to admit that you are possessed, wretch!"

"How do you understand it? In your terrible, paltry and ridiculous fashion, without a doubt?"

But silence. It will be more worthy of me, in the hour of my death, to turn my inspired face toward the rising sun.

Adieu, Monsieur Combiendefois.

THE WITCH LIBERATED

I enter the church again, but immediately I feel more desperate than a tombstone in an apse devoid of stained-glass windows.

"Let's get out of here," my soul says to me.

I resist, I sit down on a bench in order to listen to the icy depths of the holy place groan, and I breathe chilled incense in the chapels that reek of the death of white roses.

"Let's get out of here," my soul says to me.

"Not yet. It seems to me that perhaps, in a while, I'll be less afflicted here."

I touch the jealous linen with my hands, habituated to the passionate humility, the ingenuous order and the white avarice of convents. I look at the bouquets of little saints flourishing in the sensuality, chlorosis or innocence of fervor. I appeal to the saints, those who were poor, dirty and vagabond, and who made known to the vervain of the road their ulcers generative of bliss. But the saints with the figure of shepherdesses, the no-mad saints who, for my enchantment, carry staffs and beggar's wallets, those crazy adolescents, those humble lunatics, do not know me.

"Let's get out of here," my soul says to me.

I turn toward the patriarchs and the apostles magnified in stained glass. Violet desolation of pure tunics, pitiless golden crosses that reject me from the favors and the houses of the Spirit!

"Let's get out of here," my soul says to me. "Let's flee the confessional; the miraculous water is not for you, creator of miracles. It would flow in vain over your witch's face, more arid and more perfumed than the solitary heaths.

"What would you do with a vengeful and silent God, daughter of poetry and bursts of laughter? What would you do with a god who only communicated with you by means of the odor of the soutane and penitence? Oh, remember, every time . . . every time . . . that the restricted God has punished you. He made you bear against yourself accusations that had the bureaucratic redemption of madwomen. From each of your instincts a moaning tribe emerged. In the confessional, you prowled around lust with a sly expression and cursed a priest who had a hat over his eyes. Go and live, and you will be pure. Go render yourself naked, and you will be saved. Go and roll in the grass, and you are eternal . . ."

"Ah! And yet, I love God . . ."

"Yes . . . but you possess him in your dancing beasts, which browse the Golden Age in your dreams . . . For you, he is in nature with green horns, in discordant and joyful laughter, and your Satanism will save you among the butterflies whose wings fill with sulfur the fingers that have made you prisoner.

"Get away, get away from these rigid benches, from these paving stones, under which unconsoled bones still exhale sighs of contrition and Catholic dread.

"Get away from that organ, which never equals the wrath of your hurricanes and that of your silence.

"Get away from devotees and fanatics, you who have the sacred devotion of choice and pride, of the violence and hatred of everything that does not tend toward Love.

"Depart from here, you who want to make victorious darts of all the radiance of your spirit, you who know that there are only the accursed and slaves under the gaze of tyrants, you who think that wings can only be measured against wings and that the sons of Hope only respond to Infinity . . .

"Here, nothing wants you, the chairs reject you, the statues chase you away, the incense corrupts your powerful natural odor, the dolorous Form astonishes your body, which is only joy, liberty and movement.

"Get out. The ministers of this place will never absolve you . . . never . . . Even at the time of your first communion, which you made with an excessively pure soul . . . You are one of those, O predestined, whom nothing liberates except the dream, and who can only find peace in the florid revolt of universal demons.

"Go run in the wind, witch, and you will sense that your commencement was a flutter of wings and the very rhythm of sensuality."

"A little more . . . to see whether I was not mistaken, before, when the anemia of candles and the neurosis of canticles rendered convents intolerable to me. There, sighs did not move a single nightingale, gestures did not nourish a single grain of wheat . . . I had already understood that everywhere that walls loom up, prisoners groan . . ."

"You knew full well that beauty, the divine glories are, on your light fingers, matinal rays of sunlight, that eternity is yours, O Life forever transmissible, sap of leaves, sensitivity of antennae, blooming of roses . . . Blooming! Poet, poet, poet . . . Go rediscover the nameless God in free nature, and bloom in the thousand faces that have never prevented you from being beautiful, mingle with the recreation of the world, believe in nymphs, dance with the angels, caress fauns, cause buds to burst into flower alongside you, work miracles and spells, give your heart to the reproved, your soul to the holy Lyre, call poetry 'Our Lady of Satan,' throw your bare arms around the neck of all follies and consecrate your innocence, mysterious witch, to amour . . ."

"That's true. I'll immediately find my place in the sun. What am I doing here, brushing black robes when everything has the scent of carnations in my Spain, of sandalwood in my India, of cinnamon in my Arabia, when I listen to the silence of Jesus in my eternal Palestines . . . ?"

And you, Jesus, what about you? Shall we not be liberated? What have they done with your heart, which loved, like mine, lilies, children, the possessed, Holy Communion—that sabbat of purity and love—the cross, Barabbas and perfumes?

I turn my eyes away dolorously from that anatomical heart, from its sadistic and cruel crudity, and, plunging your sacred feet in the Sea of Galilee, my brother of dream and folly, I cleanse you of that somber apostolate, that accusatory redemption, that incessant reproach for having loved us too much, which does not go, divine brother, with your tresses of light and your dreams and your dreams, which the wind of Cedron bore away . . .

Soul of wheat, which doubtless only want to be the Host of an evening, in the innocent and rude caress of the Beloved . . .

In your name, you know, you who dreamed of God among men, the most inconceivable sanction has been invented: the eternal death of love . . .

Come with us! I am certain that you—you whom all poets and all dementias surround—would like to add the radiance of your eternal Mystery to the vigilance of the subterranean fire that the amiable round of the demons never ceases to stimulate, to rally around the dead the warm witches of the night.

And the corolla of sweetness and silence that represents your body and your blood, it is said, please bring it with you. It is liberated from the tongues that absolve the sins of the sacristy . . .

Ah, if the instant of God ought to dissolve ineffably in souls, say, Jesus, say that it is not with the aid of those formulae, it is not because of the conventional complaisance of one sinner for another, when a fancy chasuble leans over a submissive lip, pardoning routinely.

You would surely place the mysterious corolla, which wants to give more naïve graces, on daisies, and under the wings of birds, on the muzzle of a stray dog and the ardent heart of a wolf. And as the wolf only asks to hear your Gospel, it would listen to it, preached by you—you who have always been betrayed!—at your knees, with radiance in its ear, the kingdom of the Lord in its soul and peace in its maw, one evening when your robe would be the very lily of Genesareth.

You would offer the suave corolla that surely wishes to give itself to the most profound and most secret hungers, to the accursed who seek the Divinity in pride and martyrdom, to the reproved who are, strangely, the great Elect. And then, also—isn't it so?—to Magdalen and Judas . . . to her because she was blonde, to him because he was tempted, furtive and hanged.

THE WITCH AND LIFE

I am without sin, but culpable. Of what? Of everything. I am suspect, accused too much, and always in order that I should not be infinitely culpable. Those who love me know it and reproach me for it with a frightful persistence. They do not forgive me anything, neither a snigger of impiety nor the jaundice of jealousy. Liars, the dissolute and the malevolent find grace, but not me. People have never ceased to condemn me, including and above all in the ardent hearth of my terrible virtues.

I am without sin, but culpable. Of what? Of everything . . . and of the horror of abattoirs and the venom that forms in the glands of vipers. I know that the vitriol that is hurled in a poor and dirty face had my smile when it was enclosed in the desperate flask. The mother who murders her newborn frowns as I do when I meditate. The wolf that pursues another wolf at the conclusion of the carnage has my powerful and willful agility, and the dove that breaks its egg with a ferocious beak has a white neck like mine.

Malefactors think of me when they plunge into the shadows, and when they crush a heart in the mud, and my whispers accompany the silence of the clandestine key that opens the door beyond which murder is committed.

I wander through streets in which feather eiderdowns respire painfully, like asthmatics, in the depths of infamous ground-floor apartments. I stand up in the confessional between the penitent and the judge, a witness with a double visage, and both of them, while detesting me, implore my intervention.

I dance on the heart of acrobats on evenings of hunger and rain, and the sack of dead leaves is, above all, heavy with my weight on restive shoulders.

Oh, I know . . . I know my relationship with daggers and my alliance with poisons. The red Robe has been tinted with my blood every time the accursed have expiated, and I wonder whether I am more than a hanged man on the gibbet.

I am the blow of the fist in the brutality of wrath; in the nostalgia of women, the blue bird that beats its wings on the threshold of closed paradises, and in their covetousness, the diamond serpent that never ceases to sparkle and to vanish.

I throw roses at the winged impudence of Epicurean nights, but in the blessed ditch I am the sigh of old debilitated Christians and convicts, for none of us ever dies entirely of our poverty . . .

In beguinages I am the seraph who snows over the peace of naïve souls, but in monastic cells I make of my penitent shadow a cross on the wall, and Satan comes, weeping, to attach himself to it . . .

How culpable I am! I was an innocent child to whom malice was suggested by reproaching her for it. I was a chaste adolescent visited by the sensuality of sleep, masked by darkness and perfumed. I was a magnificent and dolorous spouse, but I departed from my hearth with maledictions, for I must undoubtedly have been, through years of superhuman devotion, infinitely culpable and worthy of the foreign street on to which I was thrown.

I only approached amour with my virtues and the faith that I had in God. I respected his brutal hands, gave to his lying gaze the sense of my verities, and in his aberration, prayed in a whisper for his redemption. What generosity was mine! I supported, in him, that which as odious to me, and adored that which tortured me in my soul. I forgave, in disgust and revolt, for the flesh is prompt to despair, and I only had, in sensuality, the refuge of the spirit. But amour charged me with worse, and I have been punished for my heroism, as the prostitute is for hers, for men make no difference between smiles . . .

And how Amour has said to me: "Go away!" and what a tone of reprobation it had! Have I, unwittingly, scorned his body or poured a bushel of stars into his soul? I don't know . . . I never know what emerges from me: lustral water or the mortal philter; or whether my wings have not the form of swords . . .

But the evening when, light, singing, limpid and musical, I spread roses over our couch, my lover and I became as somber as a night of expiation and we only sighed and remained silent in the flowers.

How culpable I am! People never cease accusing me. And when I show my valiant hands, my proud gaze, my pure solitude, when I declare of what I have been capable in renunciation, the implacable discipline, the sacrifice more exasperated than a suicide; when, seized by temporary weakness, I admit that I live without caresses, despoiled voluntarily of pleasure and deprived by my command of all terrestrial festivity; when I recount that: "I earn my bread, I pray, I am as mild as I can be, good beyond myself and—supreme magnificence!—in spite of myself . . ." when I cry: "My passions I have treated like daughters whose souls one tries to save, in furious convents, with whiplashes; my passions I have reduced to a belt of rope, roots without salt; I am for myself a torturer with an iron face; I wring my own neck—do you hear?—several times a day and cast myself breathless on to the floor of my inhuman prison . . . I am the exception and the example in the corrupt, avid, playful world . . ." they look at me; which is to say, they condemn me, and reply to me in a whisper: "You are capable of anything!"

I am culpable since I am accused. That is the great, the irremediable sin: I am accused . . . and there is surely justice in the anger with which our brethren strike us.

Everything is equitable, in sum.

What does my reason matter to those who discover the temptation of the loins of a panting dog everywhere I remain silent, my tears to those who contemplate my living eyes like those of cruel warblers, the fruits of my mildness to those who comprehend that I am the tree of violence, my perennial patience to those who divine that I am the inspired lightning and the devastating simoom?

What do my cilices matter to those who hear my inexhaustible secret laughter, the challenges that I launch and my unconscious wagers against my peace and my eternal salvation, my modest garments to those who see my poetry dancing in my shadow, as yellow as gorse charged with the fortune of the sun, my privations to those who tell themselves that the happiness of the predestined, whoever they might be, and desperate vocations, intoxicate me with the absolute and hold me upright, in the midst of everything, like annunciatory radiance?

What does my limited life matter to those who have learned that I am limitless, and that only my disdain for the mediocre and the approximate distanced me from the alliance of my peers when I wanted that of the Roman she-wolf and the divinized ox?

What do my austere habits matter to those who glimpse the ostentation, pride, scene-setting, the queens of Sheba, and Balthazars,[1] who hear the halloo of my desires in my hidden forests? And more than anyone, do I not know that I can make use of a whip as well to make

_____

1 Balthazar is employed here as an alternative name of the king known in English versions of the Biblical book of *Daniel* as Belshazzar, proverbially celebrated for the feast at which the legendary Writing on the Wall was inscribed by an invisible prophetic hand.

my passions dance and paw the ground in sparkling circus games, and that our greatest wisdom is always at odds with our profound perversities?

Blood which you shed over blood . . . reckless need to drain a breast in silence . . . to obtain the supreme pallor on the face of the condemned . . . oh, aborted crimes that bear your intention all the way to the funereal sun of a knife or the dancing pistils of digitalis, I admit you, myself . . .

Charity has for its excess, in souls like mine, despotism. What does my devotion matter to those who cry that I belong to the race of fanatical saints whose habits catch fire at the place of the heart, that to love, for me, is to take and reign, to load my cherished prey on my back and make my secret substance in my solitude in nourishing the grim heart that must always beat and to which the love that it experiences is sufficient, as the worlds he had created are sufficient to God?

My merits . . . yes . . . they are tangible but paltry, almost human. What are they by comparison with the possibilities inspired by my invisible lands and my infinite turbulence?

How culpable I am, since I am simultaneously this receptacle and this universal motor! To think, to sense, to imagine, to dream, what culpability! And how responsible I am for everything that I conceive! What a being makes are the divinities that possess her. Everything is equitable, and without dolor and without anger I accept the suspicion of all, since, as soon as I stuttered, I sensed my heart of a child-poet invaded by the Knowledge that makes you, my God—forgive me!—the great Culpable!

THE WITCH AT HOME

I

The Possessed

As soon as she had given herself to a sordid sorcerer, and then to another sordid sorcerer—they are all sordid when they have human form—the witch was purified forever. "There, that's pleasure!" she said, chewing the bushy herb that is so freshly bitter to pure saliva, and she laughed over simples, whipped by the wind. Then the universe saw the divine threat in her eyes, and the following night, she was buried beneath her own sigh.

The witch is not feeble enough—thank God!—to want to be two, she who is without number, and who can tell whether, by virtue of her dreams, in which the ingenuity of Satan of the seven laughs reigns, the perfect resource and the end of ends are, for her, in the unconsciousness and the activity of her repose?

By virtue of a flower that is presented to her and shows her that she can fecundate dust in her perfumed silence, the witch becomes a flower.

If a bush desires spring in all its thorns, already red with weeping coral, the witch is suddenly the nest in that bush—which is to say, three eggs and four wings.

If a bronze is stirred, the witch belongs to the sonority of all its slow and massive heart.

If a vegetal poison reveals its presence to the witch, she employs it immediately in an embalmed and clandestine crime, the consummation of which renders her more intoxicated than a mandrake by sunlight.

If music is lively, the witch, at the final chord, is more harmonious than water flowing over the feet of mild sylvan presences.

If a god descends, the witch rises in his place.

If a dancer wears away her languor in the sacred rhythm, the witch has the appearance, even more than her, of a serpent amorous of flutes.

If a perfume passes, the witch, whose armpits have the odor of goat and violets, sweats it, multiplying its potency and sweetness a thousand times.

If a hand touches her, the witch learns that the place of sensuality is, for her, on her pink toenail as well as her brown eyebrow.

If a kiss summons her, the witch responds via the hundred nightingales that the cage of her beak contains.

If a bellowing is heard, the witch, covered with the hide of russet cows, armed with pacific horns, listens to the melancholy call of the pastures of the nameless pastor in the cowbells.

If a garden sighs, the witch has the soul of the foliage. If a jungle groans, the witch has the loins of a she-wolf. If the setting sun plants its red cross in the pinewoods, the witch, like an owl filled with the wisdom of the kabbala, alights, with Hell in her eyes, at the summit of the radiant gibbet, which is gradually extinguished.

If spring plays with the flute and the reed-pipe, the witch becomes a turtle-dove, rolling in her throat the pearl of intoxication, and flaps her wings in the second when the gods run out of breath.

If a seed falls, the witch takes root in the subterranean earth and already sees her leafy trophies swaying in the wind.

And if the Devil is thirsty . . .

Then the witch, who is no longer anything but a golden spark, feels herself borne to the dry lips like a cup.

"By Satan! That's it, pleasure, that ridiculous haste, that despair of a marionette whose strings have just broken?" Oh, let the witch laugh! Let a sorcerer approach her henceforth! Rebellion and laughter will receive him, horns forward, like goats.

Do you know, sorcerer, the flexible branch on which I balance, which makes the tree sway all the way to the land of the dead? Do you know the ascension that transfigures me and the tidal wave that flagellates me with the hurricane of its gallop? Do you know the thyme precious to my warmth, the nettle agreeable to my restive blood, the holly that reckons with me and its cruelty, which completes me?

Do you understand? No. What do I care? But Satan, subtle and modest, who visits me in my sleep, milder and more placid than a child's, has only ever mingled me with him by means of the enchantment of poetry. I swear to you that I do not know his male vigor, but only his lyrical intoxication, and by way of the magic of the images that he presents to me, he is my most direct lover, although the most secret.

I would have myself exorcised, believe me, if my initiator showed me, at the hour of amour, the tip of his ear, his hairy chest, or what common lovers show—which, believe me, is certainly nothing much. And above all, I would dread—oh, so fearfully—to be the witch who fornicates with the lowest and most slovenly demons of the sabbat! No similar shame has ever happened to me . . . do you believe it?

How many of my peers have been subjected to broken horns, fiery and fuming tails, dangling tongues and cloven hooves, and the navel in which the suave eye of a renowned sinner is mounted! One of them—poor thing—is incessantly the prey of a one-eyed parrot, a forever impenitent ape, and a facetious pig coiffed with a fleur-de-lysed bicorn torn from the head of a dead megalomaniac.

And then . . . and then . . . the horrible complicity of the broomstick and the procuress cauldron, of the toad coupled to the bellows in which the evil spirits of sulfur and phosphorus make an insensate racket, of the curtly-clad goat which has a full brazier in its behind . . .

Oh, what a terrible vision!

But can you believe that I do not sense myself to be divine when the cry that liberates me springs from the voice of a bird?

Can you believe that, by virtue of the splendor of my dreams and the goal that they pursue, I do not salute the predestination of my being, which belongs to nothing that has a limit and knows satiation? Who can ever know what the night has wanted of me and how, in the fantastic world to which sleep transports me, the presence of a rose or the respiration of sensitive moss is sufficient to vanquish me in sensuality?

But what counts is that my soul, in the most distant realms, receives the waves of my supreme frisson, that the creative fête adds to my fulgurant moment, that the consent of the universe bears my joy as a bacchante bears a cluster of grapes, that the mystery, in taking my intoxication astray, renders it infinite. Ah, it's then that my sigh falls from the highest wrath: that of crimson flowers and wings beating the azure, that I only die of eternal vitality, that my perfection, in the instant, is realized by the profound travail of everything that germinates, flowers, murmurs, crawls, flies and radiates, and that I become, so complete is the harmony between the sensation and the dream, the spouse of ears of wheat or the pink moon.

. . . Of snakes similar to blue crowns . . . of lizards playing in the sunlight, like topazes, and meditating, like emeralds, in the shade . . . of tortoises that illuminate their miserly carapaces with the fires of their ruby eyes . . . of leopards that try themselves in human stances and stand upright in forests moist with moonlight . . .

of nightingales that veil themselves with their music . . . of tribes of ephemerae that swirl, drawing me away and die at the moment when I embrace the unspeakable . . .

. . . Of aggressive doves that I chase away with the vanquished gesture that reveals my forever unsubmissive soul . . . the second that quivers on my finger like a dragonfly that wants to open its wings . . . the silence that listens around me to things I can no longer hear and for which I search with the fervor of adorable anguish . . .

. . . Of ribbons that multiply, in my arms, the light friction of their azure . . . the wing, in the form of a dagger, of migratory swallows; their cry, which is like a rapid and harsh scintillation . . . the plaint of the grasshopper in its grassy solitude . . . a sandal crimson-tinted by the dawn, which dances for a shepherdess while, in the miracle of plenitude, I am the glory of the movement!

. . . The curlew that cleaves the thickness of the vegetal damp with a flight for which hunters lie in wait, when I too experience the intoxication of flight under the burning eyes of the ambush . . .

. . . That odor of violet when dusk is such a sweet autumn within the autumn, and me, that season filled with languor . . .

The necklace that makes the Orient ring at my neck . . . that white dress that I put on and which is suddenly the red dress that I rip in liberation . . .

Ah, sorcerer, those are my dreams. I have so many others! The marvel is that they make of me the *possessed*, in every sense of the word, and Satan, who, for my delight and his own, invents them ever more strange and charming, is, in truth, a unique lover.

*

Out of here, sorcerer! You are only rich in your appetites and your organs: paltry things when one knows a kiss more substantial than the pasture of bestial hunger, when the sunlight of wheat-fields in which quails palpitate ignites luminously over the heart of universal Amour.

Oh, the witch soon knew the poverties, the affronts and the disgusts of real couches! She emerges therefrom soiled, lessened, hateful, replete with claws and bites. And you, who call yourself a sorcerer but whom I must call a male, since you have his brutality and indigence, would like to drag the witch toward the dry litter and make yourself the enemy who remains, every time, frightened by having seen his dream stunned, his desire enchained, his dance dishonored, and his arms, which only aspired to infinities, broken . . .

Get out! You are ugly, impure, ferocious, poor, poor, poor . . . Where are your nuptial bees? I have sensed them in all the flora.

Where are your vampires with starry eyes? I am the owl the soars above sepulchers that their light corpses quit, carrying their precious ash in Elysian urns.

Where are your aerial monkeys, which throw themselves from liana to liana into the heart of the forest. Hush! I am the forest.

*

I have a familiar saying: "Elsewhere! Elsewhere!" Well, I mean by it that I am not for you, nor for the others, nor for any of the realities of this transitory world.

"Elsewhere" is, for me, the land of foliage and warm darkness where ecstasy rains in golden drops . . . the shore where the winds become furious and lyrical in listening to the promises of voyages . . . the dazzling Golden Age in which the rhinoceros emerges from the long marsh-grass and approaches me, sober and decorated like a sage charged with primitive secrets.

"Elsewhere" is, for me, those astonishing prisons full of captive swords and crucified jewels . . . it is the extraordinary world in which I hear the voice of the blood, of the thought, of the dead, of the terrible passion that no human hunger has yet devoured . . .

But you don't understand.

Only know that "elsewhere" is mine when the night exalts around my repose the eternity of things, and that the golden drop that splashes on my forehead, the wind that beats my dress and wants to depart, the salvation of the pachyderm that laughs with its entire mouth, sparkling with knowledge, the prison that offers its martyrized treasures, and the voice that speaks to me from the depths of the ages in the name of the boundless power, are for me generators of unknown delights, and that after having sensed the inconceivable in sensuality, I am disdainful of the infimal habitual embrace.

You don't understand . . . don't understand . . . what do I care? But I counted scarcely sixteen years when, already, sleep taught me the authority, the folly, the song, the glory of the Devil who makes for the senses and the soul of his creatures the great wing-beat of unexplored universes.

And yet I was so pure! But beautiful and mysterious, and always quivering like oats in the wind of the meadows . . .

And if my confessor—ha ha ha!—charged me with penances, covered me with muffled invectives, don't think that it was because of my sins—I didn't commit any—but because—ha ha ha!—of my golden eyes.

II
The Inspired

I don't know what I sing. I don't know anything that others think they know. I never interrogate anyone. When I am silent, sly and distant, it's in order to lose myself in the conversation of little girls and goldfinches, and my genius is my bursts of laughter in the faces of the wise.

"May I approach you, witch?"

"Who are you?"

"Bémolus, the poet."[1]

". . . I'm beautiful by virtue of the harmony of my gestures attached to my soul like grape-clusters to a vine. I'm mild with an entire vanquished violence and because, since that time—alas!—many beasts have been whipped. I'm mad because of all those trees that make a hurricane in my silence, a tempest of green leaves, a tempest of hope that blows in the wind, in the wind, through a thousand pure mouths . . . I'm mad."

1 This esoteric name had previously been used as that of the oldest of the spirits of chagrin featured in "Les Génies chagrins," the allegorical short story by Picard published in the "Mille et un Matins" section of *Le Matin* on 3 August 1921, translated in the appendix to the present text. Bémol is the French term for the musical note B flat, a sarcastic reference to the hypothetical poet's downbeat (or decadent) turn of mind.

Bémolus (*aside*): "So I've been told."

". . . I only have sensations and dreams. The former are the flesh of intelligence. The others are the prophetic spirit. When I touch a flower, I've understood everything. When I imagine one, I've created it."

"Listen to me, witch."

". . . I'm religious by virtue of all the forests that have cast shadows in my soul. But I have no greater glory than my fury, on the days when I think that nature is an incessant and splendid revolt and that the oaks are mounting an assault on God."

"You don't have the air of one accursed, though. Your eyes are like light."

"Shh! I am one accursed: a sign of divinity. You don't understand? Tell yourself, simply, that I have the blue laughter of lightning, the irresistible tide of deluges, the wings of which—cyclones or rebellion—swirl, rise up and fight. There's only one thing that counts: that's to have wings."

"Ah, witch, how extraordinary your joy is! Personally, I have the melancholy of forgotten lutes . . . the fearful silence of mountain lakes . . .

The Witch (*aside*): "Another one!"

"Witch, I am like a hungry beast."

"Eat."

"Witch, I am like a thirsty beast."

"Drink."

"Witch, I am like a beast that has received the entire charge of a rifle in the belly, and is awaiting its annihilation in the dust . . ."

"What is annihilation? What is dust? Personally, I only know eternity and roses."

"I'm full of usury and ravage. Over my mortal beauty, a myrtle is withering at my temples, and I sense that my lyre is out of tune."

"How pleasant that grasshopper is! It's making a tour of the forest with its song. The forest seems to have a necklace of sonorous little brown pearls . . ."

"But witch, what of the enigma of the universe. The cruelty of amour? The mystery of the divinity? The hideous snigger of death?"

"Eh?"

"What! Without trembling, you look at the world? What aspect does it have for you?"

"It depends . . . one day, that of a one-sou bouquet of violets . . . one day, that of an immense river, and I descend the flowing centuries in a pirogue of sunlight . . . One evening, that of a wood in which silence caresses, with its misty hand, the silver of olive groves . . . one evening, that of rain, which penetrates the sadness of old willows with its enchanted freshness . . . Sometimes, that of the fortunate power and strength of raised arms when I hear the storm of the Archangels beating the forests and the towers . . . But, in sum, nothing appears as simple to me as the universe, since I'm intoxicated by all its manifestations, since its light is as good on my back as on the backs of lizards, and its air as vivifying for my lungs as for the lungs of a new-born fawn. Hence my continual delight, Bémolus . . .

"Can it be? (*Aside.*) What a brute! And you are, it's said, a poet—a true one?"

"That, yes."

"I expected to see you pale . . ."

"Fleshless . . ."

"You're gazing, with a stupid intoxication, at the bracelet of juniper berries that surrounds your arm, and that dress doesn't suit you at all . . ."

"Don't be bitter, Bémolus! My bracelet was given to me by an unknown little girl who reeked of pine-woods and solitude. Only the Invisible knows what she has invented of miracles, animated of radiant shadows, added to the grace of the universe and of eternity by her soul when she assembled these wild berries. Of her babbling song Poetry was born once more—which is only engendered, Bémolus, by little girls and madmen. Let us mistrust them! As for my dress, it's indifferent to me. Adornment, for me, is a vain thing when it is not a diversion, a symbol or a folly. I like to pose crowns on my head, not hats, and also to plant horns there, and since my dress is less beautiful than my body, here I am, naked . . ."

"Oh!"

"How charming I am! Go away, Bémolus, so I can marry amorously in the caress of eglantines, the young daughters of the forest . . ."

"I implore you not to leave me alone this evening . . . but put your dress back on, in order that I don't have to blush before you."

"Imbecile! Here I am, dressed. Am I any purer? But who can see the innocence of my eyes?"

"If you knew the splendor of mine when I was struck by the dear pitiless hands! Consumed by my Déjanire . . ."

"Shorn by your Delilah . . ."

"When Leda gave me a swan for a divine rival . . ."

"And the others a hog . . ."

"How you afflict me! Have you never suffered from amour?"

"Yes . . . once . . . in my dawn . . . when I was only a few hundred centuries old. At present, when I count almost double my ingenuous age, I know that amour is *amour* and not a being for the possession of which we become idiots and criminals, and which strangles us before the manger of its absolute, where, I swear to you, there is nothing much to eat . . .

"Now I know that amour is not these eyes or some others, but all the eyes that reflect the divine light, as well as those of the dew and those of the Devil, which are rich in trillions of facets, and those of the owl hooked like a night-light on a nocturnal forest branch, and those of a shepherd dancing, with his flute in his fingers, for his goat-kid.

"Although it pleases me to rediscover a being in the odorous aridity of wild flowers, to make it young in all the leaves that grow and grave in all those that fall, to mingle it with the light that exalts me and the shadow that rends me so pensive, to give its flesh to the fruits that I eat, and its mysterious seduction to the beasts I caress, I no longer want to become the monster who, in the name of the amour that she experiences, wants to make all her suns depend on a gaze, all her plenitudes on the uncertain smile of the coveted mouth, all her harmonies on the approval of a soul that is always hostile and always foreign when one adores it as the unique divinity.

"Have you seen those grim and disgusting invalids, the desperately amorous? In their leper colony they can only weep over their ulcers and wonderstruck creation, ashamed of the vermin of their unhappiness.

"Oh, enough, let it go . . . if love were not sacred to me, more beautiful, more alive, warmer, more liberated and more perfect, if it did not teach me the infinite science of which the most pathetic expression is birdsong or the hum of bees; if, no longer a restricted end but a sacred means, it did not link me to the Beast that is enthroned above God, to the Seraphim enclosed in their wings or the Demons that I have unstitched from Hell, well, it would henceforth be no more, for me, than one of those ancient petty idols of clay at which we smile in naïve museums. They once bore all the weight of human fervor. Let us bow, but pass on, and tell ourselves that we have better things to do than die for a statuette, we poets who ought incessantly to forge the universe in our own image. And above all, let us think that we have to prepare ourselves for the other life. Let us only enter it light and perfumed, as if emerging from the bath and sleep . . ."

"There is only one certainty: death."

"Oh, please, enough. The momentary adieu? A petty challenge by which my eternity is crowned . . . I am more solid in hope than the cedar in the sunlight of Lebanon. Look: I hold out my white hands to death and it drinks the stars that fill them.

"I only inspire myself, Bémolus, but my philosophy is the basket of dreams that innocence poses every evening at the bedside of children. They are the only ones who possess it, and they are right. I have always believed that I would pass from this world into the limitless world of which we only have a confused revelation via poetry; but we give our pure caresses with our hands, collected from *down there*, and often, our shadow acquires, on serene moonlit nights, the perfect form that will one day be ours . . .

"I once heard invisible flutes surrounding my soul so amorously that I knew what music remained for me to hear . . . another time, angels that must have had the appearance of butterflies full of laughter, taking nectar from the flowery multitude of demons, entered into me and said: '*À bientôt . . . !*'

"All the dreamers who have quit this world never cease to maintain me; their words have, for me, the significance of golden constellations in a sky of divine geometry. Sometimes, in my solitude, I see tears on my hand . . . and tremble, Bémolus; it isn't me who has shed them. And those nightingales whose silence is the supreme harmony! Do you never hear them? And those books which it is only given to us to read one evening, but which make us rich forever with the certainty and torment that are the finest appeal of the beyond!

"Have you never felt that you complete God by means of one of your smiles? Have you never said, unconsciously: 'I'm departing . . . !' When those mysterious words emerge from my mouth, I am, O poet, replete with terrible wings . . . and I only await the wind, which is death. One morning, a chariot with sails and oars, which no conductor accompanied, stopped before me, and I understood how pleasant the voyage I had to make is . . ."

"Visions! Visions!"

"Our only realities. For myself, it's sufficient to think: *I am*, and I am clad in eternity, like a spring in foliage. What we sense is that the eternal is within us. When, at night, I dream that I have wings, antennae, suckers, perfume, corollas, probosces, feet, a thousand warm pelts, the soul of a gazelle, the belly of a tiger, knowledge of everything, and the little imperious head of the crowned serpent of Eden, do you think that I am not communicating, then, with the immortal life that will be mine later when, while knowing that I am still me, I shall have the delicate touch of the divinity, the inconceivable instinct of a beast, the splendid glory of a flower, and the taste in my mouth of the divine sin that the Genius, divinely culpable, committed in wanting to know . . . ?"

"Our bodies will rot, witch."

"Listen: one day when Satan was beating around me like a happy sea around a newly-discovered island, when I was full of fables and songs, inspiration and impertinence, when I saluted in the sun the solidarity of the tender pilgrimages of creation, I said to my mother—who, by virtue of her naivety and her blue gaze is a strange initiate—'I can see . . . I can see . . . I can see . . . My breath, which animates the forest, makes the bark of trees crack. My radiance visits hearts. I am, wherever I pass, the hybrid Annunciation of which the crimson is borne by two hostile and smiling archangels: one accepts God; the other, even more smitten than him, combats him. At my gesture, furtive serpents raise their sagacious heads. My vivacity is a round dance of blue flies in perpetual summers. My joy is as widespread as light and grass. I am as respectful of my amours as the oak of its shadow.

"'I am a thousand times a witch, and magnificent in all my forms. Sometimes, in the place of my heart, I have a meek grouse brooding eggs . . . sometimes, in the place of my mouth, Faust's poppy blooms, over which the warm and hairy Satan will buzz, whose sting seeks the poison of savant flowers . . . I am the veins of leaves, the mica of sand, the little pure face that, in the first violets, has the ineffable melancholy of spring, and I weep before that naïve ribbons of the wood, which make me think that once, in a green dress, I merited adolescence . . .

"'Suddenly, I am armed, headstrong, rapid, singing, durable in granite and petals, sparkling in fire and wheat, concentrated in nails. Insouciant in darts, like death . . . I only show myself in visages when I want to, and I have them all. I can offer an amphora while I hold a dagger behind my back, and I do not say beneath which flowers I have buried those whose sepulcher I am . . . I have the detours of a bird building her nest, the violent and supple cunning of a beast lying in wait for another, the meditation of water in the mud of springs, the divination of a tree that gives all the signs of human despair in anticipating a storm . . .

"'And I am wicked, wicked, in play and in folly! Spikes of holly and mahonia protrude from my loins, for I am also redoubtable to myself. I have as many antennae as instincts, as many claws as fits of anger, as much love as it requires to give birth to Amour. Oh, I can be enclosed in a coffin but . . . a quarter of an hour later, come and look; I shall no longer be there . . .'

"Well, my mother, who has never sinned against the dream, who thinks gravely that a lily is a magic spell of the Angels and a butterfly a miracle of the Devil; my mother, who knows that every jungle requires doves and wolves, and every sea pearls and shipwrecks; my mother, who is agreeable to the pure spirits of all the worlds, did not mock those insensate words. She watched them go down there, down there, light and bounding, and we both had this vision: the Fear of tombs tottering a little, struck in the heart by the Revolt that, this time took on the confident and laughing fact of an infant Hope.

"'The Miracle belongs to those who provoke it,' my mother said, simply; and she kissed my eyes."

"Know, Bémolus, that insensate words have a strange virtue. Those I have just pronounced entered into the throat of a nightingale that happened to be there and made it so melodious that my mother went pale. 'I remember,' she murmured to me, 'that my own mother, in the hour of her death, said that she could hear delightful birdsong by her bedside, And, in fact, her supreme expression belonged to the invisible music . . .'"

"Oh, witch! And the terrible black cat that the one who conceived you saw over your cradle when you were only one day old?"

"What does the appearance of our tutelary spirits matter, poet? Phosphoric eyes or amorous cleavages, what does it matter? Let us wish for the presence of such spirits for those who are being born and those who are dying . . ."

"Oh, witch, you were not as touching and innocent as you want to think when you saw your coffin forever empty of your body, the excessively living body that is all dance and sparks . . . you have given your body to the Devil, possessed!"

"Satan? I would invent him if he did not exist, And he would emerge, one evening, from my silence. And as I cannot, any longer, do without Angels, believe that their dazzling militia is endlessly born of my rectitude and will be my posterity. I am accursed and holy—which is to say, a poet. Can I not make Heaven and Hell—the Marvelous, in a word—when it pleases me, my eyes *down there?*

"God? But I never cease to hear his reckless appeal in my soul, for it is him, poet, who prays. Listen carefully, and you'll hear him. Ought we not to grant his prayer? It is the desire that I have to put my hands, with all my human tenderness, upon his inconceivable face, which the love that I give him has made

"The unknown and sensible God? He implores our tenderness for lambs by means of the candor of his pasture; he reminds us how short our voyage is by means of the cry of the migrating curlew, he demands our meditation by means of the rustle of the reeds isolated in a marsh; he admits that we accuse him with the blood of the crime and the howl of the wolf; he understands that we sometimes blaspheme before the sun, that insensible and devouring dragon, and the moon, that attentive and icy corpse . . . and in his extraordinary aspirations, his creative frenzy, how he is borne by that superb demon, our pride! How he is served by that serene beast, our strength! How happy and enriched he is when we dream in the abyss and on the summits! How he respires when we cry 'No!' for he senses, then, the great movement of wings upon his face . . . !

✻

"God? Every day he leans over me more tenderly. 'My creature,' he says to me, 'you are advancing in the truth and progressing in perfection. For you are joyful. You understand what poetry ought to be: my celebration.'

"They are fools, Bémolus, who make poetry an idle and interrogative madwoman lost in solitude who howls at pilgrims: 'Where is life?' and cries to them 'Where is God?' And the pilgrims, with reason, shrug their shoulders. They are fools who give her two masks, one wounded and the other grimacing, and attach those false faces, opposing them, to a paltry stick. 'Look at our bauble, dolor and doubt . . .' And they agitate it with the gestures of obsessed kings. They are fools who wrap that Archangel in a shroud and abandon to verse a prey of light. They are fools who drag that witch before the grimoire through which they never cease to leaf: 'We know nothing,' they groan, while at the portal of their lair, attentive and magnificent, stands the ram with the golden horns that even breaks the seals of the stars.

"They are blind fools who parade that majesty in limbo, groping. 'There are only melancholy regions,' they whisper. And yet, they would only have to exclaim a word of faith for their eyes to open and to see advancing toward them the white Robe that is as evangelical as the lily of the Nazarene. They are fools who, in the name of that priestess, insult the eternal entrails but are unable to equip their arms with the blue sword that, in the cloud of prophetic myrrh, consummates the divine sacrifice from which the great secret rises, beating its wings.

"In truth, what need have we of idle fools, puerile fools, purveyors of death, despairing, infirm fools, maladroit fanatics? Yes, yes, 'the strident cry to the caravans,' that some of them shout. Poor insensates! But know, Bémolus, that poets are criminal when they add laments to tears, when they lead the anxious tribes a little further astray.

"Let poets sit down in the grass and each distribute their share of God. Let them lean on young trees and report that a lily is born. Above all, let them not despair of the stars, since it is permissible for them to go to deploy their dance there. Let them pour out inexhaustibly the wine of hope, our untiring cup-bearers! Let them talk routinely about eternity. Who, if not them, would have the sense of it?—I ought to say the instinct. Let them project themselves upon the azure, in an ever more victorious glory, since their verity and their symbol is there. And when the Poet encounters God, let him say: 'I salute in you my presence . . .'

"Are we truly so magnificent, witch?"

"Yes, by virtue of lightness. One does not help anyone with sobs, but I save what I want when I dance. In laughing before a person in despair it is as if I were giving the clash of a cymbal at the resounding door of wellbeing, and, marching to the music, I would bring the walls down, and, like a flock long captive, I would drive the stars before me . . ."

"However, witch, if you have some reading, you ought to recall that there are desperate songs whose echo will be forever dear to the human soul, like a funereal pelican that will never cease to flap its wings over lost shores. There is a certain Musset . . ."

"I know him and I adore him. But his playfulness is more precious and beneficent to me than his poisoned absinthe, thank God! What aliments his dolors? His light and fervent genius. I repeat to you that there is only miraculous virtue in grace and intoxication, and if Musset were less blond and less dandy, he would doubtless never have written *La Nuit de Mai* . . ."[1]

"Not all poets are lovers of Ninette and Ninon. Such great ones live in despair!"

"They would not die there if they gave themselves time to grow old, the simpletons. The more a poet advances, the more radiant he is, and he only tends to return toward the fount of youth . . ."

"Well, personally, I venerate Faust, Rolla, René and Prometheus,[2] all those somber culpables who have, how-

---

1 "La Nuit de Mai" (1835) by Alfred de Musset is one of several lachrymose poems written in the wake of his doomed love affair with George Sand.

2 "Rolla" (1833 & 1840) is the eponymous protagonist of a narrative poem in two parts by Alfred de Musset. "René," in this instance, is Francois-René Chateaubriand, who was affectionately so-called by many writers of the French Romantic Movement, having used the forename refer to himself in his autobiographical writings.

ever, pronounced divine words, attempted immortal gestures . . ."

"Yes. But give them, at present, joy . . . and nothing but. In possession of that sling of light, what horizons would open to them? Faust only glimpsed the shadow of the Satanic profile in his blue or green horns. Rolla was only eloquent in blasphemy. That's not enough. Fortunately, René, when he was still at the age of a young scapegrace, rolled his carcass of an accursed Christian in the flowering gorse. Could we support, without perishing of ennui, the solemnity of his despair if he had not had leg-guards on his ankles and all of savage Armorica in his vagabond fists? As for Prometheus, do you imagine, Bémolus, that his captivity moves me less than his theft? What does suffering matter when one knows? But how I would like to deliver the vulture from his terrible hunger! It is him that it devours. Do you not think that monsters are sad and that we ought to sing for them too? I tell you that the inconceivable will belong, one day, to Hope."

Has not God, at all times, murmured to poets: "You will discover my wisdom everywhere that your folly smiles. You should suspend yourself to God, as thirst to a vase. The visage of water, fire and air will be closer to you and more tangible than that of humans. Mysteriously, you will see the rose smiling on the lips of the tomb, and before the bones of sepulchers your soul will be seized by the desire to dance with the frenzy that launches suns into the limitless worlds. In every image, even the most naïve, you will surprise the amorous and armed lightning.

"You will witness, barefoot, at your advent and your consecration, the invasion of your being by the divine combat. You will not cease to be animated by the revolt that is the first sign of predestination, and you will be the great black liberty that extends on nights of battle, over the despoiled camps and the flattened tents. You will have the sacred claws of my glorious Beasts. You will have the honor and the armor of my holy Soldiers. You will have the spirit, inflamed by pride and purity, the demonic certainty, brazen fleurons and fiery crowns, of my accursed Princes.

"Powerful eagles, Heaven, beaten by your celerity, will suddenly inhale you into its clarity, but do not worry, unicorns; you will not quit fables, and you will always throw yourself from the thatch into the brambles, like light threads of matinal spidersilk at dawn . . . Wherever you pass you will sparkle with a mild intelligence, and you will laugh at the tables of man, divine hunger, between the fruits and the bread.

"In the solitudes, you will decipher the beautiful maxim that a lily writes on a dreamer's wall. From your word will spring the sapience of the sibyls, and the rock, even more sensitive than the heather, will tremble with delight when you sing. The sap wandering in the vine will break its necklaces of freshness over your hands, and the serpent will turn its head toward Genesis at your approach.

"And endlessly, I affirm to you, body of light, the hurricane of Amour will carry you away toward the dazzled laughter of the World.

"You will find yourself again wherever you wander, and sometimes, when you are charged with the odor of privet and musical abundance, you will ask life for its amity while weeping for the flowers, and great pacts will be made.

"Around you will rise the sunlit hum of oracles when summer reigns over its tripod of amour.

"You will receive the visit of universes—O silent kings!—and you will return them, pure little children . . .

"You will smile under your eternal wing.

"You will open the secret door where your name is engraved between two triple stars, and alliances will be signed with my compasses, and prodigies will animate the writing like dragons . . .

"Meditate," he has said to them, "in my gardens of acanthus, sage columns. Grow, grow, above your mother, and your house, taller than the linden, than the black cedar, than the tower, than life, furious and tender geniuses.

"When you are perfect in initiation and prayer, you will sometimes hear me, when the hours are the pensive wheels of the stars, you will ask for pardon, so much will I have heaped you with grace and knowledge; but you will remain human.

"You will welcome, at the foot of the tree, the shadow of the woodcutter in order to caress his fatigue. In the evening, you will sell your beautiful poet's eyes in order to buy his humility and the muddy skirt of a pauper, and you will frame his poor shameful sins with unknown diamonds, but you will remain very pure.

"You will give to the lamps of those who watch and wait during nights of rain and distress, for the footsteps of the Annunciation, your gaze of faithful Satans; but you will remain joyful.

"My knights, my priests, my demons, you will liberate the siren from her prison of coral and the seas will make you an insulting and triumphant cortege.

"You will marry the bacchante of the grape, the shepherdess of the meadow, the nun in her habit, the Ophelia of the drama and the flower, the beggar-woman with her bowl, Pallas with her golden spears, innocence with her distaff and the Queen of Sheba with her rubies.

"You will keep captive in your palpitating bosom the fay who, with her sharp fingernails, scratches everything and makes life bleed from the heart of bouquets.

"You will caress, in their cells, those diabolical saints who have so innocently perverted, in the name of Paradise, periwinkles and hermitages, and all that is excessive and ingenuous, like dancing and suicide, you will love amorously.

"Then, O vegetal powers, O recreative music, you will be my lawns and my fountains, in my evening estates . . .

"Remember that it is only me that you possess, creatures . . ."

"I have just heard three very singular notes. I'm afraid. Is it you who laughed, witch?"

"If you have to ask me, you're a poor poet, Bémolus. In the same way that the words of God arrive to me distinctly, the eternal 'Ha ha ha' of the Devil never ceases to pursue me. We shall occupy ourselves more fully with him later, when I have seen him here, there and everywhere, and talked to you about his thinking horn. In poetry, you see, Bémolus, it's impossible not to frequent the Devil. Dare we poets say that we are not Magi? Let us cry, in the name of the Devil, king of adorable perversities, that we too are, and above all, fine villains. But you cannot know what I mean by that excessive epithet. I give it to the solitary who sleeps with his cheek on his guitar, to the dreamer who goes pale because the cabaret has placed his tender and dolorous face behind the dirty windows, to the innocent who think about all the curiosities of serpents and Eves, lamps and Psyches, shellfish that always group themselves on the sea-bed in order to surprise the sea, and which the sea always disperses . . ."

"Why are the innocent so troubled?"

"Because a tiny black insect has appeared in the yellow heart of the queen of the meadows . . . Oh, in truth, fine villain, the blissful curse for you is an enormous transposition, resistance and frisson, culpable and forbidden amour, delectation full of tears, strange rapprochements, profanatory inversions, savant, ambiguous and pensive interpretations of a proposition more ingenuous than the laughter of a child.

"How can I explain it to you, Bémolus? There is a certain salivation of the spirit that can only be demonic.

Poets know that particularly. A somber, sensual enchantment that we experience when the oblique eye poses upon us. Yes . . . the hymn to the Creator . . . but the tone of the color red imprisoned in a ruby robe in the crypt that we all know.

"No demonism, no Poetry. If you do not see Satan emerge from the poppy, as naked as original sin, as crimson as splendor and crime, as fervent as frenetic cities, Bémolus, you are . . . very unfortunate. That which one conceives in strict sanctity can only be seen with Poetry, that holy demon.

"The poet? I represent him as slightly sacrilegious, something of a bandit, not to say burlesque, sometimes, greatly reproved, very tender, even more wicked, simultaneously full of irreverence and amour for miracles, as proud as the Jungfrau on Ascension Day, always having, especially when he wears the robe of innocence, the desire to be damned, because that suits him so well among the sumptuous cantors . . .

"Three sous of genius more, and he is complete.

"I admit, too, that if he passes through Catholicism, the school of sadism, depravity and incomparable sensuality, he can become magnificent, on condition . . . of not remaining Catholic; for in that religion, one dies of fear, of cowardice; one calls oneself, in that case, 'scrupulous,' and it is very elegant—but I repeat to you that it is more fitting to be a poet, which is to say, a defrocked priest.

"As for you, Bémolus, I forbid you to recite the *Ave Maria*. You are not worthy of that, you who do not hear the Devil's thirst laughing in your gourd, fake pilgrim! True ones, of course, know what temptation is.

"Poetry is a great Sin.

"But listen again to what God says. Perhaps he speaks through the mouth of Satan, but what does it matter? Listen:

✳

"I had counted on my poets to assist me in the formidable labor by means of which, so painfully, I give birth to myself every day . . .

"To those who lighten the sea, dredge the salt, fill the bushels, gather the stars and the tinder, the branches and the nails, the crowns and the whips, accord royalty to whomever demands it, and divinity to those who believe themselves worthy of it; offer the cilice to those whose gaze is as pure and as somber as a cloister; beatify the possessed and the mad, say that crime is only the excess of misfortune . . .

"To those who give the absolute to the instant, soul to the unopened hour, who discover and consecrate the visages of which I want to make a lake, a lily or a dolor, affirm that life is a tambour of light, that one only has to attach it to one's loins and batter it with one's song . . .'

"To those magicians who discover the slow blossoming of the world in a flower, to those radiant gods tenderly offending the gentle modesty of miracles and dreams; to those pensive initiates directing my aurorae toward ruins, cradling the desolate angels of torrents, bringing my peace to those whose souls are crying out, my spring to those who have the feet of pilgrims, my eternity to watchful mothers, my tears to children who do not live, showing their route to birds who are searching for it, opening Hell to the sonorous Orpheus of despair and music, teaching their beloved, when they contemplate them and embrace them, what God desires . . .

"To my poets, in order for them to wake the dead and caress amour, in order for them to assist me with their genius and to situate me in my plenitude, in order for them to disengage me from this confused world that surrounds me still, and in which I wander with my excessively pensive shadow and my Dreamer's tread, which makes no sound; for them to understand that I only reveal myself entirely via the fervor of souls and the will of things; for them, my poets, to know that my Divinity is only satisfied on condition of hearing, in the human heart, a God who responds to it . . .

"But I am only sketching, dreaming and waiting. How long they are taking to come, my liberators, my barefoot apostles, my pioneers with inspired tools like lyres, my archangels vomited by triumphant lightning, my Dominations invading the stairway of the stars, guided by the insatiable and rebellious Dragon! How long they are taking to awake to themselves, the poets, my Lucifers in pure robes!

"They are, in themselves, my infinite and creative breath. What are they waiting for to make the tempest from which the dazzling and definitive universe, the saving and bounding ark will emerge —which is to say, the pure Spirit, soaring over my incomplete and dolorous work, which will finally smile?

"I lean toward the east, in the furnaces of dawns; where are they? I lean toward the west, greener and lighter than the gardens of Armide; where are they? I gaze at the magical and fragile crescent; how is it that not one among them has yet slipped away? Where are they? Where are they? Far from the sun, alas, far from that empire made fast that only asks for liberty, ascension and to reign, and it is written that, betrayed by everything since the commencement of worlds, I will also be betrayed by omnipotent Amour . . ."

III
Sainte Sorcière

Now the witch, who does not resemble anything, for she is everything, is advancing. She sits down on a rock in the buzzing brushwood, and the wind of bees and pollen whispers to her in the universal assent:

"You who have extracted yourself alive from the sepulcher of Pascal and posed your pure gaze on nature, who do not address yourself to plaster saints to whom one only shows sins and ulcers, but who gives sacerdocy to powerful oaks, to nourishing wheat, to the consolatory nightingale, you who know—O secret!—that the only damned are those who carry, against their heart, the eternal singing lyre, who are accustomed to say: "The accursed are great and the lightning is beautiful . . ."

"Precisely."

". . . You who live, witch . . ."

"Eh? What else could I do? In truth, I don't see . . ."

". . . You who are all light and all intuition, who mock philosophers along with the hares and the lambs . . ."

"And also with the blackbirds and the universal serpent."

". . . You who only seek God, but who do not admit his rigor and do not implore his love . . . You who offer yourself to him as a voluntary aide, proud and tender, and who, when he murmurs to you from the depths of a violet: 'Liberate me!' simply says to him . . ."

"Live, Lord."

". . . You who are not put in servitude by customs, nor by laws, nor by religions, nor by amour, nor by your senses, nor by your dreams, nor by others, nor by yourself . . ."

"Nor by myself."

". . . You who will even escape death . . ."

"Especially death."

"You who do not accompany any king or pay any slave, you who have separated yourself from captives and have not followed vagabonds, who have not made crowns . . ."

"Save for those I weave."

". . . You, wild and radiant, who do not say what others say when you think like God . . ."

"There are days when he thinks like me."

"Dear vainglorious! You who are your own beginning and end, your caravan and your tent, your master and your disciple, your honors and your recreations, your strength and your liberty . . ."

"Me, who, having wanted to be alone, am alone."

"Glory to you! We declare you holy."

"Truly?"

And that madwoman does not laugh, and that wicked woman has, on her face, the burning meditation of fervor, and that millenarian suddenly sets her age against her knee and, with a violent effort of her victorious hands, breaks it in two like a stick. "My age," she says, "that's what I do with it!" And she throws it into the primroses, which are an hour, among the nests, which are the eternal spring. "I shall soon be fifteen years old," she sighs, that ingénue. And, naked and pure, the adolescent stretches, the strawberry on her breast and the modest and velvet shadow down below . . .

". . . You who possess the extraordinary gift of transforming yourself at any moment, you who, as old as the Earth, suddenly become as young as a buttercup, you who, more meditative, somber and mysterious than a well, nevertheless have the playfulness of butterflies in your antennae and, in your soul, the sweet, even perfume of sainfoin in flower . . . You who combat your wisdom with caprine horns, but who also make life lie down at your feet like a submissive lioness . . ."

"For me, it is above all the tempting and powerful unicorn, and I know what blue birds pursue us in the hurricane the color of golden leaves . . ."

"You have the very face of joy and its ardent hand. Never have you been heard to murmur against the poverty of existence."

"It seems to me that it is up to us to enrich it and give to it. Is it not to act in godly fashion to add a ray of sunlight to its delight? And then, what do all disgraces matter, since the wellspring of the heart never runs dry?"

"Ah, sensible creature! Light and palpitating mill on the summit of the world . . . pure wings on the horizon . . . and—who knows?—perhaps you are good . . ."

"I'm not good at all. I'm just; that's different. I'm fraternal, which is something else again. And if I don't nourish myself on the flesh of animals, it's because they have, like me, a pink necklace of blood at the neck.

106

To eat that which one can caress, the delectable pelt of which can quiver under your hand by means of muscles and nerves, with a living and contracted heart and an open and consenting wing! Oh, how can one murder so many gods?"

"You who recognize that you are a witch. And that, your estate being yours . . ."

"Being mine."

". . . You seem incomparably more beautiful than all the others . . ."

"Oh! Yes."

"Well, we declare you holy."

"Why not? For such a long time holy Revolt has caused the whip of light to crack around me, and never ceases to say to me: "Get going! Get going" and Sainte Espérance has brought me vaster wings every day. The supreme Will is called Deliverance; I await it, and then I will rise above the world. Since I was born, Saint Orgueil has taught me that the soul is the soul and that everything that thinks and wills is divine. But hush! Don't you see that Sainte Folie is attaching her great musical laughter to my arms, more golden and more joyful than little bells? And that, in sum, Sainte Jeunesse maintains me in her holy candor and says to Sainte Eternité, by way of introduction: "She is imperishable, like the rose of my forehead . . ."

"All saints are megalomaniacs. The sign is constant, indubitable, certain and formal," pronounces a crow, whose vocation is as lapidary as it is unvaried, and which resembles Erasmus.

And with that, this cry of amour is heard everywhere: "Sainte Sorcière! Sainte Sorcière!"

*

Thus she is called by the leaves that sigh with the fresh and green throat of beautiful evenings, the stones crushed by carts, the mandrake that laughs at its cherished poison, the snake that is intoxicated by its venom, the whiteness that wants to become a dove, the cluster of grapes that imagines itself the whole vine, the nightingale that wants to have a lunar crown, the wolf that cries: "Give me the bad poets to eat, and perhaps I will no longer devour the lambs . . ."

Sainte Sorcière does not know where to put her head. She signals "Good, good," with her hand, slightly rude and perfumed by nature, but it is sufficient for her to want to liberate some and assist the others to approve of everything that lives, for the divine order to be endorsed, and for the dead, around her, to begin to breathe quietly . . .

"Sainte Sorcière," Merlin cries to her, "you have lost your soul . . ." And he presents to the astonished woman a pipe that he has found in the mint.

"Sainte Sorcière," Oberon whispers to her, "I'm taking possession of your modesty." And he shows the furious woman, who immediately laughs, the foliage, the long foliage, that is swaying in the wind.

"Sainte Sorcière." Urgèle murmurs to her,[1] "Do you not have a philter to give me? Amour is tearing my

---

1 Urgèle became the most frequently-cited name of exemplary fays in the nineteenth century; although she is not featured in the original *contes de fées* written by the salon writers of the 1690s, she appears in Voltaire's verse fable "Ce qui plait aux dames," which became the basis of Egidio Duni's successful comic opera *La Fée Urgèle* (1765).

heart." And Sainte Sorcière tears out Urgèle's heart incontinently and puts in its place a holy little bird that will never cease to sing.

Silence, mystery, wisdom, grace, joy, dissipation, dream, rhythm, space, the Golden Age, the invisible world and the dear little sensible world with the eyes of gracious animals, cry endlessly: "Sainte Sorcière! Sainte Sorcière . . . ! Daylight offers its cheek; that is in order that Sainte Sorcière might extend the beautiful velvet evening over it; a kiss begs her to conduct it to the lips of humans; the dead implore her: "Caress our bones in the black soil . . ." and the lyre presents itself. "Do you hear?" it moans. "He wants to emerge." And Sainte Sorcière, who then becomes Saint Music, liberates God, the prisoner of the golden strings.

"Canonize us, Sainte Sorcière." They are full of prejudices, these inhabitants of the bushes.

"So be it," says Sainte Sorcière, and from the berberis Saint Moineau, Saint Lézard and Saint Lis escape.

The blissful state does not prevent Saint Moineau from leaving droppings on the white collarette of a holy little child who, inflated with dominical importance, runs to buy a holy cake.

Saint Lézard, an aureole around his head, suddenly gives signs of a significant disturbance. A female lizard is looking at him with such extreme benevolence that Sainte Sorcière opens hr laughing eyes very wide. She knows that life is more precious than sanctity, and in any case, is founded in her by love.

Saint Lis, although he is pure among the pure—or, rather *because* he is pure among the pure—is suddenly invaded by a thousand strange beasts called "beetles," but Sainte Sorcière, who is savant among the savant and therefore mocks naturalists, knows that these red horned insects, which make nasty noises—zzzzz!—when their bellies are tickled, are devils.

Sabbat! All is sabbat in happy nature. Saint Lis belongs to his sonorous crimson demons, and Sainte Sorcière observes that his whiteness is perhaps more aggressive and more sovereign than a thousand lances directed at the sun. "How terrible purity is!" she murmurs, and Saint Lis takes, in her eyes, the form of an Archangel with silver armor. "How handsome you are! How handsome you are!" The radiance is exasperated around the burning heart, hearth of violence and amour.

Let's see, what is palpitating thus: the pistils animated by creative movement or the flame planted in the breast of Lucifers? Is that pollen, an odorous downpour, falling into the wind or demonic thought seeking divine receptacles in the azure and the brightness? "Stem of Saint Lis, are you the body of Saint Lis? Silky petals, are you caresses? Satan's kiss, are you summoning me by means of that flowery mouth?"

Sabbat! All is sabbat in the sunlight of poetry.

And around the lily that, in jest, Sainte Sorcière has made a saint because it is innocent, as she is innocent, a serpent sometimes laughs, with Genesis in its dangerous mouth; a tortoise seems to sow the gold of time as it passes over the sand . . . Thorns tear the soul of the rose with their coral claws; a bucket rises from the well and a nymph escapes from it, hurling the wings of her dance to the wind . . . The wheat-field sings, and on its golden lips the songs are poppies; goats bleat the torment of their meager and fervent flanks to the brushwood; Sainte Sorcière's breast is as soft as the coo of a turtle-dove, and spring-water circulates in her eyes.

Divine alarm! She senses her face scatter like the perfume of jasmine and the radiance of poppies, and now, magnificent, universal and liberated, she hears her heart slide into the river of things, like a hard and supple silver fish . . .

But suddenly, her heart, which has already changed its nature, is cleaved by the thrust of a fingernail. The ruby seeds of that golden pomegranate fall to the ground, and Satan laughs.

"Sainte Sorcière," he says, "warm spouse, who sins so much because you do not sin, everything suffices—does it not?—to give us splendor?" And he throws a woodland mushroom into the green robe. "Everything suffices—does it not?—to give us the dream?" And from a starry pipe, he causes an odorous cloud to rise up between him and Sainte Sorcière. "Everything is temptation for us, is it not? We only dream of crushing the stars like blue grapes between our white teeth . . . Everything invites us to depart, to depart . . . the gallop of your cherished beast, the Chimera, when you bestride it, is only a spark in the night . . .

"How secretive you are, Sainte Sorcière, when you fall silent, for the heavens give you their mildness to keep, so that you are tender when you bear the odor of your light dress and the immateriality of swans to a trickle of water, and that you are pure when you seek your crystal route, when the rain falls on young forests in the evening!

"How troubling you are, Sainte Sorcière, when you pass the glove of mystery over your hand, when you place the mask of caress over your face, when, like a foreign schooner you suddenly pitch, swerve, whistle and flee!

"How solid you are when you contemplate, in the depths of the horizon, your power of growth; how strong you are when you raise the setting sun in your arms over living space; how young you are when you resemble the squirrel that gambols and gnaws beyond its joy, beyond its hunger; how grave you are when, in the wood, the brown warbler listens to your heart weep, Sainte Sorcière!

"How you love everything more than with your heart, since you open your perfumed soul entirely; how beautiful you are when you traverse the multitude of hostile standards to go salute the cornflower of the fields, that blue canticle! How your breast swells with a vegetal sigh; how akin your body is to animal form, how widespread you are; air, amour and danger are not more so than you, Sainte Sorcière!

"Nourish your sensuality by eating this strawberry; let me dazzle your destiny by kissing your eyes; bite dolor on the heel, viper; sing for another thousand years, nightingale; nurse the accursed, generous she-wolf, and the one that you call Sainte Damned: Glory.

"Lash, tempest; enter into this lily, bee; populate everything, Solitary . . . and laugh."

Sabbat! Everything is sabbat, nothing but eternal sabbat . . .

SATAN

INVOCATION

Appear to me, Satan, belly open and digesting—O Gigantic!—the lust of an entire destroyed kingdom. Have in your eyes the implacable and desperate bestiality that makes you the supreme Brute. Drive before you, Satan, in the cry of penitent Egypts and the silence of burned Sodoms, the tribes of Jehovah that made Moses despair, but show that sad foundation of power that it is you who animate the brazen wand, and that you bear the tables of the Law on your formidable breast.

Let Hell emerge from the gaps in your hood, Monk who casts a shadow over cilices and the cross, and since you are the goat, O Satan, fornicate before me simultaneously with four witches coiffed with fire follets and the laughter of the accursed dead.

I await ten thousand cats weeping sulfur, as many owls with wings lined with phosphorus; and in the midst of that lugubrious militia, inquisitors advancing breathlessly—for the cross with which they stun their victims is now across their throats.

I want to see the seven deadly sins in the form of carrion transpierced by dancing pins, or butterflies that have the souls of Sardanapalus and Balthazar for wings, or madwomen with eyes of precious stone.

Show me the serpent of sin coupling with the dove of salvation, and around that sacrilegious symbol the round of your imps, all inflating with their hideous laughter a bellows with the pustules of a toad.

I summon those reprobates whose sacerdotal and preciously anointed elegance is so dear to my exasperated Catholicism, and among them, I will salute the one I love: the red Prince of the Church whose leprosy is masked in black.

I summon the accursed, of whom I am one. One has a fiery slipper sealed to her heel of an excessively chaste dancer, another a ruby necklace planted like a dagger in her neck of a seductress who always says no, and among them I rediscover the Lady of Quality whose lover died while possessing her and who hides her culpable hand in a velvet glove stigmatized by a bite.

Spread around me, Satan, the icy nights of whistling and forever-tempted penitence, the sinister blue of impious concupiscences, the frightful red of crimes committed in the entrails of mothers, the blanching yellow of catastrophic skies when, to the melodious metallic song of wars, hatred, rape and wolves hurl themselves upon the same prey. I want to see, simultaneously, the violet of chasubles and that of mental debauchery, the white of the worst soilings and that of the doves that nourish the eternity of poets. Enable me to know the green of all putrefactios: that of the drowned dog, that of the cadaver that perhaps experiences the sensuality of the caress of larvae, and that of Jehovah, who ends up, so many of those he has invented, being devoured by locusts . . .

＊

I beg you for that, Satan! Let me satisfy absolutely the detestable love that I have for the presence of poison. Enable me to sense and touch them all, in their thousand thinking cells, and enable venomous flowers, daughters of the sun and death, to incline one by one over my lips with the hissing of drunken vipers.

Open for me, Satan, the stables where the decadence of Empires wallows when, weary of anxieties and blasphemies, Nabuchodonosors rejoice in only bringing the carcass of a hog to annihilation and putrefaction . . .

Offer me, Satan, as so many Hells, the hearts that I have paved with the furnaces of my desire and throw, finally, into my arms the Being that I refused myself until now because he and I were not yet worthy of the number and splendor of my sins. Let my eyelid flutter at him like the wing of a baleful owl, and let him come, Satan, let him come, for the great Salvation is to be damned together!

"Is that really you who is speaking? I was sleeping on the blonde sheaf of my lightning bolts, and dreaming once again that the azure was mine."

"Pardon me, but I have not yet given the Devil anything but lyricism."

"Well, what more do I have, then, my naïve daughter? Why would you, a poet, make of me another being than the Genius, the musical damned soul? Why should I not remain, for you, above all, the skimmer of unreal seas who has divine pillage and fortunate shipwreck in his breast, and the death that leaps toward the stars with powder-kegs in revolt and thunderous laughter in his heart?

"Satan is what all humans have within them of the most alive and the most involuntary. Get a grip on yourself, my fervent she-demon, and continue your work by opening the wings of sacred dementia further and further. The sabbat of the spirit is far more terrible than the other, and much more sumptuous, my daughter. Dishonoring oneself with a few filthy devils when the night reeks of the priest and the witch and the rags of the shameful accursed is a game in bad taste, quite obsolete, and not worth a thrust of my horns.

"But to recreate Satan is something else. All great poetry is infernal because it has my two powerful virtues: revolt and pride. What have you done until now except free yourself and hope? Hope in the most immense pride, child of my heart.

"Let my puerile alchemy simmer in the crucibles of rudimentary Fausts. Let my frightful and ridiculous imagery continue to pervert abulic adolescents who nourish their rebel anemia, and priests who, in the fanatical sadism of Catholic fears, believe themselves already skewered by my fairground theater demons because they sometimes have fire under their soutanes.

"Child, child, I have no commerce with the horn of the young ram whose throat is cut under the navel of witches in art, or the viscera of snakes surprised by the hatchet in the moment of amour. My traffic is more serious. I am the smuggler who passes souls of pure metal from one world to the other. Already, I have lifted you in

118

my arms; soon I will load you on to my back. My mark, on your forehead, is not a patch of soot; it is a trail of stars, and, since you invoke Satan, merit him.

"But I know you; you are playing with knucklebones in the tempest . . ."

"But then, I never have enough diamonds to break the hoops. I also need the golden fists of the sun."

"I know. You've just invoked me with such astonishing candor! How you thought you were saying abominations!"

"Yes."

"Ha ha! You're not unaware, however, that damnation is elsewhere, and that sniffing a rose is the greatest torment for a poet, and thus the greatest sin. My thousand devouring temptations only surround persons who dream with arms folded over their linen garments, and one visits Hell—I swear it!—in the robe of Beatrice and crowned with laurels. As for the chapter that you're consecrating to me, what is in it?"

"O my radiant Archangel, you have seen that I was counting, in order to nourish it, on dirty magic, the somber kabbala, horrible inverted masses, the filthy witches that come to crouch around the moon while Belzébuth, hound of darkness, howls in the silence of the dead . . ."

"Fool!"

"Why?"

"Sacred tribe of poets! They suspect nothing, and how right they are! 'What about your book? When will you give it to us?' they ask. 'My book? I've almost finished it . . . hmm . . . yes, finished . . .' They only have the title. But what spirits do not flutter around the title of a poet's book, above all when it is yet to be written? The spirits form its pages of their own accord, and since you have wanted to name the second part of your poem *Satan*, my daughter, well, by Satan I'll help you!"

"What luck! But I expected it."

"Oh, divine false innocence of poets! Charming perversities, delightful accursed. I'll come to fetch you tomorrow, at midnight."

"Where will you take me?"

"Hush! But, by Satan, my daughter, I want to prove to you that Hell is much more subtle, mysterious, delicate and . . . infernal than one imagines via the catechism and Lent sermons. Consequently, I shall put you in the presence of a few more of my possessed. You have known them all, in any case.

"Tomorrow, at midnight."

THE NUNS' NIGHT

One . . . two . . . three . . . four . . .

"Voices of eternity, how grave you are!"

Five . . . six . . . seven . . . eight . . .

"Convent bells, how slowly you ring while the nuns are in a cell keeping vigil over a defunct nun."

Nine . . . ten . . . eleven . . . twelve . . .

"Ha ha ha! What a beautiful cry the screech-owl has! It seems that its madwoman's gasp is wrenched from the throat by the moon's dagger-thrust. Holy Sister Marie-Ange died at ten o'clock yesterday evening . . ."

"I knew her once, in the convent where we were boarders. She was sixteen years old, with brown curls, velvety white cheeks and the subtle smile of a musicienne. She wore over her breast the broad green ribbon of a very well-behaved child, and her eyes, with a forest of lashes, were as green as her ribbon, as tempting spring leaves . . . Her name was Marguerite, she loved me with a pathetic amity and doomed herself by pride."

"By lust too, the chaste girl! Do you remember when, under the radiance of the stained-glass window in which the Archangel armed himself with azure and anger, her long light and dark hair sparkled? Her head in her hands, she prayed and prayed. She was the edification of the convent. But you, who looked at that saint with exaltation, who sinned in the name of all amorous life in adoring the tenebrous tresses scintillating with gold spangles and the laughter of the Archangel, were less culpable than her. Even more than you she had the sensation of Satan, that daisy . . .

"Do you recall that Octave Feuillet succeeded in perverting her, giving her the artificial aristocracy of social disdain?[1] Did she play the cold and uncomprehended Princess enough, that fervent reprobate? Octave Feuillet? Ha ha! I also take the mundane and romantic form, the sumptuous imbecility of a 'poor young man.'

"When she returned from her vacation, your Marguerite was carrying in her arms a large white bouquet—she adored white, as all the accursed do—and she went to throw it at the feet of the rustic Virgin who resembled a rude guardian of ewes, out there in the chapel at the back of the garden, where all was Satanism, the nightingale of fennel and indigent violets. 'My God,' she said, 'I've met a brilliant naval lieutenant at a ball. He had oriental eyes and smelt of cheap tobacco. He talked to me about opium dens. Opium? It's a long silver veil, isn't it, that separates us from sleeping faces . . .'

"Oh, your Marguerite, your Marguerite! She never had an obscene thought, never caressed her adolescent

---

1 The popular dramatist and novelist Octave Feuillet (1821-1890) was a pillar of the *Revue des Deux Mondes* during the Second Empire; he reached the peak of his success in the late 1850s, but suffered increasingly from neurasthenia and depression thereafter.

breasts, never asked of pure water any other complaisance than to assure the strict cleanliness of her body; she took communion three times a week and collected in a flowery album a wild pansy as violet as the faces I collect in the paths of presbyteries, and the incoherent and inflamed speech of that lyricism of the flesh: Lacordaire clad in white.[1]

"A saint, I tell you, a saint!

"Yes, she was extremely virtuous and devoted, but—ha ha!—she made herself a nun. Truly, the languorous, rascally and perfumed naval lieutenant haunted her too much, and then, she had, decidedly, a determined liking for the 'poor young man.' She discovered another . . . and that one didn't let her escape. He prowled barefoot along the banks of the Sea of Galilee . . .

"When she entered the novitiate at nineteen, what did she write to you, she who was beautiful, rich, flattered, a musicienne, like all the damned? What did she write to you? 'I have a celestial *fiancé*, a *fervent spouse*, who will love me *forever and ever and ever.*' No, no! Never. The sense of eternity combined with that of ardor, that is what characterizes demoniacs. The eternal fire brooding in a narrow thorax enveloped in black alpaca. She was my daughter even more than you, and, having lived in penitence, sanctity and chastity—prophecy, like all megalomaniacs—in full lucidity, an hour before her death, what did she do?"

"She wept, giving all the signs of despair."

---

1 The reference is to the liberal Dominican preacher Henri-Dominique Lacordaire (1802-1861).

"Poor child! The God excessively hoped for, was once again in disarray, and in the funereal candles, my eyes were shining. She had seen him, you see, and that inflamed and proud dupe shed the tears of final disappointment over her waxen cheeks. Don't be sad. I wiped them away gently, and your Marguerite, who had offered the monastic God her accursed vocation on your behalf—superbly naïve!—, understanding, at the supreme moment of agony, that the sole inspirer of her seraphic existence was me, was no longer thinking about the blissful anticipated parvis . . . she was delighting in the liberty that one obtains in the act of dying . . .

"Do you remember the courses? The nuns gave directions there to very distinguished messieurs who frequented the mass, good fathers and good husbands of mature age. But youth is always on the brow of men who go through the doors of convents in order to instruct the little girls . . ."

"Yes, yes . . . I understand everything now. I can explain Marguerite's arrogant and provocative head, the infernal coquetry she put into showing as much profile as possible to those messieurs, because that profile was as insolent, neat and delicate as . . ."

"Mine when I put on the black and princely garments of Sainte Thérèse . . ."

"She looked so strangely at the chemistry professor!"

"Ha ha! Faust and the retorts! Everything is significant, my girl, but one is not sufficiently aware of it.

"Personally, the one I contemplated was the professor of drawing. He had the honest and ravishing timidity of a faun watched over by the nuns. The youngest of all, he was said to be handsome, and when he corrected, on my sketch-pad, the acanthus leaf . . ."

"His hand trembled."

"I can still see him: his thick blond hair, the golden tuft, so animal, in his armpit . . ."

"Oh, the convent educates you. my daughters! As for your Marguerite . . ."

"I understand everything now. With his precious little accent of a Gascon pedant, she had nicknamed her darling—that man with a shock of rude white hair and eyes whose irises, narrow and concentrated golden lentils, were so satanic—'the dethroned king of Poland.'"

"A taste for pomp amd decadence. All sadisms are catalogued in my house. And you remember when, the reaction having taken place, the liquid boiled and became angelically blue, the blue that makes the saliva laugh between the teeth?"

"Yes . . . yes . . . I remember. Marguerite's beautiful green eyes then took on the moist brightness of a grim solitary emerald in a secret display case, between a chaplet of nacre beads and medical poisons, meditating on the fate of damned things. Once, she uttered a long cry in the haunted nocturnal recreation hall between a hysterical Saint Louis de Gonzague and the natural history exhibit in which the venous system bled alongside medusae and ammonites. She uttered a long cry, that good girl . . . and the next day she ran like a madwoman to find the peripatetic preacher who received mysteriously, in the parloir, children who believed themselves predestined. She knelt down, kissed the apostolic hands—another fervent and passionate whim!—and said in a whisper: 'Help me, Father . . .'"

"That preacher—ha ha ha—was old, worthy and holy, but he had—look at me carefully now—my large black oblique eyelids . . ."

"Always Satan!"

"Always. Let's go up to the cell of the dead woman."

"I'm afraid."

"It's so beneficent to be afraid! Four candles are burning around Marguerite, How beautiful she is, she who died at twenty-six years of age, her breast narrow and condemned, who didn't cough once, and who, nevertheless, had hardly any lungs any longer in the torrid little cage where her angelic heart sang!

"Holy Sister Angélique, can't you hear anything? Alas, I only hear rain on a dead leaf. Where are the choirs of Angels? On the dead leaf, Sister. Listen to the gentle rain of death falling in the November night. Listen to the curlews calling in your religious gardens. Listen to all of nature, of which I am the harmony and the damnation, moaning amorously because a dying child devoid of sin—but so culpable, so culpable!—has just closed her large green eyes upon the funereal candles.

"Satan everywhere, everywhere . . . Where is he not? I defy you, Holy Sister Alphonsine, to tell me where he is not. And if he did not often take the place of the divine crucifix on your flat breast, would you give yourself the discipline until you fainted?

"Where is Satan not? Tell me. Who is the one among you who does not seek, every time she opens her window over the hopeless gardens, in the limited sky as troubling as a stained-glass window, the inexpressible odor of life with the odor of privet? Poor nuns! You are chaste, but it is because you are chaste that sin besieges you like the invisible ram, the thrusts of whose subterranean horns made Babylon tremble.

"'Holy Sister Alphonsine, holy Sister Séraphine, holy Sister Isabelle—you, the abbess of the reproved, whose thin mouth seems constantly to be drunk by your devouring eye!—why have you just fasted for forty days? Because of Jesus? Because of me? What does it matter? He savored eternal Life when I reposed my once-Beloved head on his anxious and suave heart, in the Communion of possession . . .'

"Oh, if all that were not Satan, how abominable life and death would be!

"'Holy Sister Alphonside, holy Sister Alphonsine, what do you love?'

"'Incense, that vaporous mystic; the organ, that thunder which blows the incense, the stained-glass window which is so pink, so blue, so red, so extinct, so fiery, so mysterious, so Catholic, that it is impossible to believe therein without sinking into the delectable despair of the mortal sin inspired by divine amour."

"'Ha ha! What else do you love?'

"'The breviary bound in black, florid with roses, confession in a low voice, and, as much as possible, to an Oblate, one of those melancholy monks of Spanish appearance who sighs at each of our confessions, his hand on the copper cross on his grim breast . . . Communion, on returning from which the veil falls over our faces like a funerary drape, we who are the walking dead . . . I also love the cilice, our rope couch, our brown habit, our lament in the chapel by night when Jesus refuses himself, and also the refectory where, once a year, we are childish because of the color of an apple, on a day of great liturgical celebration . . .'

"Win Paradise with all that, if you can, divine sluts! As for me, I damn you . . . What else do you love?"

"'The Angel who enters into Marie's cell . . .'

"Of course! Gabriel . . . Oh yes, the handsome Gabriel. He is my cherished double. I have my red eyes or his blue eyes, my black wing or his white wing, my royal scepter or his silver lily . . .

"Nuns, I make all the Annunciations! Good night, holy Sister Alphonsine. Keep good vigil over the dead . . . Good night, my daughter. You're smiling now?"

"Yes, because I know that Marguerite was accursed, like me."

"More than you, my daughter. More than you . . . When she returned from her vacation she was carrying a large white bouquet in her weak arms, and was about to throw it . . ."

"I found her once, almost fainted at the foot of the rustic Virgin that resembled a rude guardian of ewes . . . the nightingale of the fennel where the indigent violet . . . 'What's the matter, Marguerite?'

"'Can you imagine that the naval lieutenant gave me, in all languages, a confession of love?'

"'Including French?'

"'No . . . no . . . that would have been a sin . . . But we waltzed together. I retrieved that waltz. I'll play it for you tomorrow at dusk when holy Madame Agathe goes to care for her chilblains. It's called *España*. One can hear castanets in it . . .'"

"Of course."

"And I assure you, Satan, that in recounting these childish things to me, she fainted . . . she fainted . . ."

"The accursed! The accursed! Nothing was innocent for her. Not astonishing: she was holy. Six months later—the damned!—how she moaned, in a parloir crowded with artificial roses—diabolical! diabolical!—around the stigmatized Heart, how she moaned, always in the same amorous and feeble voice of an extenuated dove, at the preacher who had—do you remember?—my large black oblique eyelids: 'Father, I want to become a Carmelite . . .'

"Ha ha!"

THE LADY OF QUALITY'S NIGHT

"Let us enter the home of a lady of quality duly baptized and Catholic in the soul—which is to say, by sadism. Between the portrait of Madame Lafarge, the mysterious accused,[1] and an amateur painting representing those anodyne cornflowers that would pervert the Devil himself, you see in her abode a Saint Sebastian who gives the impression of agonizing twice: first in order to please his arrows and then to render homage to his ivory complexion, so yellow and so perfect. Here, too, thrown casually on the sofa, is a chasuble, bordered correctly—I mean satanically—in violet, and magnifying in its central bouquet of a pink so violent and sly, my obstinate and smiling aggression.

"What does she say, the lady of quality, lying on the pelt that she calls so passionately *my beast* . . . ? What does she say as she caresses that sweet dead antelope? She

---

1 Marie Lafarge (1816-1852) was accused of murdering her husband; her trial was extensively reported in the newspapers. Her conviction was based on forensic evidence now thought to have been dubious; the great scientist François Raspail agreed to testify to its unreliability but could not reach the courtroom in time to give his evidence.

says: 'Pooh! Pooh! Pooh!' What is it that sickens her so? The sin committed? No. The sin to be committed? No. Can you imagine that at this moment, in her sumptuous and neat bedroom where the parishioner is in evidence, she is thinking about rape?

"She is thinking about rape as you think about swallows and fresh foliage, but fundamentally, the lady of quality is no more perverted than you. She is thinking about rape, that's all. What intoxicates her, fills her, makes her so pretty, you see, is the disgust she experiences, and when you rhapsodize, crying 'Oh, that forget-me-not!' You are no more innocent than her, because what intoxicates you, fills you, makes you so dazzling before the forget-me-not is the temptation that invades you, and you know that temptation is temptation, and that if we admit its constant culpability, it is not when one shells peas that the culpability is least . . .

"The hair of the lady of quality is a very distinguished chestnut, believe me. The secrets of René the poisoner,[1] which all grandmothers transmit to one another, are supple and brilliant, and the lady of quality's chignon is the elegant and solid chignon of a woman who said her prayers this morning and took her bath in a peignoir.

"'What horror!' she says, suddenly, and the lady of quality, who is very red, gives a thrust of her elbow to the invisible brute.

What can she be thinking? About rape. Always about rape. This time, it is consummated in legal apparel. The

---

1 René Bianchi (?-1578) was Catherine de Medici's court perfumer and was widely believed to have poisoned people of whom she wanted to be rid at her behest.

lady of quality is thinking abut her wedding night. What do you expect? She has a mathematical memory, that charming woman. Do you not recall yourself, with a precision that delights me, the horns of a certain cricket that emerged from its gold-powdered hole in the pink vicinity of a poppy fifteen times multiplied?"

"Oh, that cricket!"

"'O, that . . . something!' says the lady of quality, and, ready to vomit, she swoons with pleasure.

"You, who are ready to weep, are you not also swooning with pleasure?

"Why should you be less stirred than the woman of quality who execrates, at this moment the congested haste of her husband? Why should you be less troubled than her, you who, at this moment, are adoring the lawn from which your first cricket emerged, your first demon of bronze and music?

"At present the lady of quality is burying her healthy pink face in the fur of her dear antelope, and what is she saying? She is saying: 'No, no! He shan't touch me. He shan't caress the vein in my neck with a finger that trembles and begs. He shan't suspend from the lobe of my exquisite ear his concupiscence, which would cost five sous in a bazaar if concupiscence were sold on shelves of shoddy goods. Since I refuse him entry to myself, he won't be able, that fellow who takes communion at Easter, to think in my house, sighing in anticipated contrition, about his confessor, who reeks of Lenten cod every year . . . Pooh!'"

"But the lady of quality, in all fashions, only thinks about . . ."

"And you?"

"Oh, of course, if I . . ."

"Shut up. What about the hay in the warm barn where the afternoon spider runs with sunlit legs? And the aggressive rose? And the vanquished tree? And the moss that summons, the moist mouth? And the bramble that clings, the dry claw? And the butterfly that has in its wings the implacable eyes of lust? And the lizard as furtive as seduction? And the leopard you have never seen but which you never cease, however, to embrace while its breast beats, so warm and as if so human, against your breast of a chaste she-demon? But not pure. No, no, not pure! The lady of quality and you? Ha ha!

"I watch you, you know, playful she-demon who seems free. What strikes you with wonder, above all, and thus enchains you, is the miracle that takes you out of yourself. The miracle of the avid lip bitten by the sagacious tooth. The miracle of the pupil, that perfidious prisoner of the lashes . . .

"And the woman who only thinks about her perpetual miracle, only thinks about lust . . . you all think about it!

"What does the lady of quality say as she undoes her hair. 'My hair is my own, not desire's. I hate desire because it already takes possession of me. What audacity! I have a desire to slap, with a delicate and disdainful gray glove, a serpent from Sweden, the faces of all the men in whom I see certain eyes. I know only too well that they're evoking the three velvety shadows of my body in making those humble eyes, so plaintive and so desperate, the pigs!'

133

"What! She expresses herself like me . . ."

"The delicate lady? Yes. Listen to her again: 'When I think that no matter what man—Pooh!—can, in our presence, humiliate our disdain with an ignoble thought . . . when I think that a reprobate of the lowest class can take possession, with a callused finger, of the rare reliquary . . . When I think . . . Oh, if the profanation were committed by a pale Nuncio, very mysterious and very perfumed—perhaps with a black mask—in major disgrace, each of whose fingernails would be a princely amethyst . . .'"

"Permit me to say that the lady of quality . . ."

"Hush! Listen, listen: 'The bed? It's for dreaming and sleeping, being white for its attentive pillows, being naked for its modest curtains, being beautiful for its savant mirrors . . . Pooh! Pooh! Pooh! Before . . . After . . . During . . . And the two men who have . . . soiled me, for they have soiled me—I only know two, two too many—I detest them so much that I could kill them in order that they no longer know that I have the dawn here, the night there, and a large brown tuft in the groin in the form of a crescent . . .'"

"Oh! Make her shut up!"

"Not at all. It's too interesting to hear a lady of quality thinking aloud. But listen, listen to what she's murmuring, lying belly down on her cherished beast: 'Tell yourself, beautiful Endymionne—the beautiful Endymionne is me—that those two men that you hate had such a bad education that they dared to take off, before your eyes, their underpants—as if anyone has underpants!—and their socks—as if anyone has socks, oh, the socks that trail in the bedroom!—a waistcoat in which the chronometer, the gift of a great-uncle . . . That's curious: the two men with whom you have . . . lain, each have a great-uncle—as if anyone has a great-uncle!—whose chronometer goes tick-tock on the prie-Dieu that is always at the foot of your bed . . . Those two men that you hate then unknot a cravat that cost two francs ninety-five or forty-nine francs ninety-five—it's the same thing—unbutton a waistcoat that had a hundred francs'-worth of wear here—have it mended quickly!—and the adulterated tears of a vaporizer there . . . A cigarette and a toothpick fell from the frayed pocket . . . and then, those two men—how they resemble one another, although one is almost too blond and the other almost too brown!—said to you, *O beautiful Endymionne, to you who are so refined, so haughty* . . . In the odor of eau de toilette and animality in full exasperation, well, yes, they said to you: *My adored little woman* . . . And they huffed and puffed like draughts in a poor building. And on their rascally faces you only saw one desire: forcible entry.'

"Oh, the man who, in those moments, could have the cold and willful face of a thief, the sober grace of a scoundrel! But what lover, to give himself appearance, imagines at such moments that he has promised himself to steal the papal treasure in the secret wall-panel and who has put on fur slippers and armed himself with fleur-de-lysed keys forged expressly for the contact of the nocturnal glove? How you dream of a sufficiently spiritual Being entering your room without knocking, without opening the door; material enough for you to feel him in your bed, directly against you; delightful enough to say to you: 'I'm not looking at the dawn that you have here, the night that you have there, the big brown tuft in the form of a crescent that is—oh, my love, my love!—the damnation of your dazzling flesh, its permanent confusion, its contradiction, its aberration . . . A little of the skin of a mulatress at that place—that place!—is the stigma, galley-slave; the flaw, princess; the original sin, Madame; the rainbow of the misalliance, beautiful Endymionne . . . But—don't worry!—I'm not looking at those marvels. What would be the point? While closing my eyes I can see them so clearly . . . oh, so clearly!'"

"'Shut up, damn it. You're making me blush all the way to the soul.'

"'Delectable shame! When the soul blushes, the sin is good.'

"'Who could know the sin?'

"'Oh, beautiful Endymionne, would you permit the man, who, being directly against you, might accord himself other licenses, to take your hand in his deceitful hand, brown, gilded and wicked?'

"'Yes.'

"'Would you want us to think about Theodora, or Cleopatra? One committed the sin while raising the scepter, the other while swallowing the pearl, for the sin, in truth, is not . . .'

"'Oh, no, it isn't, beautiful naked stranger, what others believe . . . Sin? Would you like me to show you how beautiful I am when I cause to run over my shoulder the dead sun of a topaz, the dead sun that remembers being alive in the Devil's eyes? Would you like me to put a velvet medal between my breasts? In jest, beautiful stranger, in jest: my breasts are white, velvet is black.'

"'Ah, sinner!'

"'Would you like us to shut up and for rain suddenly to fall on our windows, invaded by the dusk? The rain that is adorable to hear in a bed of amour when one is chaste and naked!'

"'Ah, sensualist!'

"'Would you like me to tell you what I'm hiding in that display-case? Under my sachet of scent, alongside an elegant and distant daguerreotype of a man with smooth black hair, I hide . . . a provision of arsenic. I'll never, never, make use of it, but the presence of the poison makes my eyes more beautiful, more serious than a gilded and black thought in the garden of an old palace. I've always cherished a certain kind of poisoner: the one for whom it's a fashion of loving—do you understand?—a fashion of loving . . .'

"'Yes, I understand.'

"'She said to him: *Drink!* and he drank, gazing at her with suspicion and docility. With docility, because she was tenebrous, with suspicion because the voice of the arsenic spoke to him in a whisper, in the pure crystal . . .'"

"'Ah, criminal!'

"'With regard to the pleasure? No. It exhausts our cerebral reserves.'

"'Ah, accursed!'

"'If I had known Pascal . . .'

"'Ah, literary! But all that goes together. One perversion doesn't eliminate the other. Together, they form such a rare glittering necklace. The unperverted woman . . .'

"'Pooh! A female animal. Our perversions are our aristocracies. But what do you call yourself, ideal, arrogant and fervent form? I know . . . I know . . . Your mouth is human, your eyes are animal, your beard is that of a goat, your horns are that of the dominator god . . . I love you, I love you. I love you . . .'

" 'Beautiful darling!'"

✳

". . . Well, what do you think of the beautiful Endymionne? You're not answering. Are you really so annoyed that we haven't quit your house?"

"Perfidious wretch? How you led me astray, at first! But . . . the violet and pink chasuble, the voluptuous martyr, the beautiful Endymionne lying on her antelope . . . ?'

"What do you make of the Devil's spells? Do you still hold it against me?"

"Yes."

"*Au revoir* . . . lady of quality."

THE CANCEROUS WOMAN'S NIGHT

"Have you forgiven me?"

"..."

"Oh, to welcome me, to caress me, to beat me, to try to pervert me a little more—naïve individual!—to whisper to me: 'I love you . . . I love you . . .' isn't forgiving me, beautiful darling!"

"Enough!"

"Tonight, let's go to the home of the cancerous woman."

"The home of the cancer . . ."

"Yes. She knew Satan, that one, and perhaps more than the nun with the romantic eyes and the lady of quality—*Salut*, Madame! I had taken an astonishing form in order to enslave, subjugate and doom her . . . in this world. As for the other, we'll talk about that later. I had, therefore, taken in order to possess Hortense, a born lady companion, the form of Judge. I entered into that woman's life at the age of thirty. At thirty-two she entered into mine. You remember her aggressive and jaundiced thinness, her big sad pointed nose, her little eyes, so black or so green—as you wish—and that satanic richness: her long wicked eyelashes. She was thin, very thin. Hortense, and one could have made a handful of twigs with which to light the fire with her skeleton. Brown hair, it goes without saying, and even a little naturally curly.

"From the day when I employed her, that bilious rebel became so mild, so supple and so humble that I no longer doubted my power. I was a born old bachelor. I was misanthropic and clear-sighted, with a liver complaint and the incurable melancholy of men of the robe. I lodged in a narrow, somber, dirty street, aristocratic and slightly demented too, for on the old houses, haunted by archaeologists, the stone devils never ceased to prove that, in the Middle Ages, fervor and obscenity were almost the same thing.

"My apartment was composed of an entresol that overlooked the courtyard. I never heard the tenants of the first floor walking around. I sometimes divined, up above, the glide of slippers or mice, and on windy nights, such moans departed from the room above mine that I preferred never to wonder whether they were colliding air currents or a paralytic valetudinarian surrendering himself, while dreaming, to his morose humor.

"You've seen the courtyard about which I'm speaking: funereal ivy everywhere, a clump of medicinal mint between the damp paving-stones, a dry fountain that sometimes ran, like an old woman weeping in remembering . . .

"I lived in the shadows, surrounded by my dossiers, sometimes pursued by the gaze of a man condemned to death, surveyed by green files. It's astonishing how the color green installs itself within you as soon as you're disillusioned and slightly bald. Moss invaded the supports of my balconies and my Empire candlesticks were obstinate in distilling verdigris. I remind you of the immense rep curtains that seemed to be ten meters long. Oh, the eight green curtains of my green drawing room! It was necessary for it to have four windows! A way of seeing a little less clearly there, since the courtyard was all sadness, damp, vegetation and north wind . . .

"A cat formed, between Hortense and me, a fervent and silent bond, and when that black beast, which never ceased to fabricate phosphorus in its dilated pupils, slid on to Hortense's knees she said: "Jesus! Pity! Lord!" and made the sign of the cross, for she was as pious as a damned soul.

"One evening—and with what a voice of a chlorotic congregationist, full of amazement—she sang me a *complainte* that a nun who directed a convent work-room had taught her, one of those sickly candles that only illuminate tincture of iodine and chilly humors. The kitchen in which we were sitting was one of those hovels that cockroaches run through by night like black veins, and the smoky and paltry oil lamp was lit . . .

"I understood that Hortense, having confessed that morning, was employing a sacristy maneuver against me. However, I listened to the end to the story of seven nuns who, linked to one another, were stifling in an impasse in Purgatory, and never ceased wetting their brown robes with a sweat of anguish that rolled over their green hands in sulfurous pearls. It was charming. One cannot imagine of what they are capable, those abulics who put the justice of God into litanies worthy of being chanted before the finest subjects in the Musée Grévin.[1]

"I have no need to tell you that with the aid of the poker, I left Hortense for dead in the midst of her cockroaches, woodlice and centipedes, between the dubious sink and a portrait of a propagator of the Faith, a missionary the color of bile.

"From then on, my lady companion was to me, like the fire to the fireplace, like the spider to its web, like the salivary glad to gluttony.

"Let's go into her room. The Judge I represented had just died at the age of seventy. He had only been buried the day before, and the bed was in the state in which the old wretch had left it when four of my imps disguised as humble undertakers came to fetch him.

"The enormous body had weighed, sweated and suffered there, and the Empire candlesticks were weeping verdigris around my bronze bust. I was, believe me, a fine Judge."

"Horror! Horror!"

"Put on that puce silk robe, cover your head with black lace, put on distinguished mittens, dear she-demon, and suspend the cross of an abbess around your neck. You understand that, because I'm a gallant demon, I don't

---

1 The Musée Grevin, founded in 1882, was a Parisian copy of London Madame Tussaud's, which became the model for similarly-titled collections of wax figures of famous people exhibited in other cities.

want to make the old ladies in oval frames cry out in astonishment and anxiety in the cold green rep drawing room. One of them is as old as she is damned, and her reprobation has taken refuge in her sad and stiff white hair as well as her malachite medallion, which follows you like a gaze in her narrow mouth . . . Try to resemble a little those accursed oldsters, my she-demon, and make in passing a reverence to the secretary who is full of the corrupt gold that one accumulates coin by coin, and who shelters, in addition, an Erasmus in poor condition and a deaths-head that would like to be frightful but is quite simply—*vanitas! vanitas!*—ridiculous, for the Judge coiffed her in one of his black skullcaps."

"But I'm afraid . . . I'm afraid myself."

"Come on, no stupidity. Salute Hortense."

"What a terrible vision! That shawl over her figure, those tears in the wool of that mourning-dress, that octogenarian as fat as a fist that is dying to punch but unable to express it because it's almost crippled . . . Madame Hortense, I salute you!"

"That's good, that's good. That woman has a right to your admiration, your esteem and your fervor. She is more obedient, that willful woman, than the shutter one closes every evening, the door one opens every morning, the bucket one lowers into the well and the log that one throws on the fire. 'Yes, Monsieur,' she said, and every time, she damned herself a little more.

"Ha ha! And to think that courtesans imagine that they attract Satan when they confront him naked with their thighs in the air and debauchees presume that I inhabit them! What would I do with those dandies and sluts? Milord l'Arsouille?[1] Messaline? No thanks. Not for me. I have better. I have . . . Hortense. *Salut*, Hortense!"

"Oh, that rapacious and withered face, that toothless jaw, those excessive wrinkles . . ."

"Excessive wrinkles? Yes . . . they really are . . ."

". . . Those eyes like an extinct fire surrounded by glowing embers . . .

"She's beautiful—isn't she?—Hortense. And you don't know everything. She only has one breast. At forty years of age she had the operation in the Judge's own house, very carefully. I can't tell you what had determined Hortense's tumor. To what extent did her master curse it? I don't know that either. What does it matter? The teat was affected and the cancer, after two years, as sure as I'm a stout and solemn judge, was a solid cancer as deep-rooted as couch-grass.

"It's necessary, she-demon that one day I make the rich man weep with chagrin, who thinks that because he has a superb creature on his arm, a carriage at his door and youth in his mouth, he is privileged. Vermin! Vermin! What about your soul? And its pasture? And the profound evil of the ardent? It's necessary that I confound the scholar who believes that he sometimes brushes with his horn the shadow of mine. Dust! Dust! What will you know as long as you have not made your crucibles boil in the sun of my madness? It's necessary

1 "Milord l'Arsouille" was a character created by Charles de la Battut for the Carnival of Paris in the 1830s: a caricature of an English aristocrat whose name presumably reflects an unwillingness or inability to spell "arsehole". He was featured in several contemporary cartoon drawings and was subsequently featured in a number of twentieth-century movies.

144

that I shall dance one night before the star that the astronomer never ceases to watch, because he is an idiot—which is to say, as astronomer: 'It's approaching . . . it's there . . . it's 365 centuries since . . .' Imbecile! I'll steal it from you, the star that is making a fool of you, and plant it in Hortense's heart. *Salut*, Hortense! Isn't she beautiful, my possessed?

"'One evening—he had been occupied with it for three months—the Judge said to her: 'Will you sleep with me.'

"'Yes, Monsieur.'

"Six months later: 'You'll no longer go to mass, damned devotee.'

"'Yes, Monsieur.'

"Ten years later: 'You disgust me.'

"'Yes, Monsieur.'

"'It's necessary for you to have your breast cut off.'

"'Yes, Monsieur.'

"Last year: 'Hortense, you'll be my sole heir. Are you cupid?'

"'Yes, Monsieur.'

"'Stupid animal. You don't know what you're saying. There's no one more disinterested than you . . .'

"'Yes, Monsieur.'

"'I'm giving you all my stocks and bonds, my jewelry, all my old ladies, my death's head . . .'

"'Yes, Monsieur.'

"'I prefer to go to Hell, you see. If I offered my fortune to the apostolic—ha ha!—and Roman Church, a good go-between, perhaps sincere, would assure me, between two candles, and imposing upon me a few applications of oil, that I'd be *saved*. But it pleases me to make you rich instead: rich, you who count seventy-seven years and who have—thank you, Hortense—lost a breast in my service.'

"'Yes, Monsieur.'

"'That's good. I'm going to Hell, aren't I?

"'Yes, Monsieur.'

"'You're going to join me there?'

"'Yes, Monsieur,'

"'Hurry up.'

"'Yes, Monsieur . . .'"

"Look around you carefully; look carefully at:

"The implacable green curtains, the silence.

"Cujas,[1] the street of the Gray Penitents.

"The criminal trials, the cancer.

"The deference, the Judge's eye.

"Forty-six years of accursed community.

"The supreme rendezvous . . .

"Amour!"

---

1 The reference is to a standard legal manual compiled by Jacques Cujas (1522-1590).

THE COUNTRY CURÉ'S NIGHT

"That one I possess during his sleep. I play with him, I play with him. He's my recreation. When he's asleep, I never cease allowing him to be invaded by extravagance. In addition, I enable him to live an image d'Épinal—you know that I'm the great illuminator—nothing but a sumptuousness of the end of Empire, a shameful enjoyment of sorcery.

"The man is ignorant, simple, pious—in the very gracious sense of the word—mild, pure—in the most absolute sense—and so candid! Penetrated by respect for Scripture, doesn't he call his pig 'Nabuchodonosor'? And, full of Christian prejudice, doesn't he call his neighbor's pig a 'dirty Jew?'

"But these brave fellows, country curés, can't have been nourished with impunity on Hell, Heaven, Limbo, Purgatory, mysteries, sacraments, orthodoxy, exorcisms, fathers of the Church, martyrs, sacred legislators, schisms, predestinations, councils, miracles, the Bible and its hundred thousand explosions, etc., etc. . . . and, to finish, the over-subtle casuistry of Monsieur de Loyola. Where can these poor intoxicates find deliverance, when they are not fanatics, drunkards or debauchees, and have the faith of innocents?

"And then, by dint of spreading him around and vulgarizing him, one ends up depreciating God of aristocracy, damn it! Here more than anywhere else.

"A bumpkin of a seminarist, still full of soil and potatoes, gives you lessons in infinity with an ease that confounds me, the Devil, and I can't help thinking: *A few years ago that simpleton reached the end of the rule of three thanks to his schoolteacher, and looked after his father's cows. Now, here he is strolling in the pathways of Genesis with the assurance of a distinguished agronomist, flourishing with agricultural merit. 'On the second day, God made superb plantations . . .'*

"Your execrated nuns were also victims of the indigestible Catholic aliment. In the garden of the convent, there wasn't a single bee that didn't hum that eternal condemnation: *sin, sin, sin* . . . Poor girls! You've seen them: chlorotic, moaning, fainting, scrofula here, modesty everywhere, the Devil there. Or pitiless, ferocious, persecutors with hard heels, aggressive keys, flat bosoms and loins of steel . . . poor girls!

"At least our good curé has his pig, his rabbits and that vivacious flower Saint John's Wort to purge him—if I may put it like that—the village toad and the hawthorn under which children say bonjour to him, fishing-rod in hand.

"Would you like to hear him dream aloud? But won't you find me excessive? How shall I put it . . . ? Poets never have enough. A species of heroic and burlesque folly sometimes takes possession of them, so strong in me that Don Quixote seems to me to be a coward in comparison with my imps, who, coiffed with windmills, perpetuate with claps of thunder the laughter of Sancho in the cabarets of the sun. Can one imagine a poet who is not suddenly invaded by clownish ostentation when, for example, he has just wept because of the face of a poor old woman and the rose she held . . . such a long time ago?"

"Listen:

"That Jean-Foutre[1] of a beadle is still on horseback on the steeple of the bell-tower. But he's taken care to plant a lighted candle in every lemon-tree in my garden. In a chasuble of darkness, an owl is escorting me, with Hell in its eye.

"Ding-a-ling . . . ding-a-ling . . . ding-a-ling . . . a silvery bell is sounding in every flower. Laughter of the Devil, you're everywhere!

"Although I'm fat, round, small, very small on this cedar surrounded by the false brilliants of stars and more beautiful than that of Lebanon, I'm climbing with the ease of a monkey and an inspired man. Possessed by the Spirit, I'm going to preach my sermon:

"Buck up, the incredulous! Why don't you have faith? Since the time that I could mouth 'Have faith,' you've been treating me with ill will, miscreants, and it will cost you dear. Buck up, the lukewarm! Sainte Thérèse, who bought from the Devil the very Spanish little dagger that she sometime plants in God's heart, will do likewise to you for that. That nun ought to have married

---

1 An argot term for a good-for-nothing.

Torquemada. One, in the name of divine hatred, and the other in the name of divine love, would have made the universe an immense red pyre in which heretics and the morose would have exploded like chestnuts. Oh, my children, what rejoicing! Buck up, the scrupulous! The Demon sometimes takes on a contrite, timorous and delicate face, and when, before the holy table, the faithful see him weep into a four-sou handkerchief, they renounce communion: '*Non sum dignus,*' and the Devil, while never ceasing to shed tears as large as grains of corn, makes a knot in his handkerchief: 'Good business!' he thinks, and, his day's work done, he goes to mingle with the crows who are leading a sabbat of black wings around the bell-tower.

"Oh my brethren, my brethren! Heeded, today, by Balthazar the magnificent, who, in his feasts, confused the prostitutes and the torches, by Sardanapalus, who dressed as a woman and respired salts, by Pope Innocent VIII, who, as a good father of a family, surrounded his fourteen bastards—look, the smallest wears, like my nephew Gustave when he was four years old, a beautiful white collarette—adored by satraps and Brahmins, studied by almahs and high priests, covered with ivy by druids and fans by the little Chinese saved by pigs thanks to the sou of the propagation of the Faith—let me wipe a grateful tear from my eye!—watched closely by a good number of Hottentots, Redskins and Cannibals threatened—who knows why?—by their bearded missionaries, looked up and down superbly by Moses, that horned bachelor who, with folded arms—I'll pay you back for that!—let the brazen serpent he hides in his pocket contradict me, saluted by Job, who must have had a holy dung-heap behind him, borne in triumph by Saul, who has light wings, like all madmen, approved by a very gracious mummy who is rocking an impassive Pharaoh, touched on the forehead by the enormous finger of a fakir reminiscent of an old root, disemboweled by a martyr's palm and the veils of these ladies: Semiramis, the pearl of Babylon; Cleopatra, the mask of Egypt; Dido, the demon of Carthage, Magdalen, the redhead from Magdala; and even the first female; Sarah, who, at 777 years old still made a work of flesh with profit and Abraham, a work of flesh regarded drolly—yes, believe me, very drolly—by the Antichrist, who—*retro, retro!* another trap of the Demon!—resembled unmistakably that ugly mug Jean-Foutre . . .

"Accursed! Reproved! Terrible! I will confound your arrogance. I will plunge you in boiling oil and pitch. The Eternal and I will hear the famous gnashing of teeth of which the sacred texts speak complaisantly. And do you know what we will say as we pass the hands of well-nourished prelates over our bellies? We will say: 'How all these tortures rise toward us in agreeable smoke! If there were no damned here, we would not be able to sit down on out armchairs of dark green velvet—no, garnet velvet, like well-off dentists—with such sensuality and abandon! What incomparable music! A pinch of snuff, Eternal?'

"'Thank you, my dear colleague. The Shulamite has only hidden the odor of the snuff-box from me.'

"'The Shulamite! That whore! Solomon, like some modern author that I cannot name,[1] ought be put on the Index for having recounted the turpitudes of that nightwalker. What am I saying? To prison with that pornography—and a one franc fine. And to cap it all, to the boiler with the Shulamite and her Froissart!'

"'Not yet. Later. Sultans—and I'm a very decorative one; isn't that so, Schariar?—aren't so quick to cut off the head and the big toe of their favorite. You'd like to crush, destroy and annihilate everything, my colleague.'

"'Hoasnnah! I am Sabaoth, God of armies, the great Jehovah, the potentate of the locusts . . .'"

"There, there! What did I tell you? But tonight, he isn't content to ramble. Abandoning himself to the inspiration with which you're familiar, he's becoming ferocious. Wait, I'll wake him up. Dawn is announcing itself by the frisson of the Orient,

Bang! Bang! Bang!

"Eh? Who goes there? Have you saddled my camel, Eleazer?"

"Open up to the sunlight . . . humble fisher!"

---

1 Jean Richepin, in the words he supplied to a musical piece by Emmanuel Chabrier, the one-act lyric drama *La Sulamite* (1885).

THE SPANISH WOMAN'S NIGHT

"What! To see that cavern opening in the damp rock again, preceded by that garden of box-trees where the dahlias resemble daggers planted in the languishing heart of autumn? To see that solitude again where, shivering, I gazed at the poplars of the road mingling with the clouds galloping like herds? No . . . no . . . let's not go into the house of the Spanish Woman. The Pyrenees, the greatest Pyrenees with volcanoes of snow, don't take their eyes off it."

"Let's go into the Spanish Woman's house. Ah! That low room, so dark; that crypt! And those Virgins, all those Virgins each so ornamented and supervised by the red lamp. And that black Madonna clad in gold, crowned with fire, as if she were a prisoner of emeralds and topazes! Her dear little black infant, also crowned with fire, is also guarded by jealous gems. O dear Jesus, paltry and royal, Satan would like to caress you . . . *Senorito mio*, I salute you."

"I only saw the mistress of this place twice, but I'll never forget the excessively silky dress, the color of tobacco, of that old Carmen with the grim moustache and

153

the enormous belly, the evil eye and the adorable fan, the ballerina of defiance around somber Spanish meditation . . . That woman belched ignobly, but her fan . . ."

"It was a souvenir of José, who, on a whim, went into a monastery and never quit, so to speak, the black hood. The Spanish Woman, in that epoch, was eighteen years old, José counted twenty-two. For forty years she never ceased to appeal to him, and one can affirm that the Spanish Woman has nourished her monstrous belly with the most beautiful amour there ever was. She only had one obsession: to reclaim the infidel from God, and all the holy imagery that you see in her house has only shone, only burned, only dreamed and only exalted for the man who has brutalized himself and grown old under his burlesque and macabre garment."

The Spanish Woman dipped her ring-laden fingers in infamous saffron sauces, but the pretty little gourd that is ever full, Hope, is always miraculously thirst-quenching . . .

Tarot cards reposed on the foot of the black Virgin, attentive, sparkling, contradictory, ironic and malevolent in all their colors. And there were strange dialogues between the old Carmen and the divine Negress:

"Isn't it the case, Madonna, that the knight weeping blood is the sign of an amorous visit?"

"Yes," said the Madonna reeking of myrrh, inflated by veils and crowned with fire.

"The low closed house beaten by crows, but where the eye of a prisoner looks at you through the ventilation shaft . . ."

"A sign of carnal obsession, *mala mujer*," grunted the Madonna surrounded by emeralds like vipers.

"He only made love to me three times, my José. He had my maidenhead and since then—by the Madonna—I have only slept with the Devil!"

"*Mala mujer!*"

"But can you imagine, Madonna, that the Devil has José's face . . ."

"*Senorito mio*, hide under my yellow gauze. Don't look at that woman's thoughts, in her huge belly."

And with her crown of fire, the fiery and modest Negress ignited the muslin of her ardent cloud.

"Ah, Madonna, it's necessary that I change your cloud every day. Why do you set it on fire every day?"

"Because of your lust, *hija del demonio!*"

"And you, how miserly you are, O Black One! How well you defend the jewels of your peddler's tray!"

"Yes," said the Madonna, and from the pleats of her robe, where topazes lay in ambush like little scorpions, she took a slender dagger, while her fire-crowned Jesus smiled at the idolatrous crypt as he smiled at the poor cross when he was no longer a dear little black infant but a dreamer with blond curls . . .

"Oh, Madonna, Madonna! It's been twenty years, thirty years that I've been hoping . . . however, the tarots tell me . . ."

"That he will come back?"

And the divine Negress laughed and laughed, all odorous, warm and nocturnal, delivered to rampant gems. "But *caramba*," she said, "you only think of *ti hermosa jovem*, of José when he was as upright, and as proud, as Castille and Granada . . . as gracious, and as fervent as the fan and Andalusia . . ."

155

"The body of my José, quivering more than a bull at the first *banderille* . . ." And the Spanish Woman turned toward a statuette representing her lover in his youth, a guitar in his hands.

"Ha ha ha!" said the Madonna. "But at present he's only an old mendicant monk, here, figuring fear in accompanying death . . ."

"And to think that the Devil has my José's twenty years! Every night, every night, Madonna, *Senor mio,* I see him again as when he had Spain by the mouth—which is to say, *la flor de las celosos amores*—under a fig tree under a well in Murcia."

"Isn't she an imbecile, poor thing!" the Madonna murmured to her Jesus. And then she thought: *The Devil? The Devil? He's a great poet . . . hush. He's very handsome; isn't he, my dear little black infant?*

And the Jesus crowned with fire, who heard his mother dreaming and singing about Satan eternally, said: "Yes, yes," under the gauze of the very holy idol . . .

But every evening, every evening, their garments caught fire at the green-veiled lamp . . .

"Poor Spanish Woman! She was fifty-eight years old when she was murdered. By whom? The murderer is still on the run . . ."

"He'll always be on the run."

"What is strange is that the door wasn't open, the bolt was shot and the key turned. The dog didn't bark . . ."

"Too occupied with gazing at a bat carrying a muted lantern, the dog! As for the cat, as an unknown Lady had put a necklace of topazes around her neck that night, he was dancing on the roof to annoy the moon."

"You're always joking. No sign of a break-in anywhere . . ."

"The weather-vane didn't hear anything. It said so."

"Don't laugh. The Spanish Woman in the eternal excessively silky dress the color of tobacco reigned over her bed as the dead reign there . . . Her majesty was incomparable, it seems . . ."

"She had known the sensuality of strangulation. That was doubtless why she was smiling."

"Yes, it's said that she was smiling divinely. The marks of a singular hand were visible on her throat . . ."

"Bertillon[1] would have stopped eating and drinking in consequence."

"Your attitude is indecent. We're talking about a murder."

"Of course!"

"Around her, the order was most complete."

"And most mystical. Each of the fourteen or fifteen Virgins of her crypt was leaning over her little red lamp and praying in whispers, lips sighing. As for the black Madonna, she was smiling divinely, like the dead woman. But it was quickly observed that she had gone mad,

---

1 Alphonse Bertillon (1853-1914) was a policeman and statistician who pioneered the use of "mug shots" and the use of anthropometric data in French police procedure in the 1880s; anthropometric measurements remained the standard method of legal identification in France until they were replaced by fingerprints, He also pioneered the statistical comparison of suicide rates, which revealed interesting patterns for which sociologists, including Herbert Spencer and Emile Durkheim, sought explanations.

that her Jesus, the dear little black infant, was trembling with fear, because José no longer had a head. What had happened? That didn't prevent him from playing the guitar. *Todavia una serenata!*"

"Oh, shut up!"

". . . As for the tarot cards assembled and shuffled by an invisible hand, they were playing adorable games of Andalusian seduction around the black madwoman and the decapitated charmer. *Todavia una serenata!*"

"No richness was lacking."

"None, save for a little emerald cross that the Spanish Woman was accustomed to wear in the fat of her neck, alongside the perpetual provocative carnation. What chromos, those females![1] But the little cross was redis-covered, a little later, in the throat of the joyful dead woman. I can't say whether it was her, in the excitement of dying, or me who . . . to finish it off . . ."

"What, you?"

"Eh! By the divine Negress, I was weary—you under-stand?—of hearing that fifty-eight-year-old *mala mujer* call out, for nearly half a century for José . . . José, the hooded monk. I too have sensitive nerves, so I found it appropriate—it's necessary to provide some supreme illusion, isn't it, to those one is about to strangle?—to assume, that night, the appearance of a Black Penitent.

"*Todavia una serenata!*"

---

1 Although "chromo" can refer to any colored photograph, and is used in that trivial literal sense elsewhere in the text, it is probably relevant here that the term was frequently used in early twentieth century Paris to refer more specifically to picture postcards of "actresses," the popular soft pornography of the era, while the term *femelle* [female] usually referred to female animals, often used in a fashion similar to the English "bitch."

THE SHOEMAKER'S NIGHT

That man only sleeps while trembling. He has to watch over the dreams of his wife, the sighs of his daughters, and the good behavior of his she-cat. What would become of him if he heard his redhead *miaow*, with the voice of a she-cat saluting the moon in the eyes of the tomcat who desires her? He would kill her, he would have to kill her. But as other cats the color of fire would celebrate the sabbat of defiance, ambush and dance on neighboring rooftops, he would not be liberated. At least, the presence of his she-cat, La Moune, prevents him from hearing the others wail, and his damnation, when he sees her lying between his pot of basil and the facetious hunchback of the chromo accompanying the holy-water stoup, he respires a little, but he has a fiery jewel in each eye.

That man only sleeps while trembling. His daughters, his twins, his redheads, oh, if they took it into their heads to fall for a man, or God, he would kill them, he would kill them. But as other beautiful and haughty virgins the color of fire would be in bed, either with a gallant or a scapular, he would not be liberated. At least

159

the presence of Jeannine and Armande, one sewing, her head coiffed with sunlight, the other leaning over the stove, her head coiffed with flame, prevents him hearing other red-headed virgins moaning or praying. He respires a little, but he has the ardor of red pepper on his tongue in watching his damnations.

That man only sleeps while trembling. While he was beside her, like a dead man, his wife, his Berthe, his redhead, might have been thinking that she could have married a short blond man without much hair. And if, the next day, he saw traces of that criminal dream in the eyes of that she-cat, he would kill her, he would kill her. But as other wives the color of fire commit mental adultery at all hours, he would not be liberated. At least the presence of his damnation, which measures one meter seventy-eight and is always polishing her copperware, in which she is reflected thirty times over, prevents him from hearing sin roaming like a sturdy vagabond in the russet soul of russet wives. And although, in brushing the skirt of his terrible Berthe, he is bitten in the side by the accursed dog, which always has a hair shirt in its mouth, he respires a little . . .

All arms and legs, that brown-haired shoemaker, as rigid as a log, good for a monk's hood, tall enough to make the spiders of the ceiling-beams flee when he gets up from his last, his nose harsh, his hair bushy, his eyes too bright for his eyelids, sweaty, cynical, dirty and as black as the bottom of the cooking-pot. The devil of the Catholics, what! A nasty devil, between us. Such people, whatever René the Suspect said, will be surveyed for all eternity by both God and the Devil, having no guardian angel. Of the Evil Spirit they never make the Spirit of the Beautiful, the Spirit of Good, or simply the Spirit. When they ambush him in the mass of their cathedrals, it is always in an impure, frantic, sad form . . . Ha ha ha! But which, nevertheless, gives to the carillons up there on high a free and discordant note. "That rings false," says the High Priest.

"Monsieur High Priest, I make you my apologies, but it always rings false—which is to say, in spite of you, ironic and joyful . . ."

And by virtue of a strange inversion, the Devil, under the cornices, has more seduction than the saints in the stained-glass windows, and all Gothic fervor is nothing but the triumph of the Gargoyle . . .

Let's return to the shoemaker who only sleeps while trembling. How could that man repose calmly and confidently? Berthe? A redhead with blue eyes. Jeannine? A redhead with green eyes. Armande? A redhead with dark eyes. La Moune? Russet with yellow eyes.

He has eyes that are, by turns, green, dark, yellow and blue. That phenomenon is produced by night when he prowls and laments so softly, so softly that the rain falling in the gutter astonishes him, although it is so full of languor.

"I'll kill them. I'll kill them," he moans.

"Why?" the shameful wind asks him; the wind: a "poor relative" who begs for small joints in shops and a turn of a waltz from a weathervane.

"Why? Because they're redheads, redheads, redheads . . ." And his eyes fill with amorous tears.

The shoemaker's wife has a delightful beauty spot like the eye of a mouse in the corner of her abdomen. Woe! The impious father never stops thinking that his daughters, whose twenty years have the scent of flowers and goat, each have a similar little velvet eye, somber and pensive, in the corner of her red-haired abdomen . . . and when, at midnight, he throws himself upon his wife like one accursed, it is because he is thinking with too much fury about the bellies of virgins inhabited by rodent eyes . . .

In the little provincial shop there are perpetual scenes. Its hairy Satan is not comfortable. People say that he "drinks." Ha ha! He is so sober, that man, that one glass of wine a day suffices for his shoemaker's thirst. As for his diabolical thirst, that's something else. Personally, I know that *delirium tremens* never quits that terrible alcoholic, but how can one suspect the flamboyant bottles with which that devil poisons himself?

The holy-water stoup that reigns above the grotesque chromo hears every day, every evening and every night, cries uttered that make lust tremble on its humble provincial throne. And yet, the possessed man only agitates like a despicable drunkard, a brute of a worker chained to the last. But Nabuchodonosor, Sardanapalus and Balthazar have made more than a few whores, sinners and pigs with me when I take the appearance of a great sad female . . .

And our descendants populate the earth . . .

But let us not frighten devotees and apothecaries. They too are my henchmen, though. Everything that is inspired by sadism belongs to me, and I know that

162

parishioners and bottles are snares of damnation. Sleep in peace, apothecaries and devotees; I don't mean you any harm, but if I approached a sulfur match to your anointed carcasses you would catch fire like Sodom and Gomorrah, and I wouldn't be astonished by it.

※

The other week the rumor ran around the little town that Jeannine had broken two teeth by falling against a sidewalk. Oh, credulous little town! And what do you make of the Devil's fist? But also, why did that naïve Jeannine declare that before turning thirty she might perhaps like to marry? "That's for you, my redhead?" And Jeannine, mutilated, rolled on the ground.

"Oh! Madame Berthe, do you have a stye on your eye?"

"Yes," said Madame Berthe, who also has dignity and absolves all of her devil's crimes. But it was another blow of the latter's fist that the shoemaker's wife is hiding under a modest bandage. Can you imagine that that woman had said "Bonjour" amiably to a client—and what a client! the cretin Pataud, But for the shoemaker, the insult he received had a more serious reason. While she was smiling at Pataud the cretin, all of the blue bodice that Madame Berthe was wearing was also smiling. It smiled like the copper sulfate in the jealous laboratory, the cornflowers in pious images and the angel Gabriel in the stained-glass window extinguishing in the sunset. What! Are you so candid, then, Madame Berthe, that you're unaware of the malice of the color blue, its disturbing power over the Devil's senses? And while it envelops your russet breast, you can smile! You want to provoke Hell, then, Madame Berthe? "That's for you, my redhead!" and the victim utters such a loud cry of pain that the stoup and the hunchback jump simultaneously.

Armande is in bed today. She is spitting a little blood: a fist between her shoulder-blades. "That's for you, my redhead!" But alas, why were you singing, Armande, a song in which there is a question of cherries and resedas? Are not resedas and cherries, in the soul of a redhead, maddening for a shoemaker, causing the Demon to rise up against the Demon?

In addition, the cat too is half-stunned. Has she not taken it into her head, that imbecile, to seek the Devil with her yellow eye full of treason, over the shoemaker's shoulder? That subtle man is jealous of her. "That's for you, my redhead!" and the cat, licking her dolorous belly under the holy water stoup, meditates on the passions of Satan . . .

Long live Satan, the shopkeeper, the *poilu*! What do you expect? He has decided that the eternity of his wax glue and his licentious, idiotic or bloody chromos, his nails, his leather apron, his dancing goatee, his frightful laugh, his inexplicable frenzy and his concupiscence, of which he is quite unaware, require the absolute devotion of Berthe, Jeannine, Armande and La Mouche, those four flaming torches!

THE HERMIT'S NIGHT

"What is he saying?"

"He's saying: Go away!"

"To whom?"

"To a Shadow, which responds to him: 'One only chases away those that are in one's abode.'"

"He's weeping."

"He's crying 'Go way!' again—and yet, what do you see?"

"A beggar's wallet on the wall, a spoon on the table; a litter of dry leaves on which the Hermit is lying."

"Lying? Ha ha! He's dancing, everywhere, the Hermit, even in the chimney with the owl, and on the crust of bread with the voracious mouse, and before the moon with the white sin of despair. You can see my poor body extended, but look; what is escaping from the wound that the cilice, the penitent cilice, is making in his side?"

"Golden tears. In truth, golden tears . . ."

"Cleopatra was able to weep them, and Magdalen wept them . . . From that withered breast, what is rising?"

"A rose, a veritable rose . . ."

"What is opening there?"

"A great fiery eye that never ceases closing and opening . . ."

"I forbid you to look at mine."

"I'm afraid."

"The Hermit is also afraid, for the nightingale has a brown hood, but what a voice! For the pitcher in sandstone, cold and poor, but—O vision more tempting than the others—the water of the Jordan runs inexhaustibly from its gullet, the pure water *par excellence*, distributed by the mortal hand of the apostle, a callused hand, humble and great . . . The Hermit is troubled because of that hand."

"Why?"

"Simply because he contemplates it in its passionate and sad animality. It requires no more to be greatly culpable and greatly damned. Have you never despaired of your soul because of a hand?"

"I often see one, motionless in the darkness. On each of its fingers, save for the index finger, a sharp diamond sparkles by way of a nail, but I can never discover what symbol the indicative finger has at its extremity. It remains in shadow."

"I forbid you to look at mine."

"I'm afraid."

"The Hermit is also afraid. He perceives his beehive through the closed shutters. It is coiffed in soft and weary sunlight, and there is nothing more dissolving for the spirit than surprising the languor of audacious radiance, Do you never shudder, not when the cymbals sing, but when they're waiting in a corner, or perhaps despairing there?"

"Why?"

"Because they're thinking that they will only make a poor sound, endlessly . . . and yet, the soul of storms inhabits them. I forbid you to look at my hands, which sometimes want to exalt cymbals in vain . . ."

"I'm afraid."

"The Hermit is also afraid. 'Go away!' he says. 'Go away!' He wants to chase away, with the nameless Shadow, the dust of the ground, the remains of the fire-wood, the roots that he boils in order to eat them at dawn, the hour when sin causes the frustrated pilgrim who has gone astray to shiver under the cross on the road, damp cloth on his shoulder . . . he wants to rid himself thus of those few chestnuts, one of which still has its green, piquant and bitter shell, and that sandal scratched by brambles, and that nail he has planted in his hand by way of sacrilegious and holy imitation, and that bindweed lamenting at his door, more innocent than a cherub's sigh . . . I forbid you to listen to my sigh.

"'Go away,' murmurs the Hermit, 'go away!' Do you know what he glimpsed this afternoon? A goat—a beautiful she-goat as gray as the dust and misery, coiffed with honeysuckle, between the sunlight and the rock. 'Go away! Go away!' Do you know what sobbed as he passed by? A company of quail . . . 'Go away! Go away!' he said in a sob that moved the wheat more than the scythe will. Do you know what he is thinking now? About the smoke from his roof; and he veils his face. Those who are never invaded and tormented because of smoke and a light belt are, in truth, unworthy of me. Smile, my daughter, smile, but I forbid you to look at my belt . . .

"At present the Hermit is dreaming of a golden chasuble, and seeing his heart, a fervent and ravishing furnace, burning incense for the glory of God. Ha ha! I'm planting in his forehead a Roman amethyst and the culpable papal mystery is laughing in his accursed eyes. He will never be more mine, but I prefer him with his habit faded.

"I'm carrying him away . . . look . . . I'm carrying him away . . ."

"Why? That man never sins."

"Never. That's why I'm carrying him away, that great desperado. I have lesser ones: those who succumb. Ha ha! I have the worst of them: those who are never tempted. Ha ha! What would they not give, during the long monastic monotony, to see a shadow dancing on the white wall, to see a coiling serpent in a boxwood chaplet? I forbid you to look at my chaplet."

THE ARCHANGEL'S NIGHT

"You frequently mention God."

"But as the Devil never ceases to be manifest in me, I think that he must be more powerful or bolder than God, since he is more sensible to us. As for their essence, their relationship, I confess that I can only conceive them in poetry. But no one can reproach me for having, simultaneously, the ignorance and the delight of poets, their puerility and their dazzling intuition, their child-like eyes and their diviners' soul.

"When some dolor attains me I evoke God. When some joy arrives I thank the Devil. As poets express themselves willingly in imagery I would say that, for me, God is the oak tree and the Devil the enormous, ambiguous and delightful shadow of that tree with eternal roots . . . that God is the great lily that I salute and respect and the Devil the red horned beast that, in escaping from the lily, reveals to us its whiteness and demonstrates its dependence. Nothing can prevent the lily from being so radiant, nothing can prevent the curious and malevolent beast from plunging into it with all its ardor and malice. Let's admit that one is Wisdom and the other eternal

Avidity. I easily credit God with the Dream and the Devil with Movement."

"The philosophy of a poet!"

"One can't say: 'the poetry of a philosopher.' How annoying those people are, for the most part! Can't you see the advantage that the street-urchin has over the worthy Monsieur of the Institut, the sparrow over the gamekeeper, and, at Lent, the advantage of the jester Triboulet, who believes in the eternity of the carnival? The philosophy of a poet? But don't I reason with myself, as Jeremiah reasons with himself when he laments, David when he dances, Socrates when he poisons himself, Marcus Aurelius when he is his own statue of white marble, Voltaire when he makes his little eyes of a parchmented Satan gleam, and Spinoza when he puts on his dear spectacles?

"What I want is not to adopt a pedantic, ferocious, taciturn voice, not to shout 'Since I possess the truth, I shall give you a big slap in the mouth,' as Bossuet shouted through liturgical pomp and the frightful zeal of fanaticism, who put between God and the Christian the putrefaction of a coffin, and Saint Dominic, who saw the first spark of Spanish pyres springing from the eyes of his crucifix. 'Believe this . . .' they both tell me, incessantly. What arithmetic, what catechism, has ever touched a poet? To make God a mathematical proposition! A revelation for orphans and sacristans! Thank you, I prefer to glimpse him in the golden eye of a hare when it gazes into the solitude therewith.

"Since no one has ever reasoned for the whole world, let us allow poets to wander at their ease. For myself, no one will prevent me finding the eternal morality in a tale by Hans Christian Andersen, hearing the revenge of Petit Poucet perpetuated in the carmagnole of the Sans-Culottes, and being convinced that Robespierre was more influenced by the cynical Puss-in-Boots than the entire Encyclopedia."

"Fool."

"Yes. But does a philosopher ever cease crying to other philosophers: 'Messieurs, you are in error?' For me, who hears everything, that pompous and courteous formula means: 'You who don't think as I do, are block-heads, swine and camels.' Oh, let us be poets, poets, and not read books that commence thus: *Theorem I.* Let us never pass on to the second. Let us rather go into the garden, and when we see the tortoise mingled with the fennel, the mosquito with the poppy, the sunlight's billion Queens of Sheba with the insolent cymbal, the lilac and the horns of the honeysuckle, let us murmur: 'That's our divine system' and under the tender boscage that surrounds the daughters of the dream with its light arms, let us salute Epicurus and Job, Descartes and Isaiah, the placid Renan and the demonic Joshua, the mild Plato and the slightly romantic Taine, the anxious Saint Augustine and the sage Confucius, the noble Kant and that little fool Monsieur de Voltaire; let us all embrace, shedding idiotic tears, for since the world has existed, wandered, fought, wept, hoped and suffered, the rose has always flowered."

"By God and by the Devil, you're right."

"Above all by the Devil. God? Well, I don't find him anywhere . . . anywhere. As for the Devil, there isn't a hood, a virgin's veil, a bicorn hat, a corolla or a cilice under which he hasn't smiled at me. If the Devil were suppressed, what would become of the 'other rose,' in poetry, the one that we seek endlessly, a horn on the forehead, in the nudity of the faun? What does science matter if we no longer see it with the anxious eyes of Faust? Would we deign to inhabit our Paradises if we thought that they would never be traversed by the serpent? And if music only delighted us via the organ or the harp, we might be saints, but not those demons who laugh and exalt themselves, quivering with all the gold of their physical wealth because they have seen the Devil sparkle, and who live adjacent to the Devil when two cymbals have gone *zim!* with all their singing sunlight.

"Can one imagine sensuality without the Devil, the one who turns us away so frequently from lust because temptation is his supreme game? Can we conceive of a Michelangelo who never surprised his black, pensive and formidable Double while on a scaffold?

"For myself, I'm sure that if the Devil were suppressed, Dante would throw his crown of laurels to the wind, for in only parading that austere crown before organized and hierarchical Sanctity, coiffed with an aureole, wouldn't you, Dante, be saying nothing?

"When I shiver strangely from head to toe because a color is a certain blue and a fruit has a certain melancholy acidity. I can only think of the Devil who inhabits the ambiguous blue of the color and who, laughing, refuses the fruit the abundance of juice that would make it sugary.

"The Devil is sometimes miserly, and that is one of his divine seductions. He is the pupil of our eye and the sagacious gland of our jaw. He is the inspirer of our sadisms, those elegances of or sensations and their savant deformation. What are our ignorance and our poverty when we can only eat bread in eating bread, and when we can only caress a dove by caressing a dove! The Devil, fortunately, has his initiates and makes them almost as delightful as himself.

"I swear to you that I have seen him aiding Jesus to carry his cross, that I have seen him slip into the hand of Sainte Thérèse the flaming feather that will reveal, in part, the secret of the divine passion. I swear to you that I have heard him say to Leonardo da Vinci,[1] that more than lucid demon: "My beloved," and I swear to you that the Evangelist was only demented, enormous, magnificent, confused and detestable because, on that occasion, Satan tried to lead God astray.

"If one interprets the Bible satanically, it is extraordinary.

"If one accepts the Bible in the traditional sense, it is iniquitous, grotesque and intolerable. Jehovah, in himself, that old Hebrew, so fatigued, is only a ridiculous God, avid for misfortune, and a distributor of hurricanes as puerile as they are odious. But let insensate, accursed and sumptuous Lyricism mingle with it, and we can weep over the lily clad in solitude, folly with singing strings, the adolescence of the shepherd-king, the reeds of the

---

1 The printed text has "Vincy," but I have assumed that it is a misprint.

Nile submissive to the tears of a child, Rebecca leaning over the well, like all women, multicolored merchants, the demons of odorous and brown tribes, the adorable lament of Ecclesiastes who, by virtue of destroying everything, becomes eternal, and the cedar that sways the stars of Genesis in the nocturnal wind over the silence of Asia . . .

"And, finally, we remain persuaded, however scantly, because we are poets, that the Bible is a long, incoherent and ravishing prowess of the Devil, that Jehovah is a caricature of Jehovah made by the mischief or the ill humor of the Artist who is too great not to be a buffoon and too joyful not to pose the snout of Nabuchodonosor on the knees of Babylon after, from one splendor to another, he was changed into a pig.

"The Devil? Yes, the Devil! Is it necessary that I believe in the God offended by the Devil in order to believe in the Devil? No, no!

"And by the Devil, I believe in the Devil!

"He flowers all our fervors and rends them gracious, he embalms our virtues with a very perverse little sachet—lavender or melilot—he crowns our vices, royally, with a thinking tower, a thousand precious stones, a whirlwind of perfumes or the hearty laughter of a slave. He puts culpable reserve into the salvation of a nun and the great bewildered cry of errant beasts into the exaltation of a preacher. He brings us the swallow, that suspect, voracious and delectable soul, and incessantly makes that eternal migrator, amour, depart from us.

"But he gives us even more. He gives his deceptive

and splendid eyes to our beloved, and I only adore, in them, the eternal trickery of Satan.

"He is all of our activity, all of our plenitude, and if we were equitable, we would pray to the Devil as we pray to God, and with even more fervor, because, between us, the Devil is a diabolical and practical realizer, while God—do I need to tell you?—is only a worn-out dreamer.

"God? He waits for poets to awaken him, but Satan takes responsibility—believe me!—for awakening poets.

"We are so penetrated by all the infantile imagery of Heaven and Hell that, in spite of ourselves, we employ the vocabulary of catechisms. But what do we know? Nothing. What do we feel when we feel? Everything.

"Long live the Devil, then, by means of whom I sense. As a child I already played peek-a-boo with him, and his provocative dancing shadow brushed me every time I touched flowers, sunlight, desire—that insatiable angel—or strength, that squat and concentrated demon who is nothing but silence, whereas his rapid brother is nothing but sighs.

"And whether the Devil emerged from a lair or descended from a mountain, whether he caused the star that contained him to burst by opening his wings or, in escaping from Hell, he had saluted the shade of the desperate musician, what did it matter to me? It was sufficient to know that he was there, there, there, by my side, you see, and to caress his intelligent head.

"That which we experience is our only verity. Well, I aspire to God and I possess, relatively, Satan. Are they not only One? Are they really two? The Catholics have admitted the holy Trinity; personally, without imposing the rigor of a doctrine upon myself—God and the Devil preserve me from that!—I admit—what am I saying? I worship—the holy Dualism that has been revealed to me, and those who form it, in the fundamental harmony, God and the Devil, are as precious to me as to one another.

"One is sunk in his perfection, but we will awaken him one day, we singers! The other is all agitation and folly, all audacity and imprudence, all genius and curiosity; he goes to harangue the daughters of the rain who weep, green and shivering over the celestial reservoirs that they aliment, while sighing: 'Well, Mesdames, would it not please you to rally to my red banner? Let us render a visit to the sacred fauns of the sun, whose tresses blaze and blaze and who never ceases to dance his round, the azure at his backside . . .'

"Immediately, dryness extends over the Earth of humans and the other planets. But we are only occupied with ours. There is enough toil there!

"Another time, it is four or five demonic Cyclopes that he engages: 'Get up! Quickly, in that world down there, my lads, let's make the echoes of infinity rumble, and raise an interrogative eyebrow at my Double, the serene Lord.'

"And here we are in the earthquakes, the cyclones, the hectic flight of sandstorms, the deserts . . .

"After those he shakes too rudely, when he encounters them in the melancholy hovels of mysticism—Job,

Benoit Labre,[1] Elisabeth of Hungary,[2] Verlaine and two or three fakirs—pestilence, cholera and devotion fall upon our cities, for those illuminates inevitably carry upon them colonies of microbes, given that they neglect their hair abominably, to the profit of their souls . . .

"Well, enough childishness . . ."

"But it's a matter of the petulance of the Devil! You have to remember that he didn't rest until he had proposed a charade to Eve: 'My whole is a delicious fruit' and taught Noah—the first ingénue!—the art of lacking modesty without meaning to."

"Let's not joke any longer. Who said, with an astonishing audacity: 'One only dies when one wants to'? And it isn't only a matter of our bodies. How much more powerful our soul is! Personally, I believe that those who have not ceased to aspire to the eternal light will see it."

1 The mendicant monk Benoit-Joseph Labre, (1748-1783) nicknamed "the poor pilgrim", was canonized in 1881, somewhat controversially, as he had been rejected by several monastic orders before being admitted to the Order of Saint Francis, and was regarded by many commentators as a mere lunatic. A rather fanciful biography of him written by his confessor was published in 1865.

2 Elisabeth of Hungary (1207-1231) is also said to have joined the Franciscan Order after being widowed, and was eventually canonized; she was heavily influenced by her confessor, Konrad von Marburg, an associate of Dominic Guzman during the "Albigensian Crusade," who imported a clone of the Dominican Inquisition into Germany, and played a leading role in the persecution of alleged witches; he fostered the early development of the myth that witches held orgiastic assemblies that were later labeled "sabbats."

"I salute your profound faith."

"Who can reason against the miraculous absolute of hope and desire? Thus, Cain was born a criminal, Pascal a geometer, Mozart a musician and my mother saintly; I was born supraterrestial. I regret only being able to express the splendor of that predestination in an imperfect language, but you doubtless haven't forgotten that at four years of age I gave my immortality to my doll. That didn't prevent me, however, from killing her pitiless with a thrust of a 'peignoir'[1] full in the chest."

"Poet!"

"Yes, already God and the Devil without ever having heard mention of them. Dream and frenzy: my entire existence! There are days when I imagined that it's the Devil who forbids God to approach me any more closely, out of jealousy and solicitude, and that he once said to him: 'No, you won't reveal yourself any further to the soul of that dreamer; she's mine!' And another time: 'You'll frighten her, you see, with your inconceivable metaphysics. That poor little soul can't yet nourish itself on your infinities. But I have the art of enabling her to absorb them, little by little, and in a charming form. I speak as one poet to another. I don't suddenly stun that creature with a moonbeam on the head, a blow of that icy sledgehammer, but slowly, amorously, religiously. I render her apt to receive your extraordinary aggressions when you sometimes quit the starry furrow of your wisdom, attack Pascal and render him mad . . . When, with that she-demon who is so fervent, so comprehensive a student, I have created the She-Demon, then I shall deliver her to you. You'll be dazzled!'"

_____

1 Presumably a childish misrendering of *poniard.*

※

"My beauty, although you make use of a very usual language, sometimes—but I love these vibrant familiarities—and you are too obliging in becoming extravagant, I shall take tonight my Archangelic form; but as I'm too resplendent, close your eyes."

"Let's talk. Give me your hand and tell me why people want me to roast eternally, me who desires to save the world."

"Even the nuns, priests and fanatics of your youth?"

"Them above all, who didn't know that within my radiant heart a little of their eternity beat. The true unfortunates are those whose blindness renders them unjust and cruel. While still a child I imagined that there were prisons for those who inflict harm on wings, and then, I knew that the worst torturers are liberated by the butterfly that they detach from a resin. Our redemptions always come from innocent things."

"Yes, I can affirm to you that eternal life is for those to whom birds sing in the evening."

"Once, I smiled at a hind that was nursing her fawn; well, can you imagine that I suddenly felt myself to be mother to a similar fawn. Would you like to see it? It never quits my dress.

"But why are there misunderstood dogs, grains of wheat that strike the soil with their little golden brodequins in vain, and men who never want to understand? And those unfortunate pigs that are bled in the midst of smoky torches and have never yet been able to bless men for their pity? Are they capable of it? The beauty and the pain of animals make my hips maternal, and when they caress me, and when they suffer, it's in the loins that I'm touched. If their throats are cut, I'm struck by dementia and I hide, cursing the life that nourishes its creatures on the flesh of its creatures."

"All the pigs think about you before dying, O she-demon! They know how mild you are to the frightful condition of animals, those mute gods who aspire end-lessly to the human heart. Calm yourself; tenderness is the imponderable miracle. It falls where it is necessary, when it is necessary."

"Thank you. But I pass for a crackpot."

"It's only the divine incoherence of poets; what they say is insensate and full of disorder, and yet, under their ungraspable gaze, they group the harmony of all times and the tripod on which the rambling sibyl sees advanc-ing toward her, religiously, when the crowd has gone, the Wisdom of the bronze tablets. Poets cast seed pell-mell; those who read them separate the wheat, and in every sheaf that the ingenuous reaper binds, the heart of the bushel already beats,"

"Explain to me, then, by what miracle I believe that my soul and my body are unsoiled? I have, however, sometimes—involuntarily, it's true—trailed my dream through the poor hovels of pleasure, but suddenly, my wings flap at the door and carry me away. It's sad, the carnal embrace. Every time, it seems to me that one is murdering a god, that one is burying an angel in his light robe, that one is planting a wicked dagger in a pure throat, that in voluptuous couches we are closing

180

our eyes to our suave amours. And what comes to our aid—O grace, O mystery!—is the cornflower or the sky-lark of one of our infantile tales.

"Thus, I sense that I can blaspheme, hate, even kill, knock down the Temple that outrages and darkens my thought, be cursed by men because I strike the attitude of a dancing beast, savage and alone, mask myself with the odorous veil of lies, be as detestable as sunlight upon the leprous, as perfidious as moonlight over the exodus of pilgrims, as malevolent as the sea whose desperate eruption causes shipwrecks, but that I ought to refuse myself that raucous, sweaty, frightful pleasure . . . Oh, how I would like to be able to say: 'My satanic purity!'

"Say it. It's already not so bad. But you don't know the names of all your jealous divinities, O poets! Your whiteness? It was forever desired by the dazzling snows, the armed azure of the constellations, the seraphim, those flying furnaces, daises, those little sweet sorrows of old garden . . . A mystery, as you say. You sin mentally more than the Jew of the thirty pieces of silver, more than the fratricide with hairy legs, more than Herod in the hands of the of whore, more than the Cathedrals, stone temptation with the soul of incense, more than the purple-clad who behold swords as Empire end, but you are dazzling, O Magi, and the linen tunic is yours.

"It's necessary to choose. A vast unknown equity exists. The terrible delights of the soul are unknown to those who attach themselves to the satisfaction of the senses. The great thirst of Babylon is that of the proud who never slake their thirst with the despicable cup."

"Beds are narrow for the fools who row in the stars. I've chosen. That's doubtless why I'm so joyful."

"You mean so invincible. Beings who have the unlimited before them sense beautiful victorious wings beating upon their shoulders; they are wild. Your chains are the arms that embrace you and the eyes of your too-human amours are, for you, the worst dungeons. If you only know the solitude of deserts, you also possess their light."

"What is it that I don't possess? Can I open my eyes?"

"Yes, for your soul is, at this moment, divine. There are hours in which any mortal can look into the face of the sun."

"Mortals don't know it."

"That's in order that they learn that I have released into the Universe my dearest, most infernal and purest demons: Poets."

THE SHE-DEMON'S NIGHT

"I'm going to bid you adieu."

"But you'll come back?"

"What do you mean? My presence was more sensible to you during the few nights when we have run here and there, but do I ever quit you? So, dear beauty, you are not alone."

"Ha ha ha!"

"Why are you laughing?"

"Ha ha ha! You are, Satan, as conceited as a man. But I'm very proud; I have duped Satan himself."

"You, she-demon, you are . . . ?"

". . . Hope? Despair? What poverties! And what complications, the pursuit and the goal! But to love in order to love, and sovereignly, as one breathes . . . not to want to draw satisfactions from one's love . . . only to desire its abundances . . . never to lift for anyone the odorous veil of the interior mystery . . ."

"By my horn and yours! If I had expected . . ."

"In order to thank you for having put me once again in the presence of the divine Hortense, the demonic

Marguerite of the white velvet skin, and others, I'm going to confide to you the love that is mine."

"I'm listening, lady of quality."

"I cherish a being, then, not in himself but beyond himself, in his most luminous, but most subtle, radiance. I have no need to see him to be happy; on the contrary! In order not to quit him, I don't go to meet him; in order not go interrupt the feast in which he is my white nutriment of wheat and my ever-full cup, I don't go to my window to watch him pass by. The more distant he is from me, the more complete, substantial and sacred he is for me. Near to him, I am seemingly cold and always beneath myself."

"Amour-passion, Stendhal said . . ."

"Oh, no citations, I beg you. Stendhal, obsessed by amour, understood nothing of amour. He compiled a history of boudoirs and Italian sky. My amour has other fatherlands: silence . . ."

"And Hell."

"You're beginning to understand. But I repeat to you that I have no submission, no mildness, no cowardice, no sadness and no nostalgia in that absolute sentiment. No! I don't extend my neck to the beloved so that he can surround it with a cord that I would like to see, subsequently, knotted to his wrist, but I offer him my heart, lifting it up, to make redness around him. No! He is not my prison but my liberty, flapping wings over all created things. No! He is not the pebble over which I will walk with the attentive solicitude that one puts into for bloodying a soul, but the belfry toward which I raise my head suddenly struck by a thousand azure chimes.

No! He is not the tree that makes me think of autumn, of death, of poor matter that rots and then makes the perfume of summer nights . . ."

"Enough of this old leitmotiv, poet!"

". . . He is the pride with which I slap all of life, and if I quiver slightly when he touches my hand, so much is my heart occupied with the movement of his blood and its precious rhythm as soon as he abandons it; it is of him, so terribly, that I think with despotic claws that can reckon with the most profoundly embedded nails . . .

"No clouds: broad azure. Few flowers: metal or flowers that resemble daggers: dahlias and gladioli . . . And sometimes I receive, because of that amour, a punch in the face from God, whose thunder one wants to steal.

"No! I am not the vervain and the music that dance near the pagan sea, the melodious and perfumed Sappho, but sometimes, at night, listen: in the catastrophe of sensuality, lying on the shore, I shiver, naked and icy, under a cargo of pearls. My hair is more abundant than the algae in the aquatic depths. I have perished, body and goods. The waves have beaten, bruised and rolled me in their bitter strength, and I am a wreck moaning and smiling at its disaster, and the eternal moon is shining down on me, and the voice of the ocean is still howling in my ears, and its waves, pushed by the furious trident, are still breaking over my feet . . ."

" . . . ? . . ."

"Understood! But truly, has one any need for . . . Sensuality? Sensuality, who knows it? One gives it, between us, very wretched and ridiculous means, and a zone so limited, such a paltry climate. In truth, the swoons of that world make me laugh too much!

". . . And now that the marine god finds me, that he collects me, that he searches, on my lips, for proof of life, that he hugs against his body, which reeks of infinity and salt, the victim of his desperate wrath, of his magnificent fatality, his unchained and terrible delight . . ."

"Damn!"

"That's *possession*. But no . . . Ha ha ha! how irreverent I feel in thinking about the couple that carries out a great pillage of curtains and pillows, such a foolish expenditure of sweat, fatigue, marrow and animal melancholy, and—I declare it!—absolutely unesthetic and disobliging rites!"

"Respect my modesty, she-demon!"

"Yes, Satan. You are decency itself, I know, and that's why you are so dangerous. I too am decency itself . . ."

"Sataness!"

"Let's see; what can the importance be of the . . ."

"Let's pass on . . ."

"Since it is the root of which I am the soil, the sap of which I am the vine, the staircase of which I am the tower, the harvest of which I am the bushel, the treasure of which I am the coffer sealed by hands that will not open it again?

"Live with him? Does one live, in the restricted sense that one gives to those words, with the God who makes you the mother of all life, who, by virtue of a power that has no name, offers you the children that pass and that you caress, the gardens at which you gaze with the beautiful evenings of your eyes, the spring that you hear singing when you open the windows of your soul, the stars that beat the eyelids in the great silvery silence.

"Face to face, we are only poor humans. In sum, gazes prevent us from seeing one another, our mouths from tasting one another, our hands from gripping one another, and one only hears clearly when the ears are only the most vibrant pole of the spirit. But there you go; one is tranquil when one feels that one is fitted snugly together, like the door and the lock; standing up together like the scaffold and the blade, felled together like the tree and the nest, united together like the violin and the bow, spread together like the sunlight and the golden wheat, as perfect together as the divine moonlight that gives the same suave and transparent appearance to the fir-tree and the thatch, to the ivy-clad chapel and the palace that is naked with its caryatid and its rose . . .

"What is the importance, then, of everyday existence, and the pitiful clothing of our habits, our prejudices, our mediocre vices, our imbecile fears and our egotistical trivia? What do his flaws and mine matter? We know one another—thank God!—but we have the rude esteem for one another that hunger has for bread and thirst for fresh water.

"The rest? What can it do to us? I swear to you that I can be told the worst about him; I've thought it, the worst. So what?

"Beyond us, there are our Hells and our roses, our Elysian Fields and our discourse of fortunate shadows. With him, I only see, in those enchanted worlds, those supernatural recompenses . . ."

SABBAT

THE INSATIABLE

You know the lugubrious, sumptuous and ravishing celebration of the rites of the church that is built in a corner of my soul, do you not?

My gaze has retained, of contemplated reliquaries, the somber and precious light of gold that grows old in silence and the odor of the cloistered God.

Enter that basilica. It pleases me to open, with you, its portals of terror and mercy, to show you the rose and the demon of ingenuous and terrible alliances. The incense nourishes grotesque and punished sins; the indecency of Gargoyles grimaces next to Angels who bear a torch, a scepter, a missal or a key. Each of the pearls of the lampadaires is tinkling in a sad little spring, the monstrances resemble ravaged suns and on the walls that reek of mildew and myrrh, adore the crimson lined with lust of silent Roman princes.

The centuries have augmented the horror of all those funerary copes by fraying them . . . Open those missals on which the shadow weighs of monks rotted by patience and pride. I'm frightened by the thick and faded ink that covers them more completely than any stellar writing.

Look at those windows, as blue as spring in the soul, as red as a wound in the heart, as violet as a salutation of the spirit. Adore the gold ignited by a brazier of white supplications.

Listen; the hour is chiming n the tower of the basilica . . . and think about eternity because of that silvery voice, which falls silent so rapidly.

Oh, the religious delectation of my damned spirit!

. . . I know that a swoon worse than that which comes to us from carnal music in the sonorous beds of Hell will be mine when I see accomplished, above the massive lectern in the hateful stained-glass of celestial suavity, the Nativity, the Ascension and Anne's visit to Elisabeth.

Silence.

Satan only inhabits the sanctity of things; and it is justice that our mental avidity only thickens slightly in devouring the hearts of the Seraphim.

Have I shown you my Sainte Thérèse? How she resembles me sometimes, that fiery bosom, the accursed woman who is all penitence, black veils, somber gazes, internal sighs, infecund and chaste loins, and a narrow figure striped with white!

You see, it is only the damned who are truly amorous of God.

But peace does not come. In vain we shall cause the entire river of organs to flow into the ditch that the dead inhabit. In vain we shall cast all the aerial delight of bells into the subterranean damp in which Pascal groans . . .

Let's go elsewhere. Let's go elsewhere . . . I hate this Church. Who has built it in my pagan soul? Let's see: who has given the fatal sensuality of the soul to the little horned god that I am so frequently. Who has baptized that goat-foot?

Why am I sometimes this melancholy Catholic sun whose radiance sensuality has shrunk and augmented with a wound?

Let's go elsewhere . . .

✳

Sudden miracle! My face is pink with joyous and pure blood, which pricks it with its thousand needles in its florid light. Doesn't the sun look well? Don't the branches of the mutilated forest always grow again? Don't I lack the immaterial and withered hand of a woman who is only a servant of God? Isn't it not only my soul but my body that is young, that is beautiful, into which life flows through all the veins of creation?

Oh, let's flee the Church where sinners accuse themselves in abominable refinement and flagellate their faults in order to hear them cry out around them like unsubmissive beasts and daughters of wrath.

Let joy come quickly to those who want nothing else!

Look at me; in my seduction, my soul scarcely dips the tip of its wing, like a rapid swallow in a clear lake.

I am told that there are hearts that beat more rapidly and more amorously to the odor of bread; goat-kids that follow their mother; little children who want to seize with their hand the sun's burst of laughter; streams that fall into one another in a glare of confounded necklaces and shared light; bees that go from bush to trellis and never know whether they are more intoxicated by the rose or the grape; doves that open your wings in order to say yes; goats that advance your arid and mischievous heads through bitter herbs in order to say yes; hinds that make foliage tremble in saying yes; lionesses whose blanks palpitate in the burning deserts of instinct, and salute in me the stubborn and ardently perfidious beast who never ceases to cry: "No!" even under the rhythm that recalls the wheat that is sown, the crop that is reaped, the house that is undermined, the sea that is beaten and the forest that is felled.

Hunger, thirst, health and desire are the drunken disorders of the body.

Console me.

Fortunate is the nudity that can ornament itself with a rose! Fortunate is the breast to which the perfection of an empty cup can adhere! Fortunate is the hip that repeats the curve of an amphora, the lip that wants to have the sacred destination!

But before undressing myself, I think: *Ah, the first revolt of hair in the sunlight!* I see myself when I was small. I wore, in my baby dress, the promise of future blossoming. I already possessed the pride and self-assurance of a woman who knows, throughout her existence, what the enigma is that the truest of her gazes will never betray,

I had life in order to attain life. I divined that I would grow toward you, and for you, O unknown, Stranger, enemy! Brother in solitude and torment . . . !

I foresaw that I would employ my childish health to make a stronger, more definitive, more troubling, more particular health, a health of robust breasts, amorous cheeks, a round belly, sturdy legs, a smiling, hungry and tender mouth.

But there is an *after* . . . And the rain that falls, sometimes, with satisfaction, on the November window. God! There are rancors that awake behind closed curtains, and a fermentation of the spirit that is insupportable to delicate nostrils.

Not that . . . Something else . . . What?

Meditation in a Church is accursed for me because the God that only seduces me by virtue of his vulgar pomp drives me away, and I am fundamentally too religious and too honest to confound faith and poetry, sensuality and prayer, the glory of the Lord and the Damnation that will always animate the stained glass for me, like a thousand red comets, a thousand violet comets and a thousand suns mounted by the science of Asmodeus and the ineffable languor of Lucifers with excessively blue eyes . . .

The frenzy of joy leads to the other, which has an *end* and—excuse me!—the odor of sweat and fatigue that I have never been able to forgive vagabonds.

Can one get up joyful from a soiled couch and feel like a poet? No. Sensuality ought to descend from the soul like a divinity smiling at its sacrifice. But listen; it ought to climb back up again before the knife has been plunged into its throat and its entrails are fuming on the brutal and burning altar.

I admit that as a kind of mysterious Annunciation . . . like the hope that pursues us forever of finding a green sandal in the marvelous meadows of the evening . . .

It ought to be the feast served but not the table over-turned; the beverage offered but not the amphora tipped over; the rose that the dancers do not trample.

No! It isn't from possession that the musk and hatred of feline beasts emanates at the detestable moment. No! It isn't the intoxication of those lips that kiss but mutter insults in low voices . . .

Pleasure has the rascally mediocrity of a hairdresser reeking of jasmine. And you can give me, O faubourgs, your barrel-organ and your elegiac spring, but I won't forget your dust and your rubbish bins, for—despotism of our presentiments and reminiscences!—pleasure will always be, for me, a furnished room in a suburban district.

Oh, the couple! If we want to be edified, let's approach it. For my part, I don't become queasy in the presence of the venomous lie that it betrays by its odor. It's like those poisoned plants that live between two stones. The purest of lovers are still those who purvey cheap vengeance: rat poison and vitriol.

But tell me, who has seen amour in that world? In all sincerity, not me.

I have preferred, to our caresses, the flight of curlews, and to our kisses, the perfumed seal of flowers on spring, and also, to your presence—don't smile!—the invisible angel who no longer quits me.

I have the sense and the taste of happiness, myself, and I know that it is only possible by means of the soil.

Flamboyant law of Archangels! You forbid us desire with the sword, but you delight us in Amour by means of the seven-stringed lyre.

"My darling," she murmured to me every time, after the sad embrace, "are you coming?" And don't be afraid, my child, and bless me when, leaning my radiant head against your heart, when silence has settled beside us like the supreme cup of the last night, I hold out our enlaced hands to the One who never ceases to say to me: "Are you coming, my darling? Are you coming . . . ?"

ENCHANTMENTS

You have not told me that you are as caressant as the pelt of an antelope to the nudity of a favorite slave, but what would be the point? You have not murmured to me a single word of love, but I am drowned in tour amorous language as in the Nile where the reeds weep all the languor of Egypt. You are respectful for my hand, but your arms embrace me like serpents hungry for their victim. You scarcely look at me, but I know that you see me naked . . . that, by a magic come from you, my soul takes the radiant form of my flesh and that my flesh is penetrated by the divine science of my soul, and I am more than divine . . . that the thought of you renders me, suddenly, the respiration of roses around my child's dress, and I am more than full . . . that, in remembering you, I quiver with the sensuality that stretches me toward the horizon like a beautiful day that wants to finish in the sun, and I am the more perfect . . .

I have no need for you to touch me to know, via you, a frisson with two currents: one chills me, the other burns me; one makes me think of what the sword and snow have in common in purity, the other of what a carnation and crime have in violence; and that frisson, when it runs through me, makes me simultaneously white with all death and red with all life.

For a long time I have known that our only resources are in our dreams. Here are found our dancers with thirty necklaces, our Circés more palpitating than the fresh movement of their lost isles in the evening wind; there our ostentations and our brass instruments reign, our sultanas brilliant in a noisy sunlight, and our captive, whom we have stolen from spices and wines in a hostile blue port and who is ours, with all the mute and formidable soul of a sad beast.

Do you think that I need your form when, before your evoked shadow, beauty sets my arms afire, happiness disinherits my face of its gaze, when pride multiples my heart a hundred times and gives it the victorious flutter of oriflammes, when folly inspires me with a thousand laughs, each of which appeals, seeks, contradicts, approves, adores and detests all the others, when splendor nails to my nudity the pale mask of oriental queens, joy is as sensible to me, in its intermittent sonority, as the little bells of a herd of goats wandering in the tamarisk, and music surrounds me with such a tender fervor that it equals in sighs and melancholy a rose that is shedding its petals?

Go, navigator! Hoist the sail and command the prow; your eternal voyage is being made in my heart, and everywhere, in your temples, which are under the power of the dragon or the acanthus, I engrave the direction of my figure.

When you approach me—O invisible!—there is in my soul the light and desperate palpitation of a dying butterfly flapping its wing, and you who are never there, how many times you lie me on the ground like a thickness of dry leaves that have the scent of extinct suns, and you lie on that shepherd's bed, sighing!

In the shops of the fruiterers that sell the autumn, in the sugary odor of overflowing baskets, I choose grapes while thinking about your plain and sober words, which you give me, seed by seed. I choose an apple while saying to myself that sometimes, your spirit resists me, but that I bite it anyway, that I plunge into its most perfumed pulp. I choose a pear whose hard black pips, in the depths of its streaming flesh, remind me of your most concentrated substance, the most jealous of itself.

Enchantments!

All I want of you is your reflux. It is when you draw away that your heart rolls at my feet like the booty of pirates who also count stars and lightning flashes.

How can I add your body to my celebrations when my destiny is supported by your destiny like Italy by the sea?

How can I add your presence to mine, since I know that you bear me on your heart like the red rose of your greatest good fortune?

Alone . . . I am always alone, but into the languor of our languors, pearl-fisher, you cast the golden net of your songs.

✳

Where is the mouth that has ever satisfied the hunger that we have for God?

I have never wanted to intoxicate myself with dreams in order to fall dead drunk in the knowledge of everything.

"Beyond us . . . Beyond us . . ." I always say, for I know that we only exist in our radiance.

I place your soul everywhere there is sunlight, like a diadem, and it is a sacrament that is accomplished. I take your hand everywhere there is shade embalmed by clusters of flowering silence, and it is an alliance that is made. I say to you: "Come . . ." and it is the most beautiful route that opens up. I say to you: "Depart . . ." and it is a sky full of swallows that shakes its azure scarves over the exile to which you are carrying me, it is the autumn that takes possession of the forest, the boats that seem more distant, more melancholy in lightness on the more traveled sea . . .

I say to you: "Silence . . ." and we listen to furtive footsteps in the corridors of our dreams. I say to you: "Look . . ." and in order to lean over my soul, you slowly lift up the lamp of God. I say to you: "No . . ." and you know how pitiless the glove, the mask and the rose are toward me. I say to you: "Yes . . ." and the universe draws closer to you, and the wheat and the trees and the curious and suspicious animals have the face of my consent.

But my narrow, pure and grim bed has that of my divine refusal.

Go away!

❋

Why are you still here? To embrace me in the space of a bed? Ha ha! Damnation is elsewhere, and, surely, in our silences. I have pity and not horror for the serfs of the flesh. The magnificent and the accursed are us, the chaste, and the temptation that is born of the hissing mouth and the divine flat and condemned head is not for us. Only those who rest are assailed, only those who hide are haunted. Only those who do not possess are possessed, and sacred lust is the great modesty; the crimson Lady never consents to dance before two Satans. "Only one . . ." she murmurs, and it is even necessary that he close his eyes.

VISIONS

And the vision visits me, but you who inspire it, go away! You are trivial by comparison with what you give me. You are as infimal as the acorn from which the oak emerges. Go away.

Now that you have smiled, I have my sun and I have no more need of you. Let your hands vanish that have opened doors to me, and your eyes close that have guided me where I wanted and had to go. You importune me now, and then, I have the modesty of not showing you how and how much you have enriched me, and I want to play with the diamonds born of you in black solitude.

I want to give your name to the sorceries of sensuality that have escaped from your shadow, my love, and they will be sevenfold, like you.

A crystal has resonated under your fingers, and now it is the orchestra that is whistling, buzzing and roaring: the sun of cymbals; the oboes that are moonlight; the harp that is an entire winged October; the violin, that rich golden robe; the flute, that desperate spring with the heart of a child.

You have only stirred a sensitive glass, distractedly, but how the rivers and the flowers moan, how universal and lacerating harmony is, how the brutal and luminous tempest of the Valkyries and autumn presses me and battles me, how the discrowned head of the Celtic forest laments!

You have scarcely brushed my arm, but I receive all the caress of vines perfumed by the presence of grapes. You have sighed against me; suddenly, I am now the mother of twenty doves. You have a little equivocal mist in your eyes—irony, splendor, Satanism or sadness?—and now the ram of my perditions is lying at my feet. And as you have tried to recount fables to me, here around my neck is the blue serpent whose head I crush with the blow of a flower.

Go away, go away. Yes, you have made me take off my dress; but you shall not see my nudity extended like a lyre, nor the dance of crime and golden rings.

Now that I have surprised on your mouth a perfidious and complex smile, I want to be alone and to pass over my hand a certain black velvet glove. I shall learn by means of that spell, that intrigue, silence, poison, make-up and sensuality are, in combination, pleasant and perfect things . . .

Now that you have revealed your cruelty and your covetousness to me, your grace and your domination, I want to plant my onyx fingernails in the living breast of things, like a fay . . . And since you are able to fall silent, I want to make my long necklaces of wood trail the odors of violet and vanilla, in the smoke of pipes that meditate in the lips of the Invisibles that surround me.

You will not see me invent the light, sins, roses, money, rubies, kings, unicorns and centuries that it would be necessary for me to populate with the desire you have left me, nor scythe down, with a joyous fury, as in a garden, red carnations, the gods that I owe to you and which are too many . . .

Inspirer of the Sabbat, go away!

You will not see me, now that you have filled me with ingenuity and science, entering the Golden Age and listening, with the reserved and mysterious smile of sages, to the speech of monstrous and divine beasts. Go away. After having made it possible, you shall not take part in the magnificent conversation. Perhaps you would be afraid of the witch who knows that poetry imitates, in order to seduce her and lead her astray, the stubborn heaviness of the rhinoceros, the crooked silence of long-eared owls, the mortal frivolity of vipers, and the enchanted vampirism of tawny owls crazed by musical blood and murderers of nightingales.

Hush! They have a sabbat of moonlight in their eyes and are already announcing the hurricane of witches. Life to dead wood and bones! My heart flies on its light and terrible wind, but you shall not see it whirling in the form of a leaf that has two butterfly horns and a hem of phosphorus in its green robe.

Go away. You have for radiant and triumphant rivals those adolescents that you have brought me. Armed, florid, sonorous and crowned, they collide with solitude with their dart, their rose, their flute and their vine, with all their bronze nudity, and I know via them about the unspeakable maleficence of cloisters, those museums in which one only speaks like a stone mask to a drop of water.

What need do I have of you? You have left me your preferred books, and I have planted their boldest words in the crimson of my soul like golden nails.

Go away. Once I coveted all the health and abundant nourishment of life, but now I love the empty table that I decorate with the branches, cups and grapes that I give myself, the grapes, branches and cups that one earns with one's sighs or one's meditation.

I prefer your name to you. With my most beautiful hand I lift it like a crown, with my most miserly hand I enclose it like a jewel in a sealed casket in the wall; with my richest hand I fill baskets with it that overflow; with my most provocative and most mortal gesture I throw it at my soul as the matador thrown the red rag at the bull.

It is over your enormous shadow, a vertiginous cliff, that I want to climb like an equinoctial tide. And then, I shall quit you, in order to see what I have left of you within me, in streams of azure, in unexpected wealth, and when I row back, in my grumbling bitterness, from catastrophe, death and monsters with eyes veiled by aquatic mists, treacherous algae and perhaps scaly sirens, I might be filled with you to the extent of containing a pearl . . .

Go away, you who have led me into the forest. It's all alone that I want to collect the resin in its essential golden drop, and seek the strawberry, ruby of odorous and sugary flesh, under the sinewy legs of black goats.

Eventually, I shall enter again into the night of my haunted house. I shall light the torches in order to chase away the furies of your anguish; then I shall lie down in order to allow the queens of your mildness to approach me in blue brodequins. How much more precious your phantoms are to me than you!

Privilege of limitless passions! I find that your appearance diminishes you, restricts and disperses me. But when you disappear, as you grow, as you deploy your soul, standard of my eternal victory, how you group your perfect harmony around me, how I reign in the midst of your wrath and your nostalgia, how I play with that restive beast: your joy; how I please myself in the appetizing and divine crime, our crime, as you know: amorous fraternity!

THE BEWITCHED

That's you. But don't worry; I don't have your double in breadcrumbs in the deadly niche. If I were to die suddenly, they would not find between my breasts, in the place occupied by old scapulars, a heart of soft wax that could weep blood through an imperceptible and treacherous wound. In crying your name silently at the top of my ghostly voice, with all my soul obsessed by the adroit and complete vampiric crime, I have not tortured any witch's marionette. It's truly too puerile, too uncertain, too facile to have recourse to magic when one wants to accomplish perfect rascally work, and incantation costs less effort and fervor than the smile that I know . . .

No, you are not my dishonored and despicable victim by means of the complicity of a philter, an unguent or speech that ends in the green-tinted crucible, but it has pleased me to make you turn toward me as the tree turns toward the dawn, the flock toward the fold, the flame toward the satanic visage that laughs, very blue, at the distant opening of chimneys, between the weathervane and the wind.

Scarcely frowning, the firm brown and agile eyebrow that you know was sufficient for me to think: *He will be my beast and my docile element, the mandrake that comes of its own accord to lie down under the savant and clandestine hand, the ray of light emitted by the criminal rose-bush that I represent* . . . And that has been realized, for Hope is Hope and a dagger is a dagger.

When I murmured softly, with the voice that would be that of a pearl in the depths of the sea if God had permitted pearls to speak: "I want this magnificent and incoherent vessel that is seeking its route amid contrary winds . . ." you immediately caused a shipwreck on my pirate coast.

Hush! Have you not brought me your slaves because their red collar was my delirious temptation, and have you not delivered me your idols because, I confess, the tears of your idols are necessary to the redemption of mine?

The one who is hungriest has the right, in the absolute land that is mine, to the bread of others, and your garment came of its own accord to cover me when I was naked.

While shaking my hair full of an odor of chestnuts and golden straw it was sufficient for me to say: "It's that man, and no other, that I need; at my whim, I want to enrich him rich with my resuscitated youth, between the roses, the sunlight of my abdomen, the rubies of my breasts, or to dispossess him, in accordance with the caprice of my bad days, of all his life . . ." And that too has been realized, for blood is blood, the moon is the moon, and amour is amour.

By casting my burning topaz gaze into your anxious eyes. I conquered you even more fully than by the victory of the sword, and you are more submissive to me than the Orient to the train of the Queens of Sheba . . .

No one has spoken my name with impunity before you. Every time it has flicked your cheek like a slap of light, in dreaming of my anger and my silence you have recognized that the whip is the whip and the cross is the cross.

Your superstition pales when you hear the hammer strike the anvil, or the metallic cry of the river to the moored boat, for you know the meaning of symbols profoundly, and I defy you to be in the presence of two images that combat one another in completing one another without thinking of yourself and me, who, together, are perfection and war.

I reign over you more than time over a pensive engraving . . . than the ash on a cat's ear that changes it into a sphinx beside the hearth . . .

Sometimes—isn't it so?—you are like an animal that does not know what it is and which, however, bleeds between two ribs from the thrust that it has received in the heart, but you understand immediately that at this moment I hate you abominably, my love.

Sometimes, you are as arid as a torrent that the sun drinks in its summer thirst, but you understand immediately that the very soul of the dog days causes its chariots of fire to roll in my soul in that period.

Sometimes you are wicked: that is because I am laughing in a low voice on the far side of the world . . . Sometimes you are charged with spring like the first hyacinth; I weep then a tear so rich, so pure and so concentrated that it embalms my eyes like a drop of perfume . . .

I never cease to pillage and edify you, to pursue you and to await you, to persecute you for the radiant end and the apotheosis, and to organize your triumphant salvation by complete damnation.

And I shall never, never be useful to you in this world, I who am indispensable at times, and I intoxicate myself in thinking that I cannot serve you in anything, anything at all, in everyday life, I who am your beating heart and the wave of your thought . . .

If your bed creaks, you jump and you say that at midnight, I am the starry Death that dances in the odor of your tears.

When your books excite around you a heart full of tears you are not astonished; you tell yourself that they are my warm breast.

When I talk to you in a whisper you think of nights when we could talk in even lower voices and yet, so distant am I from you in those minutes that I cannot even extend a mouthful of bread to you, my creature!

Triumphant is the man who only demands his triumph from his radiance, and a rare feast, believe me, has the man who has no need of a table, a cup, nourishment and slaves and yet fills in the rhythmic fall of roses and the Vesuvius of wines, a hunger and thirst more avid and more physical than the religion of pomp that is in the soul of demons!

And all this will be forever. Nothing will snatch you away from me, and whatever you do you will be the last to want to be free, for Prometheus can only conceive the sun any longer in the wing-beat of his divine raptor.

Without wanting to admit it, you love your nails, dear crucified, and the pink and fragile aureole that they make around the demonic and holy wound is the one for which your eternity wishes.

The earth and the earth are united on the tomb, as the wheat and the wheat are united in the mill. My soul has taken root in yours and your heart is no longer anything but the harvest of mine.

Go on, river, go on . . . you will always be coiffed with bridges, inhabited by the shadow of willows, drunk by the silver thirst of the laundress.

Sing, nightingale, sing . . . you will always be stabbed by the moonlight at your freest and most inspired note, and your possessed avian tears will fall into the evening that I am.

Run away, goat-kid, run away . . . in the depths of the remote wood, I will be the torrent of thorns that the fugitive cannot cross, and yet, that mossy spring where he bathes, moaning amorously . . .

Scatter your hours madly, desperately, clock full of suicidal desire; my finger, which watches over your gilded dial, has sometimes put order in the stars and appeared over the crescent . . .

Revolt, forest, revolt . . . you will always be, in the end, the great palpitating martyr over which the wind, which resembles me, will have cast its thousand green torturers.

Whatever your knowledge and perfidy might be, serpent, you will come, fascinated in your turn, to deposit the diamond that crowns you, and the emerald that singularizes you, in the hand whose accursed precious stones have always tempted you . . .

Yes, understand, my bewitched—I ought to say "my marvel and my miracle"—it will be thus until the end of ends. More than my eternal deliverance, I have desired that these things be, that you read them, that you recognize the truth of them, that you accept the power of them while my two responsible hands rest on your heart, for a ring is a ring, and scripture is scripture.

RESISTANCE

Why do you never turn against me? To submit is also a
fine reign. Be the torrent that descends the mountains,
traverse me like a bridge, carry me away like a tree trunk,
roll me like a pebble in your obscure strength and your
contrary currents. Fell me like the fisherman's house of
planks. Let me be, on your discordant and victorious
waves, the booty of the tempest: oars, the boat, the nets,
the frightened beast and the pitching cradle . . .

Carry me like a broken flower to the lips of the sea.
And, finally, cast me up on the calmed shore like a pearl.

Don't resist me.

"I don't want to take you or to give you; either to
destroy you or allow myself to be invaded by you. Why
are you smiling like that?"

"Because I'm a basket-weaver; I twist the rush and
weave the basket, in spite of everything, because it's my
métier and my pleasure."

"Why are you whistling while looking at me?"

"Because I'm a potter; I knead the clay and I fashion
the vase, in spite of everything, because it's my métier
and my glory."

"Why are you no longer saying anything?"

"Because I'm a weaver; I card the flax and I weave the cloth in spite of everything, because it's my métier and my vocation."

"Mercy . . ."

"Do you know the hatred that the rider has for those horse that does not allow itself to be mounted, the amorous hatred that wants to grip the flanks of the restive animal and whips it for its refusal?"

"I beg you . . ."

"Do you know the hatred that the mother has for the child that says no, the amorous hatred that demands *yes* and cuts the child off until she obtains it?"

"Oh, let me alone. It's too much . . ."

"Do you know the hated that the file has for the diamond, the hammer for the nail, the bee for the rose, the amorous hatred that seeks perfection, pursues its goal, and demands its nourishment?"

"What do you want, in sum?"

"To do you all harm, my dear soul, all the harm that is necessary, since all my good is within you. I want to turn you upside down, as a thief does a house, until I've found the treasure that I covet. I shall labor you with the cruel persistence of the plow, the terrible patience of the oxen, until the wheat that I need rises from you. I shall tie you to a tree and wait with the tenacity of savage instinct until you have surrendered your secret in your submissive sigh. What do you expect? I'm hungry, I'm thirsty, I have a soul to satisfy, and it's all the more avid because my body treats it as a vagabond. I therefore go to my bread; too bad for it if it refuses itself. I go to my spring; too bad for it if it hides. I go to my divine necessity; too bad for it if it's necessary for me to do violence to a certain number of angels in order to extract it. I am, in truth, in a mood to massacre a Throne, not to say a Domination."

"I'll flee you, I'll flee you . . . I'll flee you incessantly."

"Ha ha! I'll obtain you by means of the wings, venom, claws and golden trunks of my soul. I'll be the eagle, the serpent, the tiger and the butterfly. I'll circle above you until I've fascinated you with the sunlit flower of flight. I'll attach myself to you by means of a multiple and icy knot until the bite of my mortal teeth attains you via my flowery mouth. I'll lie in wait for you until you hear, in the jungle of our distress and our solitude, the cry with a gazelle stabs itself before having its throat torn out. But don't worry! I'll palpitate around you, charming and funereal, until you learn the grace and divine stubbornness of the great peacock that wants nocturnal corollas.

"Don't resist me. What's the point? You alone can fill my grain-lofts: I summon you to approach, my harvest. You alone can cover me with agreeable dreams in all seasons; I command you to advance, my garment. You alone can shoe my impatient and joyful foot; well, come quickly, my sandal. You alone can sanctify my accursed brow; it awaits you, my holy perfume."

"You frighten me. I've told you that a hundred times. I resist you, I resist you, I resist you . . ."

"Resist, if it pleases you, the Ocean, but not the pirate; death, but not music; war, the deluge, the cyclone, the wolf, the crocodile and the aurochs, but not amour!"

"Thinking about you, I tremble so much that I close my eyes."

"The better to see me, my child."

"I'm afraid, in truth, afraid . . ."

"How assured we are of our victory, are we not, my sisters, O great daughters of deliverance? A moving horizon and a rapid desert, we only pursue and encircle fugitives."

"I've been told that you were . . ."

"What? And who has permitted himself to talk to you about me? Your catechism, former Catholic? The wrinkles on your forehead, poor debauchee? A little white flower, my dear little heart? You listen, then, to what people say to you? But what do you say to yourself, involuntarily, in the secrecy of secrecy, in the black and profound crypt into which only God or the Devil descends, in the sacred dungeon of your soul, where captive eternity beats its wings? What do you do with it?"

"Alas!"

"I know you, and you merit a thousand malefices, since you refuse a thousand divine prodigies. Do you expect me to be the mouse that stares with excessively bright eyes at the soul of solitaries, on nights when the wind nibbles the silence? Know that I only gnaw wood, marble and iron. Have you seen me stop torrents with the ribbon of my white magic and put a leash on vanquished flocks in the mountains? Don't you know, then, that I'm the sonorous and burning hand of the thunder and the elastic conjuring trick of the lightning that can enter anywhere at the turn of the blue key?"

"By what inconceivable fatality have I encountered this monster?"

"Ha ha! As if you had *encountered* me! I presided over your birth and I wanted it . . . And since then . . . and ever since . . ."

"Raca!¹ You have the face of everything I hate.

"First confession. It promises another."

"Well, yes, yes, yes, I love you, I love you, I lo . . ."

"My dear instrument, why resist me? I'd admit your hope of recovering your liberty, some day, if I were one of those melancholy, vaporous and feeble demons who are only faithful to their possessed for three or four thousand years—but me!

"And to think that while pronouncing there terrible words, she's juggling with two oranges!

"Your soul and mine, Lord . . . and that green citron that is mingling with the aerial game momentarily . . ."

"Is?"

"The soul of Satan, my love."

"I'm vanishing."

"Under my eyes, to an intermittent spark . . ."

"How can one escape this devilry?"

"By no longer fleeing. Come closer and you will see a rose rise up miraculously in the midst of our Seraphim sighs . . . and our eternity will be accomplished, for it's written that I shall have you . . ."

---

1 This word originates from the version of the gospel according to Matthew in the Septuagint, where Jesus warns against pronouncing it; its etymology is controversial but it probably derives from an Aramaic word meaning "empty," and when employed as an insult might be the equivalent of saying "Idiot!"

THE PASTURE

They're so plaintive this evening, for they're so busy! Can you hear them? How they're moaning! They've refused the rich and sweet bread and the limpid water that, in order to weep over the divine crystal that contains it, is only awaiting a rose petal.

Oh, quickly, come in! Shake off on to the floor the mud on your shoes, which you imagine to have holes in order that the indigence of your soul should not be too humiliated; the fog that your cloak has drunk cannot, this evening, support habitude, nor toil, nor security, nor the pure gaze of your mother, nor, in consequence, its weight on your shoulders. Come on, throw on that floor, with the breath of the canals, of the suburbs, of the first autumnal frisson, your heart full of rain, somber and lax rancors, poor and impure visions of the song of the gutters over the nocturnal pavement, of the blasphemy of the carter to his nag: Life, from the sickened yawning of literature at two sous a couplet.

Mountain-dwelling colporteurs, half-brigand and half-smuggler, are less laden than you are with wretched and illicit booty. Do you still have in your pocket the waltz that you stole a little while ago from the last barrel organ? Quickly, sad and wicked Bohemian, my brother of the worst evenings, throw it on the floor.

Your soul is steeped in the wine of drunkards and your cravat impregnated with the musk of streetwalkers who address insults to life with their heels. And that tear! I have a similar one on my cheek. Our sins, which reek of the plaster of inns; our disgust, which has respired the odor of hospitals and kennels; our pity, which has invented morgues and wax museums; our sadism, which has handled butchers' knives while thinking with a delicate heart of our tenderness; our sobs, which are only saved from ridicule because they resemble the bewildered appeal of beasts on the heath; our nostalgias, which have listened to the cry of the metallic siren in the laughter of negroes and tar; our catechisms and our first verses, our forbidden and annotated books and our perversities of old adolescents, have all wept that tear.

And—name of God! as you say—throw it on the floor.

The insults that you do not think but that you shout at me sometimes, in order to have the illusion of having thought them when you have expressed them in anger, O feeble heart, throw them on the floor alongside those I think with a harsh and frowning eyebrow but do not say. The slap that you want to give me, throw it on the floor, where my baseness is beating like the heart of a laundress perfumed with basil.

And the examination of your conscience? Throw it down too. It's appropriate, son of religions whose priests say in low voices: "How many times?" Oh, you're repulsive to me; but I resemble you so much! Do I not also commit, for love of overly subtle lust, the great sin: do I not live chastely?

But how well advanced we are when we have daubed, like pork fat over a field of stars, a blazon on our mortified instincts, searched for rhymes for our wisdom with the minute care of a fairground performer delousing his last-born, when we adorn with a crown of immortelles—eternal regrets!—our poor little scrupulous cowardices!

Is that enough? No! Sometimes you are as bad, hateful and imbecile as all the Elect of the Beautiful Princess, Come on, poet, lie down on the floor. I'll lie down beside you. And, too impure to do what we call "sin," we'll think about it. And our silence will be the poison that magnifies and denounces our vitality of dangerous plants.

Is that enough? No. Have you never beaten your mother? Not with your fist, perhaps, but you have beaten her. Have you never killed your enemy, and your friend as well? Not with a weapon, doubtless, but you have killed them. Have you never overthrown a kingdom, set a fire in your neighbor's house, cursed the perfection of Satan in the jewels of kept women, thought of the bodies of your beloved that have been put in the grave, and hidden all your depravity under the wing of a butterfly frolicking over flowers?

Have you never spoken against yourself, betraying yourself three times in succession before an accusatory cock-crow? Have you never sunk, when you thought about my shadow assassinated by your treachery and your cruelty, into the wellbeing of a velvet armchair, the fireside of bourgeois quietude and your silent slippers that have—I imagine—acanthus and green wool around the heel? Have you never put on the farce of fleeing me, idiot? As if I could not run faster than you, stupid! As if I were not dancing at every bend in your route, my dear tempted! As if I did not always take the lead in our caravan, camel As if I were not you, O myself!

Let's go, brutal assassin, demolisher, arsonist, impious, sacrilegious and corrupt liar, egoist, my love, my love . . . throw your crimes on the floor with your anxious buffoonery.

And then go away!

Do you hear them? Call them. Open the door. They're so plaintive this evening, because they're so hungry . . . But go away . . . go away . . .

They're so white, and gentle, and numerous, and beautiful, aren't they? How they run toward the nourishing floor!

And you, go away. What are you doing here now that my doves have their pasture?

REDEMPTION

There was a time when I dreamed of the ardent apostolate and the dolorous redemption, but I soon realized that we were evangelizing in vain and that the salvation of those we love depends on our most unconscious divinities. What remains and acts between two individuals is the fugitive transfiguration of the smile. Let us not carry the cross for anyone, since they will only take account of the light in our eyes.

I therefore implore my poetry, and I ask it to throw beneath your feet one of its involuntary roses. My brother, it isn't with my tenderness that I can slake our thirst. In the cup, there is only the gesture with which one extends it, its significance and its value. There is nothing salutary between individuals, my brother, except music and the song of the nightingale that sometimes escapes from souls. There is nothing but grace, and its divine merit, unknown to oneself.

Everything is futile of that intended for service, and we all have no more need of butterflies than of slaves.

There was a time when I prayed for you, so seriously that I resembled the ignoble and degenerate angel who permits the sacristan to dust his chin at the foot of the master altar. A dismal effect of the modest and contrite spirit! Immediately, I swear, I became thin and jaundiced, and, rattling chaplets, I made the demons flee from your route. What imprudence! My orisons added a deadly veil to the chapels of your afflictions; I mingled with the long breath from beyond the grave that sometimes defoliates the poor autumns of poets I know not what litanies devoid of hope, and our sensitive and sick soul, treated with holy water and renunciation, fell into the funereal anemia people hardly talk about and which Pascal, in the course of the innumerable visits that he was kind enough to make us, ended up envying us.

Oh, without devils, how sad we would be! You advanced toward me, full of rancor, like a fast. I saluted you, full of allusions as bitter as penitence. Do you remember those quasi-monastic encounters? God, how frightful and paltry we were! And to cap it all, we sighed. We looked at one another intently, with suspicion, as Trappists do—and all that, my brother, because I routinely recommended your dear soul to the good old God of my old maroon scapular, that rheumatic Jehovah, obsolete and fatigued, who designed to inhabit a little piece of cloth between my glorious breasts and on my adolescent back.

Finally, we horrified the sunlight and the few flowers that still consented to frolic therein.

But now that I only have fervor in my songs and challenges, good! We're quite healthy. Still enemies? Yes, but quite healthy.

I must confess to the music of wrath that I dance most willingly, and that the maledictions that are hurled at me, given that my forehead is proud, give me ruby horns of which I'm passably proud.

A triumphant and joyful intoxication that is related to the whistle of whips and the discordant cries of the wind animates me when you have a desire to kill me—which is to say, to give me a good slap, and you have to admit then, my brother, the radiance of my cheek and the pink violence that surrounds me.

Let's leave pity to the gestures of the spinners. Personally, I'm the bounding and crazy Fate. What do the threads I break matter? My scissors are so shiny!

Yes, my brother, there is nothing profound among beings but play, the adorable game that inspires the surprise that a flower gives the sun every time it opens and the stupor that the stone causes the water when it is thrown toward the laughter of the silver god. There is nothing real among beings, my brother, but the wing-beats of ungraspable birds; there is nothing charming but the vagabondage of the desire that, while seeking Hell, lingers on Proserpine, and even on a simple poppy. There is nothing living but the fête of the dream and its enchanted incoherence, and I can extract more happiness for you from a hollow stem than a thousand chances and a thousand vessels could bring you.

But come to me, my brother. To relieve you of all the evil you have done in the ingenuity and conviction of your errors. I shall only have recourse to dance, and I am dancing for you, in my solitude, as others fast for others, gravely.

Good works are joy, and nothing else. They are the perfume of life in the hands that caress. Let's wring the necks of devotees—would you like to?—and let's lie down together, putting a little white kid between us.

Tears? Tears? You expect tears from me? Here are blows and half of my snack. We'll share the mulberries and the thorns, and if I'm hungrier than you, you'll only have my appetite and avidity. But do you know what makes one truly rich? The vitality of those who love us, the fulgurant virtues of their delight and leisure.

As for beneficence and gratitude, what is uglier, more morose, more insipid, more afflicted by chronic coryza, more provided with masks, more black-clad and mud-splashed than those poor parents who hate one another?

For myself, I'll only render you the service of being pretty, but in my own fashion and with all the fashions that please me thrown into the mystery, the track and the ambush, turned away from you by your most secret face, seductive to the point of prodigy, inconstant to the point of disaster, winged to the point of triumph, rapid to the point of victory, childlike to the point of divinity. And sometimes, for you, I'll emit one of those sighs that can move an entire forest of furze in flower, and finally, you'll know how sweet the she-demon is who makes a viper dance.

Go search elsewhere for compassion, solicitude, urgent affection, encumbering, maladroit and frightful when it arrives with a heart wrapped in cotton and a soul thirsty for syrup of gum. Get away! I no longer dress myself in rags of devotion. I've learned that duty stinks, that it's like those wretched garments that soak up the rain and provoke sweat, and I only want to make you the gift of my shadow, playing knucklebones or caressing the dead crowned with myrtle.

No soup in my house, nothing but fruits; and also, upright, tall, solid, pure, proud and sparkling, the cup that I sometimes break on the mouth of a god.

Virtues are only the hair-dos of grocers and queen mothers. Oh, let's throw our tresses to the wind, and look at me naked—which is to say, undisciplined, mischievous, capricious, mad, inspired, curious and fleeting, provocative, gentle and flowery, and thus agreeable to playful she-cats and spring doves.

And in truth, my brother, when the simple life is assured to all of us, we have no need of velvet drapes or iron-bound chests, nor rosewood bookshelves, nor sets of cutlery, nor servants to do everything, nor the advice of apothecaries, nor the favors of official obesity, nor the shivering hope that sighs at the bottom of holy water fonts, nor mausolea, nor carriages, nor this and that, nor anything or anyone . . . save for doves and she-cats.

And with that, here's my wing on your forehead and my claw in your heart.

GAMES

And I swear to you that I am everything that you have loved, and, to begin with, importunate, avid, back and thieving as the magpies that astonished and delighted your childhood. I fly low, between a rainy sky and a field of Luzerne, near the mill and the goat tethered to the axle of a cart, because I want you to throw a stone at me and break my wing, vagabond!

I circle around you in my robe of box, like the spinning top to which you credited the buzz of a bee, the color of the road, the speed of your fantasy, the victorious urgency of your desire, the intermittent folly of your soul and the crack of a whip in the time when you were a bandit who harmed everyone with too much tenderness.

And what about the straw that remained on your waistcoat when you stood up to men, slyly, injured the future bread, insulted nurturing life by striking the wheat commencing to ripen with the stick of indiscipline and pillage? And the heavy and violet sunset that inspired that hatred in you. And the faint, very faint voice of the evening that pushed you to that dementia? And the clarinet that interrupted it, sudden, crystalline and pure and left you in tears in the midst of your ravages and wrath? And the universal sigh, which taught you that every being loves amorously that which it kills?

Listen: I resounded in your life at the first slap you received, and when you rummaged in the desks of your schoolfellows in order to steal from them it was not their toys that remained in your fingers but the risk and the temptation that I never ceased to be,

And so, you have locked me in cages to learn the cruel song of captivity, gorged on berries, caterpillars, groundsel, surrounded by passionate, curious and deadly solicitude, and I died in your hand one evening, giving to your life my goldfinch soul.

Your hand? How well I know it! It doesn't shake mine, but it brushes it, imploring it, with a pensive lightness. Your warm, slow hand does not seek, but welcomes, and through it, I know the touching egotism of the wing that loves to be caressed.

And can you imagine that, since I have existed, I have adored its tender nonchalance. When I was a little girl, it attached me, alongside the goat-kid, to the wheelbarrow that went in search of wild thyme for the rabbits and for the beautiful cupboards that have the memory of its perfume.

When, at fifteen, I was a leafy currant-bush, so lively and savage, it collected her red clusters without crumpling their leaves. It picked them so modestly that my sap stopped in my branches, astonished, and to laugh subsequently, with all its golden droplets.

When, later, I had read books that had enriched me with a pride or a diamond, a fine hatred or a large crimson bouquet, it was your fraternal hand that turned their pages, for all violence and splendor are dispensed to us by grace, and I know that only furtive and immaterial hands open the massive doors of dungeons. The others break them down. But the true liberty, which can defy jailers, judges and even our own shadow, that circumspect but untiring witness, is given to us by the aerial gesture of angels or the clandestine key of demons. And your hand, your dear hand, is hypocritical and celestial enough—thank God!—for me to expect a great deal from it.

And as it is sufficiently rascally, I would like it to decapitate me like a poppy while, gorged on sunlight, as night falls, I no longer make anything but poison . . .

As simple as a little pink shirt drying in the open air, as harmonious as a beehive in the solitude of light, as perfect as the bread that enters into us when we desire it with our hungry and tender life, as divine as the rosebush that extracts from its eternal bosom the rose that it needs in its morning, as solid as the fine house whose foundations plunge into the roots of oaks, as fragile, light and gracious as the ignorant clusters of grapes that are all the joy, all the pride and all the wealth of the vine, as fortunate as the straight road that departs from the river and arrives at the bell-tower, as musical as the necklace of little bells that dances at the neck of a playful cat, as dazzling as the four aces that emerge simultaneously from the heart of chance, as fateful as the mirror that suddenly breaks under a smile enhanced by carmine, as perfumed as the unguent that the Medicis stole from the Satanism of the poisoner, sweeter—much sweeter—than the muted string that delivers the serenade of the cut-throats of Granada, and as charming . . . as me, if you wish, during our first encounter, in which, as you know, I smiled at you . . . that first encounter when I began to hate you . . .

※

I love you, and that is the noble, proud and courageous expedition. You please me, and that is the guerilla, the deception in the low dive, and the thrust of the knife full in the heart more delightful than a carnation.

I love you, but what does it matter? You please me: die, then, bewitching bird, strangled by your song!

I love you; so be it. To please me; thank you for the wisp of your hair that drives me to infinite despair—ah, misery . . . !

Madame Proserpine, in her red cabinet to which one goes to confess *in extremis*, knows what it's about . . .

"Truly, my child?"

"Yes, Madame; he's detestable, jealous, perfidious, complex and deceptive. And then, as treacherous, base and rascally as Judas, when the opportunity arises. For thirty deniers of bourgeois peace, how many times the pig has sold me!"

"Let's pass on . . . let's pass on . . ."

"He's as tender as the cabaret and the barrel-organ, as sensitive as the gutter in a faubourg that drips on the footsteps of girls . . . and believe me, he's unique . . ."

"Let's pass on . . . let's pass on . . ."

"Yes, let's pass on. But he has, can you imagine, a gold fleck in his eye . . ."

"Aie!"

"And on his forehead a great sad and soft wrinkle, of which I'd like to make a bandage soaked with my tears . . ."

"Poor creature! The door to the left, my child . . . But I warn you that Nostradamus and Merlin, Urgèle and Morgane, and all the enchanters and enchantresses, including Circe, lover of charming pigs, and Melusine, who, at every appearance of her white dress in the haunted château, liberates the dove of death, could do nothing for you . . . A gold fleck in the eye? A wisp like this on the temple? A great sad and soft wrinkle on the forehead? I see . . . I see . . . Eternal damnation, my child . . .

"I wish you well."

FATIGUE

Mildness, harmony and calm when I see you. This book is in its exact place, between the lamp and the silence, and, separating us, a flower sometimes cuts off the sunlight with its pink head.

We talk simply, and our words are as commonplace as a knife, a napkin, a white plate and a blue curtain . . . When we say *yes*, it's as frank and free as a tame starling hoping on to a table. When we say *no* it's as grave and soft as a ray of light enclosed in a cupboard full of shadows and fruity odors. When we say *perhaps* it's amusing, joyful, as light as a top rotating on its agile foot, and we know that it's only a game . . .

"*À bientôt*," you murmur to me.

"*À bientôt*."

I scarcely look at you. You give the impression of not looking at me at all. And we quit one another with a gesture as innocent, and as cordial, as one that breaks bread, picks up a pitcher, knots rope and binds firewood.

"*Au revoir!*"

※

And, suddenly, I fall back, legs and soul exhausted. Let's see: am I not going to faint with fatigue? I sense pallor crawling over my face with the slowness of a snake. I can't do any more. What did I say to you? I must have groaned, my hands over my face and overflowing with poetry, like the urn of the Nile into the reeds.

Where have all these pearls come from that are dancing a round of splendor and aristocratic wealth on my dress? Why do I have the terrible and charming weight of birdsong on my shoulder? And why does so much silence, fatality and ironic science surround them? Scintillating and deadly tarot cards are falling upon me, and everything, looking at me, has a sibylline visage.

What have I said to you? What have I said to you . . . ? Ah, no discipline. No coldness, no determination can reckon with the words and thoughts that quit us when we find ourselves in confrontation with Amour!

I've recounted everything, haven't I? And the fever was as palpable around me as a tempest.

My childhood? Yes, I've told you about it with the impetuosity that one puts into scything the sainfoin when one has the very face of dawn, a morning of delight . . . With what complaisance I have revealed myself to you, like a lizard powdered with silver, a poppy coiffed with holly, a loriot ravaging cherries in orchards that smell good in the warmth of the evening and the presence of goats! I've thrown you among those swallows—distant, such distant visions!—that resemble a tribe of little widows in the peace of funereal yews . . . I've confessed to you my animal and sighing sadness, which already marked me for amour at the age of seven! I've told you about my wrath of a vagabond—a future arsonist and perhaps a murderer of shepherds—which pushed me to throw poor and dirty gray pebbles, desperately, into the well. Hatred for wells? Hatred for pebbles? I no longer know . . . And yet, I confided to you that pity was my only neurosis, in spite of, or doubtless because of, my frightful fits of temper, that I wept over a rose fallen to the secateurs, over the secateurs that were obliged to cut the rose, over the hand that held the rose and the secateurs, over all the harm that is done to everything because life is a great indifferent and magnificent burst of laughter whose noise is the sun . . .

Fatigue . . . fatigue . . . fatigue . . . I offered you my adolescence, its fervor of the lily, its savagery of the eglantine, its singing and desperate revolt of a captive, in the depths of the convent that sometimes had the odor of a bakery and brown robes, and, too often, the asphyxiating odor of incense . . .

And my youth, more beautiful than a new sail on the traveled sea, you also knew . . . I had all the gifts that cast misfortune, and then arrogant divinity and solitude, into the self.

I have shown you my wounds. I was always pelted with stones, but their blows were rubies. I have shown you my heart; it was accursed and perfect. I have shown you my future, the route that climbs, the sky that opens; the recompense, music, that I have gained endlessly via music . . .

I talked to you then about the evening of my death as one talks about a charming recreation that awaits us among unknown and benevolent faces. "As soon as I am liberated I shall dance in the heart of violet woods scarcely illuminated by gold, and such as I am—you hear?—with my lovely winged body, desired by azure cherubim and coveted by the diabolical saints of youth. Then, having paid the tribute of joy and grace, I shall depart from discovery to discovery, and my eternal commencement will be a great cry of liberty . . ."

I have whispered many other things to you . . . oh, many other things! I have made you see my damnations sitting in a circle around me like red beasts, and, very gravely, making each one pass by in order to absorb and charm it, and to be nourished divinely by it, the absolute of sagacity, will, power and amour . . . "Behold," I said to you, my royalties; they have not ceased to sense the demonic crowns growing on their foreheads . . . Behold my hopes, which have never wearied of handling the dart, of trying their wings, of casting new foliage into the forests and giving to my heart the cooing of spring.

"I've wanted everything," I murmured to you, "undertaken everything and succeeded in everything, since, every time, I desired it completely. When I flowed into the depths I clung to the divinity of the sea. The spark was as abundant and sovereign in my soul as in the most profound furnaces, and I've borne the starry fork over my shoulder as Jesus bore his cross.

"What do you want to do," I cried to you, "with the mysterious destiny, magnificent by virtue of its possession, that is mine? I have been pure among the pure and damned among the damned. I know what I mean and if a Gehenna exists for poets, in its adorable eternal anguish, for—do you hear?—it will love me amorously, and it will want to reserve the lily that I am."

Silence! Everything is full of harmony, equity and predestination, and I swear that I have always wanted alliance with the radiant Satan, in order that his presence was always sensible nearby, and able to verify the radiance of my eyes and the shadow of my silence.

How heavy they are, how heavy they are, in the body and the soul, the peace of God and the dazzling miracle of the Devil! I am charged with those formidable burdens, fraternal although they seem contrary, and the serenity and frenzy that inspire me by turns reveal the quality of the powers that have invaded me.

But I sense, and have always sensed, that in the beyond I will be lightened—I mean similar to *Them*, doubtless, and more intelligent than the crescent in the forehead of the evening.

How weary I am! What expenditure of strength, of sacred substance! I can't do any more.

And the Genius down there, down below, has the face, the grave face wounded by the moon, of a river approaching the sea . . .

"*À bientôt*"—"*À bientôt*"—Between us, a flower is cutting off the sun with its pink head . . .

HOMAGE

Sometimes, Amour changes weapons, fortune, games, tunic, crowns, dwellings and name. This evening he does not release his arrow, but he makes of the sun, with his word, an execrated head, and in truth, death is approaching. This evening, it is not his whim to be rich, and possessed of the flower to which he sometimes gives eyes of enchantment, but of a sack full of stones to throw, which he carries fervently, like a malevolent vagabond, on his solid shoulders. This evening, he does not dance, but he laughs like a horsewhip . . .

Ha ha! this evening it is not in redemptive azure that he is clad, but hopeless crimson, the worst red: liturgical, and he refrains from showing himself naked, for he knows that the resource of the Devil is in garments, and it would not take much this evening for Amour to take the habit of a monk or a damned soul—which is to say, a hood, for he has to hide his eyes.

This evening he has an animate and venomous iron serpent around his forehead, but not the light rose, and, quitting his palace, where the illusions are laughing, in white robes, at the windows, he opens cyclopean lairs and steals from the deformed gods the rock, the lightning and the scream.

Do you know the name that he has taken this evening? What good would it do to tell you? You already know it.

But know that Amour is charging you, this evening, with all the mental crimes that I have committed, all the sins of my instincts and my knowledge, which he is putting into your eyes my dreamless nights, those nights when the dead fill us like empty sacks with all horror and all nothingness . . .

Know that he is posing on your mouth my closed fist, that he is sprinkling over your head my petroleum soul, which he will light like a conflagration and which will not be extinguished again.

Know that he is making me cry to you: "My veritable reign is commencing in you. All your minutes, including those that betray me, you will pour into my hands, for I am no longer separate from you, since I know that desperate, frenetic happiness, as the creator of seeing you stir, unworthy son of my sadness in animal loins."

Know too that, abandoning the magnificent apparel of anger and his pure eloquence, he is making me whisper to you: "Behind all your venial and mortal actions, you will rediscover my face, and perhaps you will strangle the whores of your nostalgia, weary of hearing me snigger when they have the red ribbon of complaisance and heartbreakers here, around their necks.

"Until now, one has only insulted and confounded oneself, but now one insults in order to dissociate oneself, and the time has come of the numbers on the slate, the wretched and chalky total, the bottom of the bottle, the seventy-five franc knife and sliced veins.

"The hour is beautiful, in truth, and under our footfalls we are making scorn creak like the dead wood of friend boscage . . ."

❋

"What rancor, my God, what rancor! The hour is beautiful, in truth, and I wonder if disgust is not the true splendor of the damned of amour and poetry.

For too long, you see, I have been judging you, and our mothers are weeping over the original sin of their children.

Fear, anguish and cowardice, the soul in flight like a tracked flock, the treason that is no more complicated than the skeleton key of any locksmith, that is what I have cherished too much. How beautiful the hour is!

Enter into the confessional, demonic Cain, chief of the dancing, hairy and criminal tribes; kneel humbly before the black robe stained with grease and groan the *mea culpa*. You too shall have, in the hour of your death, oil on your forehead, which Hope has made as red as the sun rising through the golden bandlet of the dawn . . . You will end up as a Catholic, Cain, you who were dishonored and betrayed by your temptation, you who were unable to choose the accursed victim and who, wanted to kill, as if it were worth the trouble, that infamous sinner . . . that poor child!

Yes, the hour is beautiful . . . and when you search for the meaning of my hostile and detestable presence

240

in every cell of your being, I shall make you hear the flail over the threshing area, the hammer in the metallic workshop, the wheel of the knife-grinder moistened by tears of rust. I shall make you see the voracious teeth of the mill, the devouring abyss of the mine, all that machines have of the conscious and the gigantic, all that industrial chemists have of the corrosive and the impure, in the hangars where water suffers, where straps cry out, where alcohol burns, where steam hisses, where carbon sweats like a black slave, where the animal hide dipped in acid commences, by the color of putrescence, to resist its own decomposition.

There! Are you content? You can be proud, poor man. And you have already understood, sensitive brute, that I have never loved you so much.

THE SOLITARY

All radiance is suspect, especially to those who radiate; all fervor is condemned, especially by those who are fervent; all prayer is combated, especially by those obsessed with God; all tenderness has fled, especially from the most tender. Rigor of the spirit and the heart, jealousy, fanaticism of elite souls, the implacable law of sovereignty and solitude! Pure foreheads veil themselves before pure foreheads, caressant hands escape caressant hands, nights that meditate do not respond to nights that meditate, and what silence has ever said to a silence: "I am your brother"? A saint does not welcome a saint; amour does not recognize amour; the poet has no thirst for the poet; bread has no hunger for bread; a flower is a flower and does not seek a flower . . .

Our only enemies are those we love; the only strangers are our fellows!

Everything that is divine is consecrated by divine disdain, and it is necessary, and therefore perfect, that fire burns and that one does not adore its flame, that the work be edified and that its tower is not starred, that a god watches and that his myrrh is not inhaled, that spring passes and its lilacs are not picked . . .

242

Without help, without recompense, without a smile? Are you thus? Yes? Then march. The man who has committed suicide, even though nothing remains to him but an empty bottle in a rag, was the greatest, because he was the most alone.

And I, knowing that harshness and pride are our powerful glories, I, the solitary, between two bloody and just robes, those of Charlotte and Judith, have held my heart aloft.

My nudity, of which desire seals the odorous, sweet and celestial wound, is like a marble statue on an abandoned cloister. So much the better. On the forehead of a genius, moss is more significant than laurels, and the white immortality that plunges its foot in humus is already part of the thinking population of the dead.

I know . . . I know . . . I have been reproached for giving God when a miracle was asked of me, and people have fled my bitter and streaming force; having expected that of the siren, they have only been offered infinity!

But what does it matter to me? It isn't on the dead tree that I want my storm to break, and against a captive rock that I want to hurl all my sea. I have—thank God!—more noble hostilities that await me.

Harmony is the great solitude, but the harp and the lute of this world, imagining that it is the great distress, refrain from having pity in making the soul of their breaking strings. That which is not itself an absolute is nothing, and may I be preserved—O God!—from ever asking for rain like the soil; grapes, like the vine; the crimson, like a carnation; sacredness, like a king; blood, like a knife; anyone, like a desert!

It's true, then, that you love me! And that is the strangest prodigy. Listen: one day, the man to whom I sacrificed my radiant youth, after years of common dolors but singular understanding, said to me, as he was smitten with I don't know who: "I've never loved you . . ." One evening a man who had committed for me what are called "follies" told me, as he was smitten with someone else: "I've never loved you . . ."

Well, I thought, *that's the second time I've heard my condemnation,* and I turned toward my mother. I can't think about her without my soul quivering with superhuman passion. She is Poetry; I'm only a poet, but I've gazed profoundly into my mother's incomparable azure eyes.

Then I discovered that she cherished me less, much less than her other child, who is mild, weak and gracious. "You," she told me, once, when I no longer had a hearth, when I had no money and no tomorrow, and I was smiling at my misery beside her, "I don't lament . . ." And she went to cuddle my sister, who had a toothache, with maternal fanaticism.

Well . . . , I thought, and suddenly, I sensed the barrier of roses around me and the regiment of swords above my head, and, without puerility, I saw the Devil's fork to my left and the lyre of the Seraphim to my right.

One of them cried to me: "You are a furnace . . ." The others murmured to me: "You are a tabernacle . . ." And solicitude blew over me from the mouths of all the

accursed and the breasts of all the blessed. I understood
. . . I understood . . . And since then, I have held to my
particular condition, telling myself that no blessed or
accursed individual of my species would come to bring
me her heaven or her hell. And yet, you're here. You have
crossed the odorous and spiny bush, you have marched
under the scintillating menace of the arrows of the sun.
That's good. I have your crimson, devoured by mine as
a she-wolf devours a she-wolf. I nourish the insatiable
angel of my perfumes with the inexhaustible cinnamon
of your thought and your heart, but I do not thank you,
and when I accept—for I am equitable—that you add
the gold of my damned idols to the gold of your holy
divinities, that you make broad commerce of my infinite
produce, O magnificent trader, you do not thank me
either.

We only look at one another from a distance. We
never salute one another. We do not sign the Alliance.

The only strangers: our fellows. The only enemies:
our beloved!

PRIDE

Dear beautiful passion, you never see in me the chilly humility of the trees that November strips in its squalls, or the suppliant immobility of the blind man who holds out his begging-bowl to the dead leaves of the avenue.

I have a strange liking for pirates, and also for their more modest brothers, thieves. In those who lie in wait and rob people I salute my patient and avid soul, my sparkling somber eyes in the depths of which no one, no one, sees with what alarming light coveted booty can cause them to shine.

Have I told you that I have never received? Have I told you that I have never asked? If, perhaps, two or three times, I have employed that manner, I confess that it was an infernal maneuver. Vagabonds know it; they beg for a hunk of bread at a door that opens. Woe! The door is open . . . and you have understood . . .

It is always by forcing myself that I have collected a heart. I only like the hearts of which I take possession. I have, therefore, no need to tell you that it is of no importance to me to be loved. Fundamentally, I only have the desire to vanquish. The submission of females in flocks has always saddened me enough to let me laugh freely—which is to say, in solitude—at the game of the swift and murderous arrow and the "I am me!" more resounding and more salutary than thunder in the heart of fine climates.

While still a child, at the significant and profound age, I fled the tenderness that came to me: "I don't want anyone to love me!" I cried, doubtless already sensing that someone would dispose of me as soon as they chose me, and I launched vehement kicks at the affectionate and usurpatory shadows, as I launched them at the wind when, blowing too strongly, it violated my skirts and took possession of my hair.

I wanted, already, to *choose*, and I turned my face, which gave birth satanically to a rose, away from human faces.

I have not changed.

So come or don't come. It's all the same to me. If I want you, I'll summon you with a hiss sweeter than that of the serpent of the seven days when it danced on its power and saw the shadow of its blue head divinized in the sunlight.

In truth, I have the royalty of desire, and I wouldn't permit myself—for I'm very honest with myself—the frenzy of temptation, if I didn't have skill. I possess it, and the audacity as well; I dare to pillage and destroy, and I don't hesitate before the terrible mental crimes that one commits by driving the cold blade of one's thought into hated breasts.

Mine is a strange duplicity! I seem to have the perfume of my joy when, above all, I have its venom.

How I laugh when I see scorn naïve enough to display itself! Who has ever suspected mine? It is absolute, like everything that hides, having the modest and royal pride in oneself.

So, when I hear our feeble Musset cry: "What does the bottle matter?" well, I have my demonic disgust and I go to make silence on the mountain.

But such malaises pass, and very quickly. What does not pass for us, the charming Lucifers, is our princely elegance and breeding, the breeding that gives us an ambiguous gaze and soft laughter.

Life? I slap it with my song. Others? I move them aside with my wings. My errors? I crown them like the most precious idols. So they warn me when I am on the point of deceiving myself again. Others, others have remorse, for myself, I only have divine vigilantes and accomplices. "Look out!" they say to me. Thus, I learn to smile at those I shall soon kill.

My pride pricks fate with its hard and powerful thorn. What does it matter to me if I make books indignant that have veils of mildness or resignation over their lovely eyes?

I have learned to weigh myself heavily since I am so light and Ascension envelops me in its flamboyant cloud.

I have learned, by not taking my eyes off the supreme goal, to adore all my vehemence, to exploit all my follies and to meditate all my blasphemies.

248

There is only one thing that counts: a heart that beats abundantly.

Peace to the accursed.

And do not try to smile in order to appease me and to take me by the hand in order to render me gentle, in the sense in which your mother taught you sanctity.

I set fire to the white curtains of my childhood bed in order to make the angels scream, and I swear to you that I didn't want to offend them; but our most active miracles are not in our acts of tenderness, our perfumed deaths and our amiable religions. Every being that wants God must commence by only occupying itself with itself—which is to say, pitilessly, with its liberty.

And finally, I shall say to you: "Leave me alone . . ." Leave me to my silence, lulled by a silence that only I hear. Leave me to me bare feet, but to my head that receives the sacrament. Leave me to my inconceivable pride of a Poet, to all the vessels that I corrupt and seduce by means of the promise of demonic Conquistadors. Leave me to all the suns that I attain, all the fatherlands that I give myself, all the Columbuses who disembark only to depart again, their shoulders full of tar and stars. "Hurrah! How many of you have invented New Worlds out there, out there toward inaccessible shores? Go . . . put to sea. There are always, always, inaccessible shores . . ."

"And New Worlds! Glory to us . . ."

Leave me to all the infinities into which I plunge by means of the sword, and wings, and unlimited power.

Leave me to my virgin forests, where I charm and dupe the ape by taking on the appearance of a liana and, by dancing, spread like a nutritious snow the yellow flowers of the cotton plant . . .

Leave me . . . that I might discover there again, upon the warm, deserted, gilded stone, the flute-playing serpent, the Tempter with amorous eyes.

Leave me, leave me alone. I only like my Presence, and weep once more, you who never cease to weep, delicate and sacrilegious forget-me-not; all I have wanted of you is the substance that has nourished my Satan. And now, his head heavy with roses, his breast swollen with detestable Hope, he is asleep on my sinless breast.

We shall have what we want, both of us, our curiosity listening to strange silvery sonorities from the direction in which divine unicorns are passing.

Go away. Leave me to this extraordinary dream that visits me often in my sleep of one predestined:

Alone, all alone, I am advancing in the Universe while cloudy standards flap overhead the wings of great exiles.

The world—excuse the megalomania of joyous insensates when they sleep!—has no other inhabitants than me, but the sky before me is of clear topaz, the color of divine sumptuousness and celebration.

I advance into the music . . . always the music! The trees are agitated by a muted and grim tempest of the end of time. I go on . . . I go on . . . The earth, the entire earth, quivers beneath my feet, for Orpheus, lyre in hand is wandering there, in its most unfathomable subterrains, in my victorious and tranquil footsteps.

I go on . . . I go on . . . And I know that I am the Poet and that my mortal course will come to an end, for the more that harmony becomes sensible to us, the more we understand that our reign is nigh.

But I fall silent.

Folly—the beautiful bird of fire—sometimes flaps its wings in my strange eyes.

Leave me alone,

I clasp my solid hands to my heart, to my loins, to the hidden lair of my soul. I close upon the invisible world my eyes full of infernal dawns.

The possessed woman does not want to surrender her demon.

THE COMBAT

I have fallen back, into order and rhythm, every time I wanted to do so; but at every encounter, my standards have been more soaked with the blood of roses, and their shaft has hardened in my Archangelic hand like the sun of the Sporades who watched the Evangelist describe his end on his mortal knees.

I am enriched every time by what I have left in the battle, and I know only too well that when the adversary refuses to surrender, our power develops, as the hammer concentrates its strength when it solicits the spark. I know only too well that everything has divinity as soon as it possesses stubbornness and does not cease to aspire to the day of glory.

I had only to wait for you elsewhere; but I have cried "Mercy!" because, after days of struggle, in the august solitude of reflection, patience and darkness, I furled my wings in order to love you.

Of your eyes, when I coveted them, I only had the flame; but as soon as I understood, in seeing them steal away, that I wanted something more certain, I knew that I would have their soul.

Of your heart, when I touched it, I only had the warmth; but as soon as I understood, in seeing myself betrayed, that I wanted something more ungraspable. I knew that I would have its life.

Of your existence, when I possessed it, I only had the hour; but as soon as I understood, in seeing it flow away, that I wanted something more durable. I knew that I would have its eternity.

Thus, what you call your triumphs have ensured mine, and I have learned that it is in escaping us that our beloveds learn how much we want them. From then on, they are ours.

More skillful, you would have obeyed me, and in that fashion, my satisfied domination would have been complacent within its limit, like the kings of this world But, imprudently, you resisted me so many times! Now I am redoubtable. Broken swords have the nobility of suns that have fought, and I make use of the steel of my spoils to sharpen my new weapons.

Vanquished at ***, beaten at ***, wounded in the heart at ***, left for dead at ***, have no fear; I know what war is—I mean victory.

And now, now that, having abandoned to you the closed field, the free space, the rampart, the fortress, the bell-tower, the mountain and the cloud, now that, as a scintillating and helmeted militia, I have retreated all the way to the sky—and who has ever done as much?—beware!

THE POOR LITTLE WITCH

THE POOR LITTLE WITCH

In an everyday dress, sitting on the threshold of the somber cavern, she has a nutshell in the palm of her hand and she is looking at it sadly.

Always, the souls go away, whether they are those of the woodland fruit, the light rose or the lover who comes to fill her cup at the last spring . . . always that lament, always! The most pathetic is the lament that the dead add to the song of the mole-crickets in the subterranean depths. Always that appeal of the departed, always! The most mysterious is the appeal that falls from the voice of the curlew when the forest has the odor of a marsh and October rain.

Oh, the poor little evil witch with her savage heart! It is by instinct that one shows oneself so comprehensively, when one is only a poor little witch, and truly, innocent souls have much for which to console themselves down here. . .

Not everyone sees the mourning of the forest when a hind falls, weeping to quit the foliage where the fawns dance for the somber gold moon of the end of summer. Not everyone hears, when full nocturnal silence falls, the cry of the great vehement hours that hold the ax, the hammer or the sword. Not everyone thinks about the cowardly and wicked returns of life, the vengeance with clenched teeth of that slut endlessly occupied in evil work . . .

Oh, not everyone has before their eyes the face of ingrate Amour, which is more bitter to behold than a field of bones under the moon.

And the poor little witch who is leaning on a dead tree also desires to lose all her sap through a large black wound . . . And now the bramble quivers and the one who watches retreats into the ages and the wind . . .

Not everyone knows that the hare never ceases to murmur; "I curse my ears that listen to all sounds, and the shadow of my shadow, which frightens the soul of my soul. Where, then, is the paradise of hares? When will those innocents be able to play in peace, and wreak great carnage in the sainfoin, and dance gaily on the grave of the last hunter?"

The poor little witch smiles dolorously. All the distress of the world is moaning in her heart, more sensitive and more reckless than a leaf in the evening breeze.

Not everyone has the visit of a cricket while the bark of oaks is creaking in the somber anxiety of the night.

And the cricket recounts that chubby-cheeked monsters with torn trousers—"Here and there, Madame, but especially—excuse me!—here . . ." are surrounding its burrow every day. "And they'll have me, Madame, they'll have me! My cousin, who was betrothed and about to marry imminently, is presently a prisoner of that tribe.

The mother cricket's family is in despair. As for her, the unfortunate . . . Please, Madame, don't you know, for me, of a cavern like yours but much, much smaller? A fissure in the rock and I'd be happy."

"Oh, naïve individual," says the poor little witch. "Do you believe, then, that one can be sheltered from the world forever? A thousand pilgrims besiege every day the most grimly solitary door, and their sticks beat strongly and shells rattle in their wallets, and their gourds beg to be filled and their feet want to be washed, and their brown robes want to flower with the lilies of the Lord, and their souls want to expand, for they are such captive springs, always so captive . . . Oh, if you knew, if you knew!

"And when by a miracle, the wanderers of life have left the solitary tranquil for once, the wood of his hearth complains because he burns it, and the smoke complains because it vanishes right away, and the ash complains because it resembles the dust of men, and the robin on the roof complains because it does not have enough material to build its nest, and the nest complains because . . . You have no idea to what point one can be tormented on this earth when one only has the human heart of . . ."

"A Poet . . . Oh, yes, Madame."

And the poor little witch and the poor little cricket fall silent and gaze into the far distance before them with their golden eyes . . .

. . . In their everyday nudity, lying on her solitary litter.

"Hou! Hou!" goes the wind, and the dead have great difficulty sleeping.

The poor little witch is poor and unhappy, like everyone else, this evening.

"It isn't cheerful, Madame, it isn't cheerful," cries an owl through the closed door, an owl that has lead in its wings.

Fortunately, there's the arrogance of squirrels, she thinks, not being asleep. But now one of them comes to expire in her arms, because it has an acorn stuck in its throat. And the poor little witch observes that the mole, which is pursuing its blind and mechanical task, and the squirrel, which shows off the sumptuous and sad color of autumn in the wood with sacrilegious grace every year, and the man, who philosophizes with regard to the leaves, and the leaves that fall on the man's head when Death puts on a robe of pale sunlight between the marsh and the horizon, have nothing that distinguishes them particularly from one another, since the universal humus will make its fatal pasture of all of them.

"My God," she says, "my God, where are you? How can I explain that you are only sensible to me when the Devil possesses me? You don't know, then, how I suffer from the poverty of nursing she-wolves, from the scream of the lamb whose throat is being cut, from little feet that get cold going to school and even colder returning to the dwelling where the cat only counts, in order to eat, on mice that do not appear? Distress! Distress! The trees that weep in the night think, as I do, that our greatest misfortunes are our petty despairs, and that we are almost dying of dolor when we say to ourselves that there are invalids abandoned, culpable individuals who expiate excessively, wretches who are born with a knife in their hand and have only scented around them, all their life, until they commit the crime, the odor of the crime.

"Terror! Terror! I know that my mother, who is so tender, is afraid of dying, and that sometimes, her blue eyes fill with those infantile teas that contain all reproaches, begging me to hold them back from her.

"My God!

A field of heather, in the wind, is as sad for me to contemplate as human destiny.

"My God, how ill poets are when their enchanted dementia quits them! How dark it is when I no longer carry my torch, how silent when I no longer sing my hymn! How the spider looks at me from the corner of her web, and how cold the shrouds are! How the termite calls to me from the bottom of his hole, and how lonely the tombs are! How the star implore me from the depths of its abyss and how empty the heavens are when the poet no longer populates them!

"Ah, miraculous dawn when I am so alive, so alive, so alive that, in the coffin in which I have been laid momentarily as a simulacrum, I only leave my veil—the modesty of the dead—and the light and ironic sigh of the eternal heart that is going to beat elsewhere!

"Ah, the extraordinary evenings when Satan, the magnificent God of the worlds of crystal and science only gives me the charming radiance of his eyes in the emerald or the topaz of fable!"

"By the gracious and puerile symbol," he says to me, "communicate with the Invisible, dance with the mystery, like the laughing child enlaced with the child who does not speak. Here is the perfume of myrtle and solitude; is it really only a perfume?"

"Oh, it is already the unimaginable forest where, later, I shall be naked, terrible, radiant and sagacious, like the original Shadow that sees, beneath every profound leaf, the flat and furtive head hiding that wants to know . . ."

"This is a rose; is it really only a rose?"

"Too bad for those who cannot see the demonic face appear in its multiple faces, the infinite smile circulating and contradicting itself."

"Here is a drop of dew; is it really only a drop of dew?"

"My future suns live in it and set fire to it. Another fable, Satan!"

"A fable? Ha ha! I have just introduced universes to you. Do you want more? Musical and pure regions? Let us descend into the sonorous and accursed regions that the color red strikes with its horn of a demented bull, and come with me to touch the forehead of the possessed, as Jesus, clad in linen, touched them with me, who was crowned with holy human indignity.

"My daughter, approach my sons and my daughters, who are hungry and thirsty as you. What do the food and drink to which they aspire matter? What counts is the hunger and the thirst, and the more devouring one is, the more one becomes the prey for which one lies in wait, and divinity is for those who seek God in Satan, his brother . . ."

✻

Precious nights in which I make a shadow a reality so that the blade is less present to the hilt of the knife and the silk less present to the pole of the oriflamme than my soul to the cherished soul . . .

Where are those perfect nights? From what heart nourished on strength and embalmed resins am I speaking to you, my beloved? My soul detaches its petals over yours like a dome of roses over that bath that awaits your nudity in the shadow.

Then I return to my primal destiny, to the violent and joyous canticle in the azure, go the jealous armor confronting amour, and—who knows?—perhaps, by reason of its fervor, hostile, for all that loves is armed . . .

My power possesses, then, all the virile splendors of the Archangel. It was sovereign hardness beneath its pure helmet.

But this evening, alas, this evening . . . !

How my misery crawls toward yours, like a serpent lost in the night, torn by the brushwood, in vain! I no longer know how to dominate you, seduce you and lead you astray divinely, I who, like you, await consolation and the star.

Where are we? Who are we? In the bleakest Sahara, two pilgrims whose cloaks scarcely recognize one another, make a signal and pass by, are not more pitiful and estranged from one another than we are, my brother— oh my brother!—on the nights when the nameless Fête no longer animates us.

263

＊

Sabbat of poetry! O sole magnificent delirium! What! Your folly can sometimes abandon us? However, when we are prey to its inconceivable felicity, it seems absolute to us. We welcome it as the eternal recompense of our demonic vitality.

My heart, which only any longer belongs, this evening, to the obscure force of my blood, frightened me now that the goddesses of frenzy and the witches of sensuality have let their warm and violent hands fall.

I'm naked. I have nothing on me: neither the undulating tunic of illusion, nor a mantle tightened by secret detours, nor the armor of beautiful challenges, nor the foliage of perfidious modesties, nor the arrogant roses of what one invents, what one believes and what one wants, nor the culpable and ravishing crimson of demonism, nor the azure of perdition that one sees in presbytery flowers, and butterflies even more accursed than the lust of stained-glass windows, nor the implacable and conquering gold that falls from cymbals, nor the prodigious light of dreams born of their luciferian malice and already searching infinities with its quivering antennae—for it's necessary that I admit, once again, that in inspiration, for me, everything is occult temptation, savant and subtle, fiery and sinful curiosity, transposition within the infernal miracle, satanic interpretation, the triple heart of the Devil, the sun of his brain, the irony of his dance, the adorable sadism of his conceptions, the poison of his offerings, the snares of his beauty, the magnificence of his laughter, the candor of his insolence and dandyism, the thunder of his genius, the lightning of his dementia, the thinking horn of Belzébuth and the starry belly of Absaroth!

"Ha ha!"

". . . But this evening, alas, my visage no longer has the royalty of sparkling diamond, and now the aridity of deserts weighs upon my mortal eyelids, the anxiety of the old world is extended at my feet, somber and voiceless, like a pilgrim vanquished by cypresses. Everything crumbles when poets are in ruins, and when the lyres are dead, nothingness commences . . ."

And the poor little witch, closed, this evening, to the scintillating enthusiasm of Lucifers, weeps, weeps like all those awaiting the somber shadow, the soulless urn . . .

When the Sabbat is over, what remains? A nutshell in a perishable hand . . . the adieu of the curlews . . . the plaint of the dead . . .

Ha ha! Are you lamenting too, the fine miracle of exulting when a sonorous damned soul quivers in your hand? No more music, then, no more delight?

You confound religion and exaltation. If the latter abandons you momentarily, your most adored, most certain, most recognized gods are no longer anything but black cadavers on the ground.

And yet, what do you make of the things that surround you, of that brown earth, as possessed by the invisible breath as the light umbels of the stars? What do you make of that doubt, even, which has just brushed you? Ingrate! Doubt is the meditation of the dream, the ambiguous and profound shadow that only envelops it in order suddenly to throw it, naked and more radiant, into its eternal march . . .

Satan, is it or is it not yours, the poetry that dances in the heart of poets?

"It is. But sometimes I quit you, singers, and it is by means of the plaints that you exhale then that I know my power over your accursed and divine souls. Come, let us fly here, there, everywhere . . . And laugh, my living witch."

SATAN'S NIGHT

THE FISH: . . . And if Satan does not inhabit my round eyes, ablaze with gold, circled by azure, my fins subtler than the wing of a dragonfly, my belly swollen like a gourd, and, full of ironic laughter, fleeting Amphitrite, I declare that he does not exist.

THE OYSTER: Atheist! Personally, I see him in the pearl that I incessantly await in telling myself that I am the nacre of solitude, of the yawn, immobility and quietude, on the remote rock . . .

THE MEDUSA: Get away, Madame Guyon![1] He can only exist in my unreal splendor, which penetrates, like that of the chameleon, all fleeting appearance.

NEPTUNE: By my beard, which flows in the wind of the tempest, and my trident, which reigns over shipwrecks, I swear that I shall annihilate all that miserable small fry that aspires to Satan. Where does demonism lodge? Satan? What about Neptune, then?

THE THUNDER: Silence, father of the waves, I carry Satan in my black belly.

---

1 The widowed Jeanne Guyon (1648-177) was a mystic who became an important figure in contemporary theological disputes by virtue of her controversial advocacy of the philosophy of quietism.

THE LIGHTNING: Satan is never noise, but broken laughter, crawling, fatal and very blue.

THE WIND: Oh, let me pass, the rest of you! Satan is in the caress that I bring to islands on behalf of captive poets.

COLUMBUS: There are no captive poets. Who says Poet says wanderer. Who says Poet says navigator. Who says poet says Christopher Columbus, the Satan who laughs every morning at the New World!

FERDINAND THE CATHOLIC: Who says Poet says accursed, oppressed, enchained, instrument of the Devil.

THE CHAINS: And if Satan is not forged with our thinking links, we wonder what is the point of the Cyclopes.

THE CYCLOPES: To plunge the red stem in the eye of the king of Hell.

SATAN, *aside*: Imbeciles! It isn't you who will puncture my eye. It sometimes has the suavity of a violet hidden beside a gray stone, and more often, the immortal gleam of . . .

THE SUN: Bonjour Satan.

SATAN: Bonjour, bonjour my dear eye. For a while, I've only been hearing extravagances. I know that they all, especially tonight—quickly, hide!—want to be possessed by my inconceivable divinity.

THE CARESS: So sweet . . .

THE TURTLE-DOVE: So tender . . .

THE LEOPARD: So tender? She's mad; Satan is, in us, a beautiful wily beast, florid with blood and dappled with black.

THE VULTURE: He can only be a somber bird, rapacious and finicky.

THE WOLF: Only the dog that I am, hungry and lean.

THE LION: Only the king that I represent, superb and solitary.

THE ANTELOPE: Only the victim that I love to figure, the fleeing victim, tricky and plaintive, with the eyes of a cherished slave.

THE SERPENT: Leave tranquil the one who only frequents me. We have the same venom, the same sagacity, the same perfidy, the same grace, the same silence and the same persuasion, the same shining gaze and the same royal topaz here on the forehead, and the same accursed destiny, we whose delightful mission is to slip away as soon as we have lied.

EVE: Satan? I conceived him; his name is Cain.

ABEL: I adored him; he killed me.

NOAH: Satan? I saw him escape, in the form of a dove, from the captive ark.

MOSES: And I felt him raising, on my forehead, two horns of flame when I descended from Sinai, staggering under the formidable and vain weight of the tables of the Law.

ABRAHAM: Satan? A burning bush.

JACOB: A golden ladder.

JOSHUA: The Sun stopping before the face of demons.

THE ARK: The Deluge over which every Demiurge wants to have free winds on the shoulders in the guise of wings . . .

REBECCA: Thirst, the eternal thirst of souls . . . An amorous halt at the well . . .

RACHEL: The one for whom one waits for seven years . . . and then seven more years . . . and then seven more . . .

NABUCHODONOSOR: The bestial and unrepentant pig into which I was changed.

THE STATUE OF SALT: Satan? Divine curiosity! I was punished for having satisfied him. What does it matter? I satisfied him.

THE MOON: Satan? A diamond serpent coiffed with rubies who prowls in the nocturnal sky and sometimes . . . swallows me.

THE STARS: And us.

JESUS: Barabbas, Barabbas, thank Satan, I love you.

MAGDALEN: Jesus of sinners. Jesus of the saints, which is the one for whom we wept more bitterly at your feet, Nazarene?

JESUS: You who embalm them.

SATAN: O my accused sighs: perfumes . . . perfumes . . . perfumes . . .

THE ROSE: Satan!

SATAN: Who never ceases to think about you, my rose.

THE ROSE: To you!

THE FORGET-ME-NOT: I am the most possessed; I am the most celestial.

THE PANSY: I am the most alive. My velvet mask thinks,[1] therefore I am . . . Satan!

---

1 The French *pensée* [Pansy] can also mean "thought."

THE LILY: And I spread the poison of whiteness over the feet of saints in the Church . . . Satan? That's me.

THE TORTOISE: Whatever he is, I keep his miser's treasures in my millenary carapace.

THE RAIN: I spread his generous poverties over the buds with coral horns.

THE CHURCH FATHERS: Tempter! Tempter! Malice of malices! Would you believe, O Christians, that he sometimes takes the form of a cilice, the odor of vervain, the smile of Gabriel, and even misery, lassitude and the sleep of the pilgrim?

SATAN: If tortoises and the Church Fathers get mixed up in it I shall have no more peace. But what is it that they all have? What is it that they all have to . . . ? Have no fear, Cambronne,[1] I'm not one of those comedians who spread sublime words in all directions. However, I'd really like to know why they never cease to sigh after me, tonight and throughout life.

CAMBRONNE: By his little hat! You're almost as beautiful as Him.

THE STAR: Sometimes, I confound you.

SATAN: I made his tent tremble to the song of my machine-gun . . . Oh! There's an alexandrine that has some allure, it seems to me. But I didn't do it on purpose.

---

1 General Cambronne became notorious for what he was supposed to have said when called upon to surrender at Waterloo. The "official" report that he said: "The guard does not surrender; it dies!" was contradicted by one of his men, who alleged that he had actually said: "Merde!" He denied that he had actually said either— plausibly given that he did surrender—but *merde*, a more forceful obscenity in French than its English equivalent [shit], became known thereafter as "Cambronne's word."

GENIUS: You didn't make me on purpose either, and yet you caress her, your beautiful bitch, Glory!

THE BIBLIOTHÈQUE ROSE,[1] *to its young readers*: Let's see, my little friends, has your catechism really given you an idea of Hell?

A YOUNG READER, *a future sadist*: Hee hee hee! It's in Sophie's crinoline that the Devil is!

ANOTHER YOUNG READER, *a future Catholic coward*: Have you seen the knout? (*He passes his hand over his backside fearfully.*)

ANOTHER YOUNG READER, *a future candidate for mystical lypemania*: We are all Torchonnet, you know . . . [2]

ANOTHER YOUNG READER, *a future Trappist with big blue eyes*: Yes, wash the dishes, wax the boots, never eat jam . . . (*He raises his shining gaze toward the heavens,*) But look at General Dourakine!

SATAN: Saint Martinet, this is for us.

RISK: That's right! I'd throw myself in the water to give pleasure to Satan.

GAMBLING: And I'd put my last sou on his red horn.

THE WITCH: Well, I'd rip out my entrails and . . .

SATAN: What! What!

---

1 The Bibliothèque Rose is a classic collection of children's books founded in 1856 by Hachette, a descendant of which still exists.
2 Lypemania is a pronounced tendency to deep melancholy. Torchonnet is an unfortunate orphan, a character in *L'Auberge de l'Ange Gardien* by the Comtesse de Ségur, a pillar of the original Bibliothèque Rose, to whom the knout is administered on the orders of General Dourakine.

THE CURÉ'S MAIDSERVANT: Satan? Beware of him in the corridors; what a tribe, cockroaches and draughts!

BYRON. I drank Malvoisie from a skull, invoking Satan.

SATAN: That's curious, as Romanticism was harmless.

BAUDELAIRE: Satan? Look at me: a green-tinted and desperate trickster.[1]

SATAN: Dear Albatross![2]

FRA ANGELICO: I painted virgins so pure that Heaven didn't want them.

SATAN: Of course; they were destined for me. The Middle Ages understood me.

THE COURTESAN: This necklace has ten rubies; I'm putting the laughter of Satan around my neck ten times over.

THE TOPAZ: That's a revolting injustice! When I think that I'm the very gaze of Satan . . .

THE EMERALD: And I'm his glorious mildness when he meditates!

THE DIAMOND: And I'm his insolence with a thousand glints!

SAINTE THÉRÈSE: There are black diamonds that only think of God, in cloisters . . .

SATAN: What! That nun too? Who will come to my aid?

---

1 Baudelaire notoriously once dyed his hair green.
2 "L'Albatros" is one of Baudelaire's best-known poems, often used as an exemplar in schools because its subject-matter is less sensitive than that of many other items in Les Fleurs du Mal.

A MAN WHO BELIEVES HIMSELF TO BE VERY STRONG: Behold! I'll tell you why he revolted: they wanted to make him an Archangel. Think about it! An Archangel . . . You can understand that when one has within one the cloth of the Devil . . .

THE UNIVERSE: Oh, as soon as they sensed the breath of the Devil run over them, the leaves danced with delight and the wild beasts licked the blood of their wounds.

THE MAD: Satan? The magnificent hypocrisy of sages.

THE SAGES: Satan? The radiant dignity of the mad.

THE INFERNAL MILITIA: Satan? Hope, that dazzling form of pride.

THE CELESTIAL MILITIA: Satan? Hmm! We sometimes miss him.

THE ARCHANGEL MICHAEL, *bitterly*: I've always thought that the Dragon remained more sympathetic than me.

SATAN: My dear Saint Michael, in the disaffected arsenals of Jehovah they have made of you a very proper captain, in charge of false cataclysms. Alas, there are no more deluges and Amalekites and, in response to the horror of holy Jewish wrath, no more frog choruses. No more rogues, possessed, musicians and accursed of high status—I'm alluding to Absalom, Saul, David and the charming statue that melted in the first downpour. No more Pharaohs whose old age crackled like dried myrtle-wood in the fire of precious stones. No more combat between you and me in the epic azure. In employing yourself as best you can, therefore, and in accordance with your reduced capacities, degenerate Archangel, forget that you have trodden beneath your feet my person, helmeted with a firmament and armored with wrath, and who consented nevertheless to be defeated, for a Dragon-martyr was necessary—come on!—to the splendor of the world . . .

THE ARCHANGEL, *subjugated and intimidated*: What ought I to forget?

SATAN: That in my person, which was nothing but dance, sparks and temptation, you trod underfoot the ardent Sodom and Gomorrah; the voluptuous Nineveh overlooking the Tigris; Byzantium, that bazaar selling the eyes of slaves and the suns of Emperors; Babylon the debauched, extending its shadow every evening over its odorous Balthazar; the Earthly Paradise where my thousand eyes shone more brightly than the trillions and trillions of jewels sewn in my scales, more than the smiles of all the female sinners of all times who kissed my pink lips at least seven times a night . . .

THE ARCHANGEL, *thoughtfully, aside*: Why was I not the Dragon?

TEARS: Satan? Joy.

HAPPINESS: Satan? Tears.

MUSIC: Satan? The last major chord.

B FLAT: I won't say very much, because I'm very small . . . but there are young men who are as pale as . . . Satan when they listen to me falling from the fingers of Chopin, by candlelight, in the perfume of linden trees . . .

BEETHOVEN: Back! Back! Chopin? That consumptive, languorous and nocturnal . . .

CHOPIN: He isn't seen, that one, with his mask of a deaf and resigned demoniac.

SATAN: There are times when it can't hold together. But what are they all, then, tonight?

JESUS: When I only came into the world for Judas and John, the apostle with the brown hair . . .

SATAN, *apart*: I cherished him too much.

JESUS: . . . I blessed my crucifixion.

SATAN, *apart*: Oh, my brother! How I betrayed you! How I reposed on your shoulder!

ALFRED DE VIGNY: He is the one that one loves and does not know.

ME: If after all this frenzy exhaled toward Satan, anyone is indignant that I have consecrated these very convinced pages to him, well, believe me, I'm like RISK, like GAMBLNG . . .

SATAN: But not like the witch . . . witch!

ME: Is it true that you were Judas?

SATAN: Shh . . .

ME: Is it true that you were the apostle John?

SATAN: Shh . . . Isn't it nice on your shoulder, my brown-haired head?

THE END

APPENDIX

THE SPIRITS OF CHAGRIN

How sad and somber the lair of the spirits of chagrin was! It opened in the rock on to a deserted plateau where pale grass swayed in the lugubrious wind of sunless solitudes.

Every evening, the spirits, who had been traveling the world since morning, returned home tiredly. Each of them bore a heavy sack, which he deposited on the ground with a gesture of infinite weariness.

"This," said one of them, "is what I found in the house of Envy." And he displayed extinct topazes, dead bouquets and frightful beverages.

"This," said another, "is what I found in the house of Pride." And he displayed smashed mirrors, broken swords and scepters corroded by the secret destruction of termites.

"Yes," groaned the most handsome among them, "humans are hateful, with their lamentable and terrible passions. But why are we condemned to go and see them, to bring back to our lairs the symbols of their evil and spoiled existence? What unknown power is edifying, in a world we do not know, a realm of ruins, desolations and shames with our evening's booty? Oh, chagrined spirits, my brethren, what bitterness is ours!"

And that spirit, who was a languorous and tender adolescent, shed tears that no one wiped away.

The heather quivered around the remote lair, in the breath of a pitiless north wind, and sometimes, a chorus of frogs told the echoes that life is a poor dream, and that human destiny always reeks of humus, putrefaction and forgetfulness. Nothing more frightful could be seen and heard.

However, toward midnight, the spirits of chagrin adopted more courageous poses, and the tender and languorous adolescent raised himself up on his white feet and went to apply his ear to the door of the desolate lair.

"Can you hear a noise?" he asked one of his brothers.

"Yes . . . it seems to me . . ."

And the handsome spirit put his charming hand over his quivering heart, desperately.

Gradually, all his companions became animated, and they all listened avidly.

"Can you hear a noise?" repeated a suppliant voice.

"Yes . . . it seemed to me . . ."

The spirits of chagrin were never disappointed. When midnight chimed, a knock resounded in the door of their lair, and immediately, those unfortunates found themselves clad in warm and joyful colors. Their gestures were those of beings who love life, who welcome the flowers, who savor bread and who salute light. Their sacks, which had only brought from the city of humans rags, masks, baubles, vermin and dust, suddenly emptied of their contents, collapsed in the shadows.

The damp and icy ground was covered with moss, the fresh silver veins of which extended toward an enchanted tree. And there, the king of the night, the king with the harmonious crown, the delightful nightingale, the eternal cajoler, was singing . . .

Soon, stars ran across the obscure vault with a lightness full of music and harmony . . .

And the door opened . . .

This time, the spirits of chagrin had not had time to shout: "Come in!" when a knock was suddenly struck on their door. A second rap was heard, and then a third.

They looked at one another in astonishment, but a fourth and fifth rap resounded. And Lamento, the handsome adolescent whose eyes were so blue and so profound, hid his face in his hands.

A sixth blow shook the door, and the spirits of chagrin were clad in moonlight and odorous mist from head to toe. Wings palpitated on their shoulders, and their arms and necks shone with the soft assurance of pearls.

They had never seen themselves so radiant at the blissful moment of their nocturnal metamorphosis.

Reassured by their beauty and magnificence, they shouted: "Come in!" and their surprise and delight were boundless.

Before their eyes six messengers were smiling, who had only previously penetrated their abode one at a time, and only by night. They were Illusion, Hope, Desire, Dream, Amour and Happiness.

"What is happening, dear divinities?" exclaimed Bémolus, the oldest of the inhabitants of the lair. "By what supreme permission are you all entering together?

Why are you so radiant tonight? What news have you brought us from the abode of humans to console us for having been there, and what divine songs will soothe us until dawn, O divinities?"

"Spirits of chagrin," replied Dream, "when all six of us found ourselves at the door of your lair, as we do every evening, the severe and lucid spirit appointed to guard it, and who designates, in the interests of the story that each of us tells him, which of us ought to reach you, was very embarrassed . . . All six of us had witnessed the same charming event, and I shall not hide from you that each of us believes that he had played a principal role therein . . ."

"We're listening, Dream," said the spirits of chagrin, striking poses of sensuality and abandonment. "Send us to sleep in enchantment and beauty. Alas, it will soon be time to wake up, the hour when we taken on our melancholy forms."

" . . . A poet was asleep in the forest. He was young and charming. A queen of the same age passed by. Everything about her announced misfortune, grace and tenderness. She stopped in front of the poet, and suddenly, he recited verses while pursuing the most intoxicated slumber . . . Then he fell silent, but the queen kissed his melodious mouth . . ."

"She was right," exclaimed the spirits of chagrin, "but we understand why you believed yourself to be the most authorized, among your companions, to come and tell us that adorable story."

"Yes," replied Dream. "The poet was asleep . . ."

"In the abode of the gods," said Illusion.

"He smiled at me," said Hope.

"I saw him blush," said Desire.

"I heard him sigh," said Amour.

"He woke up," said Happiness.

"Dear divinities," murmured the spirits of chagrin, "each of you was, indeed, gratified by the delightful adventure, and you could only enter our abode together. When each of you has had his entire part of a similar sweetness, come back again, all at once. How you have vivified and rejuvenated us! Tomorrow morning, we shall have more strength in order to descend to the abode of humans, of which, alas, we only see the turpitudes and vanities . . ."

"Don't criticize them too much, spirits," said the six light divinities. "They enable us to live."

"And you prevent us from cursing them," replied Lamento, closing his large eyes over his poor sack, which was filled with roses . . .

www.ingramcontent.com/pod-product-compliance
Lightning Source LLC
Chambersburg PA
CBHW020403110726
47899CB00006B/1845